AN IMPRINT OF PUSHKIN PRESS

"Meng Jin has so much to say about the legacy of the past, about families and secrets and journeys of the body and the heart. She has a sharp eye for transformation: subtle changes of feeling, huge national and international changes… She represents the best of international literary fiction"
                                                            Bidisha

"Enthralling. Crisply told and seductively crafted, *Little Gods* plumbs the depths of the immigrant story to reveal something sharp, intricate, and true. I didn't want to put this book down or part with the brilliant, maddening woman at its center"
          C Pam Zhang, author of *How Much of These Hills is Gold*

"Prepare to be swept away by the global reach of Jin's sharp eye, the intellectual depths of her characters' minds, and the twists and turns of a love story between wounded people, and a wounded nation"
          Lillian Li, author of *Number One Chinese Restaurant*

"Meng Jin's beautiful debut novel is ambitious in the best ways: meticulously observed, daringly imagined, rich in character and history. Ranging across continents, cultures and generations, Jin poses profound questions: how might we know ourselves, or the people we love? And what truths, if any, travel with us?"
          Claire Messud, author of *The Emperor's Children*

"This stunning, lyrical debut explores the intricate ways that grief, identity, sacrifice, and love all weave together to create a bond between mother and daughter"   *Refinery 29*

"It's a page-turner — but all the while it winks, reminding us that possible explanations in our universe are as varied as the beings who populate it"   *Paris Review*

"Artfully composed and emotionally searing, Jin's debut about lost girls, bottomless ambition, and the myriad ways family members can hurt and betray one another is gripping from beginning to end. This is a beautiful, intensely moving debut"   *Publishers Weekly*

© Andria Lo

MENG JIN's writing has appeared in the *Pushcart Prize Anthology*, *Threepenny Review, Ploughshares*, the *Bare Life Review, Vogue*, and *Best American Short Stories 2020*. A Kundiman Fellow, she has an MFA from Hunter College, and received the David TK Wong Fellowship at the University of East Anglia. *Little Gods* has been shortlisted for the *LA Times* Book Prize, the Balcones Fiction Prize and the NYPL Young Lions Fiction Award. Jin was born in Shanghai and has lived in the UK and the US.

We hope you enjoy this book.
Please return or renew it by the due date.
You can renew it at **www.norfolk.gov.uk/libraries**
or by using our free library app. Otherwise you can
phone **0344 800 8020** - please have your library
card and pin ready.
You can sign up for email reminders too.

ONE
An imprint of Pushkin Press
71–75 Shelton Street
London WC2H 9JQ

9 8 7 6 5 4 3 2 1

ISBN 13: 978-1-91159-045-3

Offset by Tetragon, London
Printed and bound by CPI Group (UK) Ltd, Croydon, CR0 4YY

www.pushkinpress.com

For my family

The past is never there waiting to be discovered, to be recognized for exactly what it is.

The past is not for living in . . .

—John Berger, *Ways of Seeing*

THE END

JUNE 3–4, 1989

FROM ABOVE, THE HEART OF the city is easy to see. Beijing is a bull's-eye. Concentric ring roads close in toward the old city walls, now paved into wide avenues. The avenues form a tight band around the heart: the south-facing gates, the moated palace, the desert square. On a map, diminishing circles draw in the eye, as if to say, Come.

Bodies have come. In the square, bodies sit, stand, and lie on the hot paved stone. The square was built for six hundred thousand bodies; for weeks, there have been more. Rats sniff between folds of newspaper; flies regurgitate on sunburned shins; roaches scuttle across sleeping toes. Women in white uniforms weave through carrying metal tanks, spraying disinfectant where concrete shows. From above, this movement looks like a primitive organism, breathing. In the nucleus a burst of color radiates and contracts, radiates and contracts, as bodies leave the square, return and leave again. West of the outer ring, a dark mass gathers: troops preparing to enter.

In every city and circumstance there are those who will go on with living. In the east quadrant, an old man circles his hutong courtyard for a morning stroll. By the northern lake a young couple wakes to *Tian Mi Mi* on the radio. South of the train station, three boys race to catch a hen escaping her coop. Between the second and third ring roads, a woman crosses a canal bridge on her walk to work. The woman has a round and candid face, and her hair, striped with white, has been brushed neatly off her forehead. She carries a sensible black purse over her shoulder that has served her for the good part of a decade. She is not chubby but her bones are sturdy, and she commands more space than a woman should.

Normally this woman, a nurse, bikes to the hospital where she works, her lightly permed hair clipped at the base of her neck, a thin shawl draped over her arms to protect her skin from sun. In recent weeks the streets have been too crowded; she has had to take her feet off the pedals and toe her way through. This morning she has decided to walk the two kilometers. She clutches her purse to her side and steps through the people standing in her way. She advances slowly. Sweat beads on her lower back.

She walks past a complex of luxury apartments. In one of the top windows she imagines a woman not unlike herself looking down and shaking her head. She heard once that wives of deposed government officials are given rooms here as a consolation prize, and ever since, she has thought of these buildings as the widows' towers. Whenever she sees them she is reminded of how she wouldn't mind so much being a widow. Being a widow would give her a simple answer for the question of why she has no husband.

The faces crowding the nurse are young, the faces of children. The nurse has never been so foolish as to have children of her own. She learned long ago that she does not like what children grow into. She remembers herself as a high school student, how her grown-up heart felt trapped in her adolescent body. Looking back, it is clear that the opposite was true: her body had been more mature. As a result of this mistake, in the early days of the Cultural Revolution she and her classmates stoned to death their high school physics teacher, a reasonable woman who wore her long hair in a bun at her neck. This is what the nurse sees in the faces of the children around her. A hunger for revolution, any Great Revolution, whatever it stands for, so long as where you stand is behind its angry fist. Little gods, she thinks. Desperate to turn their own growing bodies, their own aches and despairs, into material that might reset the axes of worlds. What did it boil down to but children, giddy with breaking rules!

She arrives at the hospital three minutes past seven and heads to the end of the north corridor. In the nursery her colleague is counting the newborns. There are eight, five boys and three girls, and they are lined up next to each other with the tops of their heads along the wall, swaddled under the incubation lamps like loaves of warm bread.

The nurse cares for infants in a way that she cannot their grown counterparts. Perhaps it is because they are so helpless: nothing more than potential. She cares for them with the hope that they will grow not into humans but rather become something entirely new.

Did you hear—her colleague asks—last night a car ran over some students?

The question comes bursting out as if the girl has been holding it in all night.

No license plate, nothing, she continues. And they say they found guns and helmets inside. Already there is bloodshed! What will it come to?

Her colleague is a slim girl who wears her hair in a pert ponytail and just finished school the year before. The nurse finds her overly excitable. She hangs up her purse and changes into her frock.

I guess you'd better go check the delivery unit, her colleague says, and the nurse exits through the swinging doors.

The delivery unit is at the opposite end of the building, adjacent to the operating rooms. To reach it the nurse must walk through the maternity ward. Here, at seven fifteen in the morning, a handful of pregnant women are waiting with their families at the check-in windows for their numbers to be called. The nurse walks quickly, fixing her gaze ahead. But before she can reach the door at the end of the hall, her path is blocked by a face.

It is a small face, with small, plain features, so plain, in fact, that the face resembles a blank paper, on which anything can be drawn.

The mouth on the face moves, dots of sweat filming the edge where lip meets skin. For a long moment the nurse does not understand that the face belongs to a person—a woman, pregnant, nearly full term. The woman's voice is soft and pleading and the nurse does not hear what it's saying. She cannot stop looking at the woman's blank face, at the mouth moving—the lips shaping, the wet tongue swelling, the slivers of teeth emerging and disappearing. Finally she steps back, blinking, and hears:

Ahyi, my name is Su Lan, please help me. Here is my husband—the woman pulls forward a man—we are not from Beijing, we arrived just last week—

The nurse pushes past. A shudder moves up her neck. It is not that she has never been accosted for help in the halls of this hospital before. No, something disturbing cuts through this woman's voice, a desperation so bare it's indecent. The nurse does not take a good look at the couple, but she has the impression that they are handsome and well-dressed. City people, even if they aren't from Beijing—not, in any case, the type of people who should beg.

SIX OF TEN beds in the predelivery suite are empty, along with the delivery room itself. In the operating rooms the first cesarean has begun. The nurse slips in and waits, preparing identification tags and linens as blood-soaked cloths line the floor. Then the baby is out, a boy, and he is in the nurse's arms on his way to the nursery before the surgeon's needle has begun to mend his mother's wound.

In the nursery there is just one window, a small rectangle carved high in the wall. Some mornings the sun reaches through on its way to noon and fills the room with light. The faces of the newborns become so bright that the nurse can't stand to look at them. The sun passes quickly, but in the minutes before the room returns to bare fluorescence, everything inside insists so baldly on its life that she must look at her shoes in embarrassment.

This day is cloudy. Light presses on a sheet of gray. The nurse looks into the glow and tries to replace the images in her mind with that same static colorlessness. But one persists: the blank-faced woman, her moving lips. *Ahyi, my name is Su Lan, please help me.* In a flash she sees the husband pulled forward, his pupils narrowed, his lips thin. The nurse shakes her head. Briefly she wonders why the couple came to Beijing, if they were drawn by the same excitement as the other young people flooding the city. She picks up a boy who has begun to howl. She prepares to return him to his mother.

WHEN THE INJURED come, the nurse is bathing an infant girl. It is past midnight and her shift has ended. Instead of standing in the nursery wiping dried amniotic fluid from this newborn's red skin, she should be at home, facing the wall and trying to sleep.

No replacements have arrived. She does not mind. Walking through the corridors, passing under open windows, she has heard muffled commotion straining the walls. She is not eager to push home through all that. She dips a cloth in warm water, washes and dries the infant, checks the tag on the foot. On the tag she reads 苏兰: Su Lan, a familiar name. Before she can place it, a yellow-green flash lights the window. Then a human noise hurtles into her ears, and in her eyes it is the woman from the morning, mouth in the shape of a scream.

The nurse stands still, holding Su Lan's daughter in both hands.

The daughter begins to cry.

The door opens: her colleague with another child.

In the moment before the door swings shut, shouting in the hallway outside.

God, her colleague says. His mother was just pushing him out when they—right into the delivery room.

They?

I've got to go, her colleague says, and hands the newborn to the nurse, who quickly wraps the new arrival and sets him under the lamp.

All around the nurse the newborns are crying, red faces pinched against white cloth, wet lips open wide. All but Su Lan's girl, who has suddenly grown silent as herself. She picks up the child. She knows it cannot see her. The newborn brain understands shapes and light but cannot process images farther than two lengths of hand away. Still she watches the child watch her, wondering what it dares her to do.

BODIES ARE LINING up in the halls. They come on cardboard stretched between two bicycles, on the flat beds of watermelon carts, in the arms of shouting strangers. A man in blue pants with a wound in his gut lies coiled on an unhinged door, hand curled around the knob. Mattresses are improvised, IVs inserted with bare hands. Nurses triage while wrapping wounds; an off-shift doctor runs through the gate. Trails of blood dry on the floor. In the morgue, volunteers step between bamboo mats, preparing a list of names.

The delivery unit's operating rooms have been taken over by urgent care. Scalpels that earlier extracted babies now extract bullets. Ten of ten beds in the predelivery suite are occupied, along with the floor space between them, by the wounded waiting. New and expecting mothers are moved into two rooms on the top floor. Their families trail behind, looking at their feet. The mothers are silent as they're wheeled through the halls. Some pretend not to see. Some close their eyes and pray.

Su Lan sits up with her eyes red and open, staring coldly into the faces of the wounded.

The nurse stands in the center of the nursery, not knowing what to do. She has stood here for hours, checking vitals, preparing birth certificates, listening to waves of clamor erupt beyond the walls and ceilings and floors. Two more newborns have been brought in, the first by an overnight nurse from the inpatient building, who tells of the maternity ward move, the second by a teenage girl who calls herself a volunteer. The nursery is running out of space. By now, over half the babies should be back with their families. But no one has come to stay and the nurse cannot leave any newborns unattended.

She checks temperatures and heart rates again. There have been no major complications all night, no early babies the size of her palm, no blue-skinned babies whose lungs need coaxing to breathe. Death, she thinks, is elsewhere occupied. She digs in the closet for the largest supply cart with high sides she can find. Syringes and boxes of gauze clatter to the floor. She pulls out the cart and presses her hands and arms on the metal trays to warm them. She pads the top and bottom layers with linens. In this way she squeezes all but one newborn onto the cart. She straps Su Lan's daughter to her chest. The girl starts crying as she pushes the cart out the door.

The hall stinks. Bodies lie perpendicular to the wall, bleeding and burned black. The nurse has seen plenty of blood and should not be surprised by it. In the operating room she has learned to dissociate blood from the human. But these people are not inside an operating room, and their blood does not seem material, like flesh or bone, but rather like a too-human thing. It is almost pretty. The nurse looks at the people along the wall and sees their blood as a painter sees paint, coloring in who they are. She pushes the cart through the hall. The living look up, blinking, at what she brings.

THE MAKESHIFT MATERNITY ward is a mess of beds and chairs. Cots crammed in every space, families squatting on the floor. The nurse enters the first room with her cart. New parents and grandparents sit up and crane their necks. They catch their joy and hold it close, afraid or ashamed to hope. Outside, it is finally quiet. For the first time in months, the adjacent street is deserted.

The nurse picks up the newborns and reads off the mothers' names. Families come forward and collect their babies one by one.

When her cart is empty she calls out the name Su Lan. There is no response. She sees a woman alone in the corner cot, a body turned to the wall. She unwraps the girl from her chest and walks over. She sits at the edge of the bed and waits.

Finally the woman turns. Again the nurse is fascinated by her face, how each feature taken alone is plain and unmemorable: the small and single-lidded eyes, the straight nose, the pale lips. It is attractive but not pretty, not quite, and it strikes the nurse that it would be a good face for an actress—the kind of face that could become anything with just a few lines of makeup, that, like a mirror, reflects the viewer back upon herself.

Su Lan's eyelids are swollen, her eyes glassy. She looks at the nurse and says: Do you believe in time?

Time?

Do you believe, Su Lan continues, that the past is gone and the future does not yet exist?

For a moment the nurse is quiet. Then she says, Yes.

Su Lan stares. She begins to scream. The screams are short and breathy and sound like a repeating mechanical alarm. The nurse covers the daughter's ears. Someone else's mother-in-law leans over: Su Lan has been hysterical all night, calling for her husband. Apparently she begged the doctors to let him inside the delivery unit, but of course this was impossible. Afterward the man could not be found. The mother-in-law lowers her voice and looks meaningfully at the nurse. She says, When was the last time you saw a yunfu at the hospital all alone?

A woman, all alone. The nurse wants to touch her. She wants to cover the screaming mouth and smooth the damp hair from the face.

She wraps the daughter to her chest and stands to leave. Her legs buckle. She sits back down. For a moment she feels her exhaustion. She has not slept in over twenty hours. She has not eaten in ten. She shakes her shoulders and stands again, breathing slowly, and heads for the second maternity room.

In the second room are women in labor, and one who just arrived, heaven knows how.

NEAR DAWN, SU LAN takes her child. She holds her daughter's neck in her palm and does not smile. The nurse wants to say something to Su Lan, something final and wise, as if she is at this woman's deathbed. She opens her mouth, closes it, stands up, leaves. She goes to a washroom, splashes water on her face, and steps outside. It is raining. She does not look at the stained ground or the smoldering carcasses of tanks and cars. She does not look at the elderly couple burning mourning money at the steps. She lights a cigarette and listens to the hiss. The front of her frock, where Su Lan's daughter was strapped all night, is damp and suddenly cold.

Su Lan will live for another seventeen and a half years—not an insignificant amount of time. Enough to turn an infant into a woman, a Chinese into an American. But the nurse's feeling is correct. Today, Su Lan begins to die.

2007

ZHU WEN

YOUR MOTHER RETURNED TO SHANGHAI in June of 1989, a few days after the event. She was not wearing proper shoes. Instead, she had on these pink rubber slippers, the kind you can buy for half a yuan off the side of the street. They were too small, and dirty—you could tell she'd been wearing them for some days. This was unusual for your mother. Su Lan was the kind of person who presented herself carefully to the world, regardless of circumstance.

She had left the longtang ten days earlier with her husband and one small bag. When she returned she had neither. In their place was you.

Ten days—that's how long it took for the swallow eggs to hatch too. That spring, a pair had nested above Su Lan's window. Of course she hadn't noticed. Perpetually insulated in the world of her work, Su Lan barely seemed aware of the protesters that passed daily under our windows, hollering slogans and singing songs. But I had seen bird droppings on the windowsill in early May. I watched the swallows build their nest, flying back with little bites of mud in their beaks and sticking them to the wood. When they were done they'd made a brown cone the size of my palm. The same day Su Lan and her husband left for Beijing, five white-flecked eggs appeared in the hollow. The parents perched on the ledge of the terrace and turned their heads this way and that, little red throats flapping as they sang.

These nests had been a common sight in the neighborhood when I was a girl. I was afraid of them then—they looked like hornets' hives. Until one day, as I walked home from school, following my big brother, my hand trailing the longtang wall, a baby bird fell from the sky. I'd caught it in my hands, almost dropped it in surprise. It was delicate and ugly. I could crush it with a little squeeze.

Su Lan didn't say anything when she saw me on the stairs. I followed her lead. Later, I boiled water so she could give you a warm bath. The next morning I woke early. The air was crisp and fresh, like it had rained, but it had not. Su Lan's door was open, so I went in.

She was sleeping. You were too, belly down on her chest. You were both naked. When I turned to leave she opened her eyes and spoke, a soft and pleading sound, the first she'd made since she returned.

It won't stop crying, she said. I want to rest, but it won't stop crying.

I thought she'd gone mad. I thought she meant you. You were not crying. You were fast asleep, and for a moment I wondered if I should take you away from her. You hadn't even cried the night before, not while I bathed you and not while I slept (fitfully, listening). I remembered I had thought it strange, wondered if it was normal for infants to be so placid.

Then I heard it, the sharp, shrill screams. They were coming from the window. I slammed it shut. It was no use.

Outside, on the terrace, I counted four swallow chicks inside the nest. One egg had not hatched. The chicks were featherless, with translucent membrane for skin, beneath which could be seen webs of purple capillaries and the ridges of tiny bones, angular folds of what would become wings. They sat in a line and shrieked for food, necks stretched out, little beaks opening and closing like hands. Theirs was not a pretty birdsong. It was a call for attention—for survival, aggressive and loud. On the other side of the window Su Lan covered your ears. Through the glass, her figure and yours appeared warped, your bodies flattened and geometric and yet revealing layers, as if I were seeing you from many directions at once. That was when I realized—in the cavity of your distorted bodies—that her husband, your father, was not there.

I went to the kitchen. I pulled out my chopping knife. Back on the terrace, with one hand cupping the grainy round bottom, I sawed the mud nest from the eaves. It felt like a ball of dirt. I grabbed my cane and went down the stairs again and out the door. In my hand the chicks continued to shriek.

Along the stone wall surrounding the longtang are little holes that were once used for candles and oil lamps, and had since been filled with garbage and pieces of loose stone. I walked down the alley cradling the nest in search of one of these holes, and found one not too far from our building. I scooped out the filling and tucked the nest inside. When I returned to the terrace, the swallow parents were hopping about the window ledge squawking their own song of alarm. I threw some rice over the ledge in the direction of the nest and told them to go look over there. The swallows flew away.

The next few days, between looking after your mother and you, I went to the nest once a day to check that it was still there. I counted the chicks: four, four, four. On the second morning I saw the parents perched nearby and sprinkled some more rice on the ground, a reward, and clucked to them of their cleverness.

I don't remember if it was the fourth day or the fifth. One morning I found the hole empty. The nest lay on the ground at the base of the wall. Beside it crouched an enormous black bird with blue and white underwings, a magpie, which pecked at the mud cone with its sharp hooked beak. The magpie pulled a chick from the nest and thrust its beak into the naked neck, then continued down the body, ripping open the stomach and extracting the entrails. It pulled out a second chick and a third, opening each body in turn. The chicks' skin broke easily; the magpie's head darted out and back, its black beak shining, not red with blood but blacker, almost blue. I could not tell if the magpie was eating or simply probing; it moved with disinterest, like an investigator sorting through a cabinet of evidence. It turned and looked at me with one beady black eye, then pulled the last chick from the nest. When it was done it trotted a few steps before flying away.

I watched its shadow move over the wall. I had thought magpies beautiful once, had admired their long, graceful tails. I hadn't realized how large they were.

For a few more moments I stood there. Already the pulp of purple and gray at the base of the wall was barely distinguishable as baby birds. The only evidence that remained was eight little feet that hadn't yet sprouted full claws. I was a girl again, I'd just caught a bird in my hands. That time, I had felt how delicate the tiny life was, had felt the thin warm skin against my own, and had imagined closing my hand tight and hearing the crunch of bones in my palm, the hot blood dripping through my fingers. Instead I fastened the bird in a pouch around my neck and painfully climbed a ladder to the roof. I crawled to the edge and slipped it back inside its nest. Sharp pain stabbed my hip, and on my way down I slid, kicking a few shingles and nearly falling off. You see, I've always had this limp, even when I was a small girl.

I walked quickly back to my room, where next door Su Lan was still asleep. My hip ached.

The magpie had looked at me in recognition; the magpie was myself, the girl I'd almost been. I had no doubts: it was I inside that tapping beak, I in the cold beady stare, I in the beats of the wing, in flight over the longtang wall. Since I was a girl I had known the fragility of life and the power to extinguish it in my own hands; I had no right to feel anything; not horror, not grief, not even surprise.

IN THOSE DAYS I found myself thinking often of the first time I had seen Su Lan, when she moved into the neighborhood a little less than a year before. She and her husband were strange newcomers— two intellectuals from the provinces, newlywed, young and fashionable—the longtang didn't see many like them. In that first year, before what happened, they were spoken of with admiration and envy. Even I had felt that things were changing, that the course of possibilities was turning from one road to another.

She had come first, a few days before she brought her husband. I watched her arrive in the morning, walking down the lane in a pale yellow dress and red high-heeled shoes, carrying a bucket of what turned out to be white paint. I was surprised when the stranger walked all the way to the end of the lane, and more so when footfalls made the back stairs creak. For many months the room next door had been vacant. I had spent the years after my husband's death cultivating loneliness; I liked to think I was the one who had driven prospective tenants away.

She was there to paint the room white. Not just the walls but the ceiling and the floor—she kept painting until she stood in a white box. If you squinted your eyes, the edges disappeared and the space looked like an empty plane expanding in every direction. I had never seen anything like it.

There was something alarming about her. Even before she began throwing paint on the floor, her presence unsettled me, though I couldn't say exactly how or why. She had this way of looking at things, an expression if you could call it that, with such focus and intensity you would think she was trying to bore a hole through with her eyes. She painted in ferocious but controlled movements. Barefoot, skirt tied above her knees, she pressed layer after layer of white paint onto the walls as if aiming to annihilate every trace of what had been there before.

When she finished, she stood in the middle of the room holding the empty bucket, breathing heavily. The paint, still wet, gleamed. Later, when I went in and out of the white room, I would feel how even though the space now looked larger than it was, there was something oppressive about it, as if all the air had been squeezed out. But right then, containing just your mother, who stood there examining her handiwork, blinking with surprise and relief, the room looked brand-new. So did she. She walked out, cheeks red, eyes fresh, like she had been born in this field of blankness. Here I am, she seemed to say, starting my new life.

She gathered her things and locked the door. When she turned and saw me watching, she gave me a long look, her expression startled but not unkind, and mumbled something before picking up her red shoes and turning to go. I think she said, You look like someone I've always known.

Her feet were caked in a layer of dried paint. I watched their white soles pad down the stairs.

It wasn't until a few days later, when she returned with her husband and other belongings, that I learned her name.

This is Su Lan, her husband said, she forgets to introduce herself.

If her husband noticed the recent paint job, he didn't say anything. He opened the door, looked around, and said, Very nice! He ran his hand down Su Lan's hair. Do you like it? he asked her. She kissed him on the shoulder. They looked very much like a young couple in love. As far as I could tell, he believed she was seeing the place for the first time.

I nearly believed it too. She behaved so differently from the other time I'd seen her (now talkative, now effusive, the sullen intensity now dissipated into charm) that I wondered if she was the same person, wondered even if I had somehow imagined the events of the previous week. Had the room always been white?

SU LAN WAS a physicist. It was possible she had an extraordinary mind. Certainly her husband thought it. In the evenings he could be heard addressing her, with admiration and a note of disbelief (she's mine? she's mine!), as *my brilliant wife*. Perhaps as a result, there circulated rumors in the neighborhood about where she had come from, how she had graduated first from the top university in the country, how she had been interviewed on a radio program featuring the brightest of her generation. She was pursuing an advanced degree in theoretical physics at Fudan University, where, it was said, her colleagues called her the Chinese Madame Curie.

She was studying the behavior of the tiniest particles in the world— many trillion times smaller than a rice grain, she once told me in an effort to explain—the bits that make up everything we know. She was trying to tease out a mathematical principle that could describe their behavior, a principle that would hold even when applied to the behavior of their opposites: entire planets, entire worlds.

According to Su Lan, in physics it is far easier to understand the behavior of massive objects than that of minuscule ones. You would think it should be the reverse, like how it's more difficult to hold down a large man than to carry a newborn child. But then I thought of children, how they were more surprising and unpredictable than adults, and how as I aged, I felt I was settling into a rigid form, becoming if not someone I understood, then someone whose moods and reactions fell increasingly into patterns I could predict. I thought too of the stories in novels and history books I'd read, stories about nations and empires, stories that spanned centuries, how sometimes it was easier to imagine large pieces of land animating and moving against each other than to comprehend one day in my own insignificant life.

Su Lan agreed. She said that when something was massive, we could still imagine it. Undoubtedly we simplified it, made it stupid, missed some important things. But imagining what we could not see? Where would we even begin?

It was when she spoke of her work that the intensity I'd seen on the day she painted the room returned to her eyes; it was then that I could be sure she was indeed the same person. Her relationship to physics was not like a typical person's relationship to their work. There was a religiosity in it, which is to say a dependence. In the weeks after she returned from Beijing with you, the weeks she spent strapped to her bed by weakness and grief, trapped in a language that could not, like mathematics, be manipulated into pattern or logic, she was lost. I'm tired, I'm very tired, was all she said. She spent her days half asleep but unable to reach a place of true rest.

She never told me what happened in Beijing. The most she said was on a night she woke screaming from sleep. I had not thought hers a human cry; in my own dreams a scaled bird had stuck its black neck out from the fleshy earth, waking into existence. When I went into her room her eyes were two wide lights in the dark.

That night, she spoke of a conversation she'd had with her husband, what I assumed was one of their last. It must be so terrible to see through everything, he had told her. She repeated his words to me in a fit of lucidity, nearly spitting:

It must be so terrible to see through everything like you do. It's a form of blindness, you know. It gives you an excuse to do nothing while feeling superior, when really it's just selfish, which is another way of saying stupid, lazy, everything you say you hate.

She turned the words over.

He's right, she said. He wasn't right then—I didn't see anything then—but now—now I see and it *is* terrible. I see skin and beneath it muscle and bone and organs, and beneath these, blood, water, mucus, filth. It is all so clear that I feel as if I can reach inside and wrap my hand around a vein, and it is all so, so ugly.

A bolt of terror seized her and she became frantic.

What if I never want to look again? she said. What if I turn away and close my eyes for the rest of my life?

The next day she asked me to bring her a pen and paper, and wrote very quickly, her words running into each other until they filled the page. This was not the neat, controlled script that I had once seen in her notebooks, describing the behavior of those particles she studied. This handwriting was wild; the only words I could decipher were *dear friend* at the top of the page. She folded the letter and sealed it. The envelope was addressed to Beijing, to someone I didn't know. A former classmate, she explained, someone she hadn't spoken to in a long time, but who would do anything for her. She said this very confidently: *He would do anything for me.* She asked me to post the letter.

Two weeks later, she received a response. She opened the envelope, read, and for the first time since returning, began to weep.

After the letter Su Lan reverted to a near-mechanical state, becoming a collection of human components that did not quite add up to a person. She was neither happy nor sad. She was simply an observer— less than an observer. An observer with no stake but sight, who had lost her ability to care. I tried to engage her with small talk, with little stories I'd heard here and there, even with questions about the nature of things, hoping to startle her into scientific interest. It didn't work. If she responded her answers were dispassionate, even mocking, so that when she spoke of gravity or refraction or the laws of motion she seemed to be saying underneath her words that the entire enterprise of knowledge was ridiculous. Often she simply ignored the question and said: It is better not to know, it is better to be innocent. Once I read to her a mathematics puzzle I'd found in the newspaper, a silly little problem involving marbles and a scale that seemed simple but had me thinking in circles for days without finding a solution. She listened, head cocked to one side, and said, The answer is nonsense and death. Nonsense and death until death. Then laughed, and brought her hand to her mouth.

She had lost her instinct for science. I think this was more devastating than losing her husband. Without that desire to see through everything, she did not know who she was.

It was only after she pushed everything present (including you) to one side and prepared to return to work that the spark of life returned. Time happened, I suppose. One day, two or three months after the event, she came to my room and asked what type of scale it was in that marble problem I'd found in the newspaper, the kind they use at the vegetable market, with a weight tied to one end, or a two-sided balance, like the scales of justice. Scales of justice, I said. She thought for a moment, then began to solve the puzzle out loud. The solution was quite involved (later I would not be able to re-create it), but as she presented it I followed each step with perfect clarity and ease. She asked if I could watch you for a few hours and I agreed. Soon after that I began to see her sitting at her desk, bent over the physics publications that had piled up and gathered dust, and soon after that, she returned to the university.

Her eyes were no longer dull, her cheeks flushed in the heat. Urgency returned to her voice when she spoke of her research, and she was invested again in the pursuit of scientific truth. But something had changed. She was too invested. Whereas before she approached physics with a sense of delight and play—an innocence, as she might say—now she was severe, serious. She worked as if driven by a force outside herself, as if her life, or its vindication, depended on it. She frightened me.

WATCHING YOU WAS boring. You slept, ate, peed, pooped. While your mother taught classes and attended meetings at the university,

I fed and cleaned you. When you were awake, despite the fact that you could not do much, you required a minimum modicum of attention, entertainment of some form or another so you did not start wailing, observance so you did not roll off the bed or otherwise harm yourself. I had not cared for a child before. The most similar thing I'd done was care for my husband in the years before he died, bedridden and also in need of feeding and cleaning.

It is remarkable that you don't remember me at all. For nearly two years, keeping you alive and placated occupied most of my days.

I remember the golden yellow stink of your waste. I remember Su Lan bent over a metal tub in the mornings, squeezing the milk from her breasts before putting on her makeup and gathering her papers. I remember winter afternoons, in that season when the sun set before you expected it to, bringing with early darkness a sense of malaise and doom, when you nuzzled your head into my armpit and I felt for a moment that caring for you was not like caring for a dying man after all. That it was a comforting feeling to hold something so small and so alive.

But I could not be perpetually charmed by your helplessness. I didn't need to think hard to take care of you, but you still demanded a kind of attention that drowned out all my thoughts. The work was tedious and unrewarding. At the end of the day, my arms and back and thighs ached, my head was dull and exhausted. At night I slept like a rock.

Around midday I took you on a walk around the neighborhood. This was the easiest way to quiet you for a nap. My uneven gait produced a rocking motion that without fail put you to sleep. Often on these walks neighbors would approach me to look at you. They commented on your looks or size, asking how old you were, if you cried a lot, if you ate and slept well, eventually winding to a comment about how they hadn't seen your father around in some time.

The brazen ones leaned in and said with false commiseration: What a shame, for that woman to enlist the services of a cripple.

It was in these moments that I understood I would do whatever your mother required. No matter that we were no one to each other. No matter that I was not a natural caretaker, did not particularly like children, and had a bad hip. You see, there was a delight in the neighbors' gossip that made me want to hurl my cane through a window. They did not try to hide it. The ones who had been friendliest and most welcoming when Su Lan and her husband first moved to the longtang, looking like youth and wealth, now kept the farthest distance, addressing Lan only with formalities, disappearing quickly, whispering cheap falsities among themselves while she was gone. The younger women shot her openly dirty looks and pulled their men close. Worn as she had been by pregnancy and all that followed, Su Lan was still beautiful. And after she returned to the university she began to dress beautifully again as well, wearing the fashionable clothes and bold lipstick and bright earrings (hardly any women in those days would even consider piercing holes into their ears) that had once spurred the other women to praise her elegance and style, and now gave them a reason to call her whore. In the neighborhood, a beautiful, confident woman without a husband was a dangerous, hungry beast.

If they had known her at all, they would have seen that Su Lan had eyes for no human. She was not interested in her beauty. In fact she did not think herself particularly attractive, and believed her features to be small and inoffensive, nothing remarkable on their own. Rather, she felt the strength of her face was its neutrality; like the white walls of her room, it functioned as a blank palette that was enhanced (rather than made garish) by makeup and jewelry. In this way she conceived of her beauty, like her other attributes, not as an inherent or inherited quality, but rather as another aspect of her self-invention, the hard-earned result of her own work and will. At times I wondered if she thought of herself as two people: the one that moved through the world, and the one that created that other apparent self.

It was for the sake of her work that she made herself beautiful. It scares them, she told me once, poking earrings through her lobes. By them she meant the other physicists in her department, who were mostly men. She had introduced herself at enough institutions, research groups, and conferences to see how her appearance affected her colleagues. It started with surprised confusion—initially she was asked, addressed as xiaojie, what she was looking for, if she was lost. Then came shock and dismissal. She didn't mind being underestimated. It was a satisfying feeling to prove someone wrong, to know that she would not be underestimated again. After she revealed her intellectual superiority, the result was a kind of terror. Physics professors are not comfortable around beautiful women, she said. She strapped on her high-heeled shoes. It was important to be as tall as the men, so she could make them look her in the eye.

Perhaps she heard what the neighbors were saying about her after she returned to Shanghai alone. Perhaps she didn't care. To break through the shock of those first months, she had wrapped herself so thoroughly in her physics that the little time she wasn't at the university was spent bent over her desk, cradling you in one arm and scribbling and erasing with the other, so focused she often didn't notice when you cried. She had started work on an ambitious project for her dissertation, the project that would eventually take her and you away from Shanghai, and which, I now believe, would hound her for the rest of her life. It had to do with the most fundamental laws of nature, and its question was one she had long pondered without the proper vocabulary, the kind of question she had pursued knowledge in order to know to ask.

HER SUBJECT WAS time. The arrow on the horizontal axis of a graph, pointing beyond the edge of the page, the little t found in nearly every fundamental equation describing the workings of the universe. And yet we barely understood it. Less than a century ago, physicists had believed in absolute time, some god-hand beating out the seconds as our three-dimensional world was pushed from past into present, present into future. Human nature was to blame for this error. We centered our experience too readily. For the same reason we'd once believed the stars revolved around the earth, we believed time to be static and irreversible.

What strange torture it was for Su Lan to be limited to a linear experience of time. Imagine being constricted in space, a cartoon drawn on a page. This was how Su Lan related to time: as a prisoner. She was determined to rewire her brain so it could comprehend—and eventually intuit—reality as it actually was. In this reality time was more complex than we could imagine; far from static, it might be bent and twisted and tied in knots. And during one of those nights when she stayed awake reading the physics journals that had piled up by her bed while she convalesced, a breakthrough came to her, a new way of conceiving the restriction of our temporal experience. This reconception, impossible and wild as it was, provided a small opening through which she glimpsed the beginning of a theory.

The reconception had to do with energy. Specifically, it had to do with the theoretical conditions under which the second law of thermodynamics might reverse.

According to the second law of thermodynamics, in a closed system disorder will always increase with time. This is also called entropy. When Su Lan taught this concept to first-year physics students at the university, she used the classic example of the partitioned box. The two sides of the box are filled with two inert gases, and there is a small hole in the partition. After enough time has passed, the random motion of molecules bouncing off the walls and each other will result in the two gases distributed evenly across the two parts of the box. The gases will be mixed so thoroughly it would take quite a bit of energy to separate them back into their original pure states. In other words, the box gains in entropy; to decrease its entropy requires work. To further illustrate the concept, she asked her class to imagine two bowls of water, one hot and one cold, which are then combined. Passing your hand through the water, you wouldn't expect half to be cold and half hot; rather, it would all be warm. In both scenarios, it would be impossible to imagine the reverse sequence occurring. Nothing starts in disorder and moves without intervention to order.

Su Lan argued that the second law of thermodynamics was why we experienced time at all. While the rotations of the earth around the sun constituted our relative measurement of time, the tendency of the universe toward disorder was what created our experience of irreversible events. Irreversibility in turn created the feeling of moving in one direction versus another—that is, the experience of moving through time. The second law of thermodynamics re-sounded so strongly with human intuition that many physicists believed it to be the most fundamental of fundamental laws.

Did Su Lan believe there existed a place where the laws of physics would not hold? Not exactly. She believed it might be useful to theorize the physical consequences. To articulate the strange relationship between entropy and time, she would develop both a physical and a mathematical theory for what might happen under the circumstance of reversal. That's what she told her colleagues at least. In private her imagination ran wilder. Imagine if you could manufacture conditions under which the universe tends not toward disorder but toward order—she said to me once—you could watch time run backward.

One morning she'd found a student sleeping in her class, and to wake him, grabbed a glass of water off her lectern and threw it down. Wet shards sprayed across the floor and the sleeping student sat up with a jolt, tucking his feet beneath his desk. Explain to the class, she said to the student, how you would put the water back inside the cup.

For the rest of the term she hung this impossible problem over her class.

The answer, of course, lay in the idea of entropy. Only by reversing the second law of thermodynamics could we expect the glass to come back together and the water to fly back into the cup. Of course this was physically impossible.

Or nearly impossible. Su Lan corrected herself: actually, it was only extremely improbable. When you considered the question of why the second law of thermodynamics existed at all, the answer was simple: probability. It will always be more probable, given a set of heterogeneous components, for the components to arrange themselves in a disorderly way. In the case of the broken glass, there was only one way for the pieces to fit together in the original glass, and near-infinite ways for them to lie in a disorderly heap. What people forgot was that probability had nothing to do with possibility.

So you're building a time machine, I ventured.

She laughed: That sounds too exciting.

She began to speak then of human memory, calling it *the mind's arrow of time.* In her thought experiment, under the reversal of the second law, the thermodynamic arrow of time would run backward, toward order instead of disorder. The mind's arrow should run parallel to it, so instead of remembering what had already occurred, we would be able to predict what was about to occur. The cost of seeing into the future, however, was that we would lose our memory of the past, and with it, any explanation of how we arrived at our present state.

Again she used the example of the glass of water, the scenario in which the broken glass comes together and the water flies back inside. If this were to happen, while the glass was still broken we would be able to remember it becoming whole, but once the glass was whole we would forget that it had ever been broken. Though the mind now remembers the future, order is in the future now, and disorder in the past. It's so strange, she said, that even when you turn the laws of physics on their heads, we're still blind in the direction of chaos.

Perhaps Su Lan would cringe at my understanding of her work. Perhaps she'd say that physicists defined things differently from you and I, that a thought experiment was just that, meant to manipulate the mind into thinking differently. She might shake her head and laugh, dismissing her ideas as wordplay and mind games. But I saw their grip over her, and wondered what the project really meant for Su Lan—what exactly it was that had made her so desperately want to remember the future and forget the past.

SHE BEGAN TO study for the TOEFL, the English exam required for admission to American universities. She never said explicitly that she was aiming to go abroad. But as your cries and murmurs turned to strings of syllables and then to words, your mother was also forming her mouth around new sounds. She practiced at every opportunity. On the weekends she held you on her lap and sat on the terrace, and the two of you spewed nonsense noises at each other, each staring intently at the other's face with bewildered eyes.

Human language was not among Su Lan's talents. She had asked me once to teach her to speak Shanghainese like a local, and it was immediately apparent that her instinct for mathematics worked against her ability to master language. The patterns in language were not perfect and consistent like the patterns in numbers, in fact nearly all the time they were false patterns, breaking down just when you needed them most. Language was messy, unpredictable, inelegant: in other words, too human. It was this human logic that seemed to elude her. Solving a mathematics problem, she said, was like entering a room filled with clear light: the air is crisp and fresh, the mind is free. On the other hand, trying to say something—trying to say exactly what you mean—was a foray into darkness, where your fears and failures hid—a foray into hell.

So she resorted to rote memorization and repetition, and her memory was much weaker than her intuition. You could tell it pained her to know there existed some deep current of linguistic understanding she could not access.

Su Lan had always spoken with a strange accent, so much so that I could not place her—even now I don't know where exactly she was from. Initially I'd believed this was intentional, part of her effort to present herself a certain way. After I watched her struggle with Shanghainese, then English, I wondered if it was actually her failure to properly learn Mandarin.

By then you had entered your most charming and pretty phase. You'd grown a full thick head of hair and your singled eyelids had doubled. You sat up on your own and looked around, blinking, making little o's with your mouth, opening and closing your chubby hands. For a long time you had not had proper clothes. It was easier to wrap you in diapers and blankets or keep you naked during the hot days. But after returning to the university Su Lan purchased a handful of nice baby outfits, tiny shirts and dresses that she fitted over your head with care. Sometimes she took you to work with her, and on these days she dressed you as meticulously as she did herself, once even dabbing a dot of rouge on your lips. I think she was using you as a kind of prop, similar to her high-heeled shoes, a way of forcing her colleagues to contend directly with that for which they might judge her. I imagined her striding into a laboratory full of balding men in glasses, with silent smiling you staring over her shoulder, and that hard look in her eyes, a fearsome and impressive sight. With me you fussed and cried and grabbed whatever you liked, ignoring my scolds with a stubborn willfulness that astonished me. But with her you were perfect and obedient, as if you knew your role in her game. Even then you had developed an instinct to please her.

It was spring, nearly two years after Beijing. Su Lan checked the mail often. The other time I had seen a similar impatience, she had been waiting for the letter from her university friend; I assumed she had written that person again. Now you could stand up and carry your body across the room. You called me po-po and gleefully mimicked the sounds of cats and dogs. When Su Lan finally received the letter she was waiting for, she ran up the stairs and went into her room without stopping at mine to collect you. Later she came in and announced that she had gotten what she had been working for. She would be going to America to complete her PhD. She had passed the TOEFL, just barely, and she had been granted a fellowship to work with an American professor who had visited Fudan the previous year and was impressed by her work. She would be leaving in a couple of months and did not know how long exactly she'd be gone. She picked you up and asked me to look after the room while she was away. This was her first home, she said, the first home she chose, and she did not want to lose it. I saw a flash of fear.

Besides, she continued, it was possible that her husband would return—the room was his too, after all. It was the first time she had mentioned her husband since Beijing. Months later, when I went into the room to air and dust after you'd gone, I saw that she had left his clothes hanging in the closet, his shoes arranged neatly beneath them. On the back of the door was his doctor's coat and stethoscope.

She handed me a key and took you away.

THE LAST REAL conversation I had with your mother took place the night before she left for America. In the three years she'd lived here, she had somehow accumulated many things, and so she spent her final week in Shanghai packing what she could into two suitcases and tossing or storing the rest. After she finished the room was immaculate, with books and bedding and clothes perfectly organized on shelves, in trunks, shut behind wardrobe doors, the kind of order that could never have persisted amid life ongoing. She buckled her suitcases and pulled them upright. When I came in she was sitting in the middle of the room with you, looking at the white walls, which now gleamed again as if new. We sat there for a long time without speaking. In the silence I felt all we knew and did not know about each other. How strange time was indeed, this human time, how it could bind people, pull you away from yourself. There was too much to say so I said nothing. I could feel that Su Lan had more to tell. She bobbed you on her lap and stared at the wall behind my head.

When she finally spoke, she did so compulsively, without interruption, the words pulled from her throat.

I have always had a talent for leaving, she said. I began to cultivate this talent when I was very young, barely old enough to dream. Most of all I wanted to leave my mother. Leaving her, I thought, I might finally leave myself.

I know you think of me as this bright, talented person, a person who will no doubt become something. I think you're wrong. I'm ambitious, yes, that much is true. But my ambition runs backward, not toward anything but away. In fact, whenever I've tried to become something, I've failed, because I've only really ever managed to care about what I'm not.

I left my childhood home early, when I was still a child, and then I left the place I left for, and then that place too. In secondary school and university I would return home for the new year, because that's what everyone did. Eventually I stopped going back. For years I haven't seen my mother, I don't even know if she's alive or dead. And yet, she's still here, her spirit, her ghost, she follows me wherever I go, even into my mind and thoughts. I think I am alone, and then the room fills with shadows: my mother, my waipo, my tai-waipo—I can see her limp body, calling out from her deathbed. My father too, sometimes, and other men I know only from names carved on stones. They all watch me, closely, waiting to laugh in my face.

Sometimes I ask myself why I am going to America. Isn't there more for me here, where I already know the rules? Isn't Shanghai big enough, rich enough, new enough?

But my mind trips on itself, repeats, comes up again and again with different versions of the same story. It orders the space around me—which should be new and dynamic, full of its own patterns and pains—with outlines of everything I need to forget, so that no matter how far I have come, how old I've grown, I am stuck in a reel of the same irrationalities and insecurities that plagued the first decade of my life. Even my husband—I see them taking him, in order to drag me back. I am leaving, again, to populate my world with unfamiliar, indifferent ghosts.

Su Lan looked down at the patch of white floor between her legs. She had never before spoken of her childhood or of her family, not even in this vague way. I realized that in all the time I had taken care of you, I had implicitly accepted that you had no blood grandmother, no blood aunts or uncles, just as I'd accepted you would have no father, and I saw again your mother on the day we met, standing in the center of the totally white room. Despite all her talk of time, I had accepted her as she presented herself, as a person without a past. What had she seen in the paint that day, where I had seen an expanding emptiness?

I said goodbye and goodnight. Her eyes were far away, imagining the white walls of her future. In my own room I took the key she had given me out of the drawer and threaded it onto my own chain. I understood she would be gone for a long time.

FOR MANY YEARS after your mother left I thought about what she'd said that night. You see, I had come to see her as a sort of authority, whether I realized it or not. Perhaps it had to do with her education and the relentlessness with which she pursued it: you could trust her not to say anything unless she had investigated it thoroughly. She was a generation younger than I, yes, and there were times when the foolishness of that youth was too apparent, when I could see that in fact she was still coming of age—nevertheless I felt a deference to her that I've never been able to summon for my elders. I was reluctant to touch whatever it was that was growing inside of her for fear of altering it.

Su Lan had spoken of ghosts, familiar and unfamiliar, of seeing things that were not exactly there. How jarring it was, to hear a science-educated, reality-minded woman like her speak of such things, and with such nonchalance. She did not present these fantasies as unbelievable or surprising but rather as mundane phenomena, as ordinary as this chair or that broom.

She had spoken, I realized, with the same casual certainty as my mother. Uneducated and intensely religious, my mother lived in a world inhabited not just by humans and their depravity but by all-powerful beings and their invisible notions of good and evil. Throughout my childhood she enforced this world on me with great tenacity and skill. Despite her efforts she failed to convince me—from a young age I had considered myself science-educated and reality-minded too.

I had assumed Su Lan would have taken my side, knowing as she did the scientific explanations for all manner of seemingly inexplicable things. I wondered then if perhaps it was not a matter of education at all; perhaps people were born with pious or wicked dispositions—my brother too, despite his literacy, had been like my mother. Both were the kind of people who liked to be praised, and especially liked to be praised for doing well what they were told to do. They took pride in being seen as good and kind and self-sacrificial. Did Su Lan have a small measure of that desire to be good too?

I, on the other hand, am wicked. There is no instinct in me to please. Even after things changed, during those years Su Lan and you were in America, when I entered voluntarily into that world of spirits and ghosts and became a woman like my mother, who burned incense at her altar every day, I believed it was the wicked person inside me, acting against my own disposition toward disbelief.

IT STARTED WITH Tao Kun's ashes. For as long as my husband was dead I had kept him under the bed next to old quilts and my red wedding shoes. I thought of his remains only as what they were: bits of significant dirt. Now a presence made itself felt there. It was physical—it pressed against my back as I slept, not like a hand or a push but a simple light upward force. If Su Lan had still been here, she might have described it as gravity, applied in the opposite direction. It was enough to arch my back in discomfort and toss me in my sleep. The next morning I pulled out the ashes and placed them on the table next to the window. A film of dust covered the box. Particles moved in the light and came to life. I wiped it with a damp cloth. That night I slept soundly.

But Tao Kun looked lonely on the table. So I searched in my trunks and drawers for things to keep him company: a marble bust of Mao he'd once been awarded by the neighborhood committee; my mother's Guanyin statuette, which we had kept hidden for her during the Cultural Revolution; and Tao Kun's flute. The flute was made of bamboo and had a little crack at its lip from years of sitting in the trunk. I picked it up and felt its weight. My fingers slipped over the grooves over which his hands had moved, on summer evenings when the neighbors played mahjong in the alley and he stood by the door like a sentinel, feeling for a tune. I put Guanyin and Mao next to Tao Kun's ashes and laid his flute in front. Behind his ashes I propped up a black-and-white portrait of him at thirty, a photograph he had taken for me. He'd had no use for photographs, he'd been blind. In the portrait, he looked surprised, as if he had just turned his head toward an unexpected sound.

Slowly, I found myself gathering more gods for the altar. In the alley stacks of old cardboard boxes leaned against a crumbling wall, so I took one and cut four plaques out of it, and, wetting my stiff brushes, wrote on the plaques in my best script the names of my and Tao's deceased parents. From the wall of an abandoned room I peeled a poster of the five revolutionary heroes and pasted it to my own wall with pinches of mushed rice. I cut out pictures of past and current presidents from newspapers and magazines, Deng Xiaoping and Jiang Zemin, then Hu Jintao and a handsome black man the newspapers said might become America's next president, and glued them on frames of cardboard. In the alleyway dump I spotted a small painting of the white man's pusa, a woman in pink and blue robes holding a yellow-haired baby with a golden crown, and a perfectly intact plastic figure of the monkey king. All these items joined Tao Kun and kept him company. They kept me company too. There was a strange pleasure in the work of this accumulation. I still did not believe in spirits or ghosts or pusas or gods, but what was the harm in pretending, just in case I was wrong? If it turned out that my mother and Su Lan were right, if gods were indeed real, then a wicked old woman like me needed as many as I could get.

WHILE I ASSEMBLED my altar, the neighborhood changed. The living fled (your mother's departure had marked a beginning); the dead returned.

I remember the year 2000. It seemed such a large number, much larger than one plus 1999. Even now it seems larger than the numbers that came after. How inappropriate my continued existence felt, in this year with so many zeros. The future had been thrown backward, trapping me in a place I did not understand. I hoped I would die soon.

The red shells of New Year's firecrackers were swept from the alley. That same week, large posters appeared on the walls of the longtang, and people gathered before them, talking and craning their heads over each other to read, as they had in the months before your father disappeared. This again, I thought, and paid them no mind.

But there were no ensuing protests or marches. Instead the long-tang quieted. The neighborhood began to empty. The clutter lining the alleys accumulated a layer of dust, and I saw that it was mostly piles of junk. The clotheslines no longer sagged with clothes, clods of exposed electrical wire hung unconnected and dangling, dusty windows flapped open in the sun. Where had the people gone, the ahyis with bags of groceries, the children racing up and down the block, the men coming home from work, all those people I had had to jostle around just to go to the market or the latrine? It seemed that even the stray dogs had wandered away to neighborhoods with fresher garbage.

On the outer wall of my building was painted a single red word: 拆 (chai)—to tear down, to take apart.

The word had a red circle around it, with a line slashing across its middle.

The 拆s were painted up and down the longtang. Windows and doors were boarded up. Three rows down, near the southern entrance to the neighborhood, one building had already been reduced to a gap of rubble in the row of houses. In the pile of splintered wood and bricks, partially buried in crumbled cement, were items left over from lives: a pair of pants, a hanger, torn pages of magazines, smashed bowls, broken brooms, and mops. I picked out a fat-bellied buddha and dusted his face with my sleeve. I brought him back to my room and lit three sticks of incense. My window fogged with smoke.

I SANK INTO a way of living in which forgetting and remembering tumbled around each other, floating me in their midst. I abandoned a linear relationship with time—I forgot about the 拆. Days passed quickly and slowly at once. One got comfortable on a stool, and then it took a long time to convince the body to move. An hour disappeared considering whether to open a curtain. If the curtain was opened, it was possible that sunlight would expose how the window needed to be wiped, which then required finding a rag, wringing it out, rubbing it over the glass. After which other things in the room (the stool, the window frame, the bed, the table gods) might look dull compared to the newly brightened window, or dirty in the light now barreling in, and have to be wiped clean too. Sometimes the stomach rumbled and food had to be made, which meant deciding what food to make, as well as buying, cleaning, and preparing the food, then storing and cleaning the remainders. Relieving oneself too required time, as well as washing the chamber pot, though there were no more lines at the latrines or sinks. After all that, I wanted nothing more than to sit peacefully on the landing and just be.

One day, while I sat there doing just this, catching a cool morning breeze, Tao Kun came up the stairs. It was summer. He was wearing his white undershirt and plaid boxer shorts. With one hand pressed on the dark wall, he tapped his fingers lightly, as if feeling for the rot that had softened the wood in the years he had been away. His face was quiet with concentration. He was counting the stairs.

I understood that he was a memory, but as the memory walked by me and passed through the door, I felt a brush of air. The memory walked around the room, it touched the furniture and opened the cabinets. I heard the chafing of shoes on wood and the sigh of skin over cloth. For a long time Tao Kun stood in front of the altar, facing his photograph, and I could feel his amusement, not just about my new habits but because besides this table, everything was in the same place as it had been when he was alive. Even his sunglasses case still lay half open on the covered massage table; a small critter had crawled inside to die. What a kind sight it was, Tao Kun feeling his way through our home. For a long time I hadn't known why I'd acted in the ways I had; I understood now it had been for this.

He stayed in the room all day. In the evening I stood to enter. I did not try to speak to him. When I went to sleep I made room for him on the bed and heard it creak as he lay down. The next morning I knew before opening my eyes that he had gone.

I lit incense and dusted his portrait. I pulled my stool to the landing and waited for him to return.

Waiting became a ritual. Halfway through the morning his hand appeared on the railing and his body came up the stairs. I left the room to him during the days, sitting outside as I had when he'd run a private practice in our room, and I'd managed the books on the landing. We went to sleep together and sometime in the night he disappeared down the stairs. I slept deeply, not wanting to catch him leaving. I didn't bother with wondering what he was. I didn't think of him as the first ghost until the others came.

SOME OF THE ghosts were alive, living human beings. But despite being alive, they were intent on making the longtang into a place for the dead; everywhere they went they brought with them destruction and death, death that came in the form of hammers, shovels, and money.

One of these ghosts came to my door after the 拆 circles appeared. He wore a polo shirt tucked into nice pants and had his hair slicked back. He waved a piece of paper in front of my face and read it to me; it said I would be given 100,000 renminbi and a new apartment in Pudong if I vacated my room. I took the paper from him, confirmed that he had read what was written, then tore it into two. He gave me pamphlets decorated with photographs of tall buildings that resembled the new ones being built around the neighborhood, which cast the longtang increasingly into shade. He said the 拆 was happening, demolition was inevitable, terms would be best for those who left early, voluntarily.

I told him I could not. He was the first ghost of this kind to visit, and so I explained myself with patience: My husband had returned, and this was the only home he'd known. He was blind and he was dead, so it didn't matter how big or pretty the new apartment would be, in fact the larger and more beautiful it was, the more impossible it would be to teach the ghost of a blind man how to get around. Even if I found a solution to this obstacle, how would I inform him of where the new home was?

When the government ghost returned he was bigger and meaner, with broad shoulders and a stone face. He stood over me with an enormous hammer in his hand, ready to strike down the walls the moment I gave a sign of assent. He said vaguely that it would be better if I signed; I saw then on the paper he held that the number had gone up; now I would be given 150,000 renminbi. Shame on you, I said, threatening your grandmother. I hit his shins with my cane until he went away.

The bully ghost left me alone but he returned to the neighborhood, bringing with him noise and dust and taking in return whole sections of the building: a wall, a room, an entire floor. In this way the building was amputated to its present state, where only my room and your mother's remain, standing parceled and whole in the wrecked shell of the house.

The next government ghost took the form of an ahyi who had lived nearby. She brought a plate of red bean cakes and spoke with syrup on her tongue. She took my elbow and said, Nainai, 200,000 renminbi is a lot of money. She spoke exaltingly about the shiny new house she had moved into: it had a bathtub, a toilet, a washing machine, a new kitchen with an electric stove. I sent her away disappointed.

That evening I discovered my light would not turn on. I lit a candle and climbed down the stairs. The kitchen lights were out too; the electric rice cooker Su Lan had left for me did not heat up.

In the alley I looked up and saw a ring of lighted skyscrapers around the dark emptiness of the neighborhood. So the electricity had been cut; I understood it was meant to drive me out.

I walked through the hollow rooms. They lit up around me as I walked, each step revealing spaces that for years I'd only presumed existed behind curtains and doors. The ground was covered in dust and little chunks of rubble, small and large splints of wood. Enclosed by shadow, I felt I was not only traversing a foreign terrain but creating it with my light. Su Lan had told me once that light did not age. Light could travel only through space, she said, not time, and if we could travel as fast as light, time would cease to exist for us too. She went on to speak of a particle she had imagined—only imagined, for she had no proof—a corollary particle to the photon, one that was the opposite of light: dark. This darkness particle, as she called it, would be stationary, frozen, lacking the ability to travel through space, and so lacking almost all physical capability, except that it could move through time.

Soon I covered the entire space of the first floor. How small this building was, even in the dark, now that all the walls were on the floor.

Every time the ghosts came, they knocked too on Su Lan's door. When no one answered they slipped the same notices and pamphlets beneath that they had given to me. A few times I tried to shout them away, and they smiled at me knowingly before leaving.

I went back to my room and lit incense. I prayed for Su Lan's return.

IT WAS IN this environment that you appeared to inform me: Su Lan was dead.

YONGZONG

MIDDAY, WHEN WE LAY IN the hot sleep of noon, my father stalked the house with a flyswatter. *Splat. Splat.* Little corpses dropped to the ground. I pressed my ear against the bamboo mat and listened for the sound of crushed wings. I heard—

My father's foot crashing down.

My father creeping steadily across the room, flyswatter up and alert, his shuffling broken by another *splat*.

My father had good reason. The house was big and pristine. The walls were painted white, the floors tiled. The windows were lined with glass to keep dust outside. Who else had a house like this?

In the mornings while my mother boiled porridge for breakfast, my father ran a damp cloth over each piece of furniture. His ragged finger penetrated every groove—he kept even the carved designs on the backs of the chairs dust-free. He had worked hard to earn and keep all this, he reminded us. He took nothing for granted.

For my father, I was another one of these things—the house, the furniture, the glass windows—to be kept fly-free.

I didn't understand this until I was much older. As a boy all I knew was that at times I envied my two older sisters. My envy confused me. I had no chores. I picked the best pieces of meat at meals. If I even got a cough, my mother and grandmother pampered me with attention. Why was I so unhappy, to be so loved?

My father threw out the dead flies before I could look at them.

A bamboo mat rustling under my ear, a broom bristling against a smooth floor—to this day, these sounds will lull me to sleep.

A FATHER LOOKS at his grown son and cannot understand how that man, now bigger than he, was once an infant. Not only *was once* but *is still*—that the man is the *same person* as the infant. So I am with myself, unable to recognize who I was. It is not only that my body has changed. Each time I stop to take measure, I feel not as if I have grown, but as if I have left behind many corpses of former selves.

Today I am 1.79 meters, with bony broad shoulders and long legs. I am thin. No one would call me muscular, but my muscles do their job, and their movement over the years has etched a certain shape into my skin. My skin, pale and hairless, has just begun to sag. My bones are stiffer in their joints. My hair is full and thick but peppered with white.

Bodies I have shed: plump white babe; sturdy toddler with a square face and rosy cheeks; runtish boy, his body smaller than he felt; gangly teenager with legs that shot up daily and a torso that could not keep up; tall young man with long legs and a full frame, sprightly, not chubby, but with meat on his bones. This middle-aged body, rougher, weaker, beginning to shrink. I shed my bodies for something uglier each time.

I shed their memories too. The meat of them. So when I read the bones of my past, I feel as if plunged into a terrifying book, identifying too well with a story about someone else.

Picture the sturdy toddler. He was just tall enough to see into the bowls of old yellow wine his grandfather left around the house. It makes the flies sluggish, his grandfather said, easier for your father to kill. The toddler's father waved him over and drew on a corner of old newspaper the molecular form of ethyl acetate: four carbons, two oxygens, the triangular plane formed by the double bond, followed by the ethyl tail. If the flies were trapped in a glass with a spoon of wine, his father said, the air would fill with this, and the flies would choke and die.

It was summer in Hangzhou. In the evenings after dinner I walked to West Lake with my big sisters to watch old men play chess and tourists drink lüdotang on the banks. If we were lucky, Mother gave us a penny and a handful of raw rice for the baomi man to pop. On one such evening, walking home from Xihu and eating from Dajie's bag of popped rice, we found the road ahead lit with pinprick yellow lights. The sky was purple and it looked as if the stars had fallen down.

Fireflies! Dajie cried.

I stood still and listened for the buzz of flight. The lights drifted around me, blinking on and off in the branches of the peach trees lining the sides of the road.

Dajie and Xiaojie poured the popped rice into their mouths. They danced around chasing fireflies with the empty paper bag until finally Dajie raised her hand, triumphant. The bag glowed, a lantern.

We ran home. Xiaojie sneaked a glass jar from the kitchen and we dropped the captive inside. We huddled around it in the corner of the garden. Dajie covered the top of the jar with paper and poked holes in the paper with a needle. I took the jar in my hands and was surprised to find the glass cold. The firefly was still emitting bursts of yellow light. Our father called, and Xiaojie tucked the jar behind a potted orange tree before we ran inside. At the door I stopped and turned. A weak light pulsed against the ceramic base of the pot.

The next day after lunch when everyone was asleep, I went to the garden to check on our firefly.

At first I thought it had disappeared. In the dark I had imagined it as a floating flame with wings, and I saw no such thing. Instead, a black beetle sat motionless at the bottom of the jar. I wondered if the firefly had burned up and died. I shook the jar and the beetle slid to the side. I tapped the glass. Suddenly it flew up, crashing into the paper, wings whirring. I tucked the jar between my knees and, cupping my hands to shield the light, looked inside.

Yes, it was glowing!

The bug was ugly. It had a long, sectioned body and black wings folded over its back, two curling antennas, and three sets of thin crunchy legs. The bottom half of its hard body glowed faintly. The picture of hundreds of these bugs flying around me replaced the picture of walking through stars. Suddenly I felt sick.

I went inside for one of my grandfather's bowls of old wine and brought it to the garden. I dug my finger into an airhole and widened it. In a swift movement I poured all the wine into the jar, until the insect was drowning.

The firefly's legs twitched and flailed madly. Its wings opened and closed. Its body spun in circles, curling and uncurling. It writhed for a very long time. Then all movement stopped, and it hung stiff and suspended in yellow liquid.

I poured the wine onto the earth and picked up the dead bug. I peeled its wings, layer by layer. I pulled off each leg. I pinched off the head. Finally I squeezed the juice out of the bottom, where the glow had been. White pus oozed onto my fingers.

I buried the evidence in the dirt. I covered the jar with a new paper, punctured new holes, and left it behind the orange tree. When my sisters returned in the evening to retrieve their glowing pet, I didn't say a word.

I HAVE NEVER thought of myself as cruel. Most of the time I think I must be ordinary. When I was younger, the prospect of being ordinary tormented me, but now it is comforting, almost a relief, like the first breath of warm air in the spring.

Yes, I am ordinary! I lay out the facts of my life and there is no other word for it. I have been married to my ordinary wife for ten years. Five days a week I go to an ordinary job translating foreign books at an ordinary office. The books I translate are ordinary too, neither trash nor great works of literature, detective stories and mystery plots that ordinary people read to escape from their ordinary lives. I collect my salary and return home. My home too is ordinary: a two-bedroom flat in a six-story loufang. It could be anywhere in Beijing.

I have one child, a six-year-old daughter who has just started school. She is thin and shy; she has a boyish haircut and thick glasses. Most days, she wears her school uniform: teal pants and zipped jacket, with a white polo shirt underneath. She wears the uniform happily; she is carefree and unselfconscious. On the weekends when my daughter may wear whatever she likes she pulls on shorts and a T-shirt, whatever is easiest to reach in the trunk of clothes her mother has filled, though she refuses to wear anything with flowers or frills. Prints of cartoon animals she tolerates. She pulls on her clothes without thinking about them, rinses out her mouth, splashes water on her face, and comes into the living room full of contentment and ease. Every day I am amazed by her peace with the world. I watch her anxiously as she grows, afraid that she will lose it.

She inherited these qualities from my wife, who is a practical woman. Practical and perfectly competent, my wife is everything I need and as much as I can stand, the kind of woman who makes me content in my ordinary life because she is so content in hers. She does not goad me to be anything more than I am: that is the beauty of her practicality. She is organized and efficient, an accountant; her clients' lives settle neatly like her own. She wakes every morning at six to turn on the washer, boil six eggs (two for each of us), put out slices of sausage and bread, hang up the washed clothes on the balcony to dry, and shepherd us through breakfast before striding out the door with her smart work bag in hand. After work she swings by the market for vegetables and meat. I clean up after meals, but there is not very much to do. When my wife cooks, she cleans as she goes along. Every moment of the day she is doing three things at once. This is how she likes it. If I try to do any more housework than I've been assigned she hovers over me, wringing her hands, impatient, and I know she is thinking how much better and faster she could do it. She is warm, but always efficiently so. There is nothing desperate in her kindness, nothing at all desperate in her energy. I cannot imagine my life without her.

But mathematically, that was most of my life, without her.

Who have I been? I am an ordinary man, but would my past, put down on paper, make me look cruel?

For a year I have woken to the gasping urgency of this question— for a year since the text of an old skin resurfaced, while I was browsing in the Wangfujing Bookstore after work.

I DO NOT often go to the bookstore. It is close to my office, but I must walk ten minutes in the opposite direction from home to get there. When I left the office I'd felt restless. The day was still bright— the winter was just beginning to let, for months it had been dark at this same hour—and I must have felt the possibility of it, must have wanted to use my legs, to feel the pumping of blood in my veins.

At the bookstore I scanned the shelves for something I had worked on. I took the escalator to the third floor and browsed in the foreign language section, flipping through titles in English. In the center display was a table of Harry Potter books. I considered getting one for my daughter, who would soon start to learn English in school. I picked it up and began to read.

I had sunk into the easy world of imaginative pleasure when I was struck by the feeling of eyes on my skin.

A man was staring at me. He stood two bookshelves away with the new Han Han book open in his hand, and he did not pretend to read. He was short and graying, with a substantial gut, rectangular glasses. He looked at me pointedly, his eyebrows furrowed in amusement, or was it confusion?

I'd seen him before. I thought he was some colleague of my wife's, or perhaps, another father from my daughter's school.

For a full minute we stood there with books open, staring at each other.

Then it struck me who he was.

I put down my book, turned, and walked to the escalator. Hearing steps behind me, I quickened my pace. I brushed past shoulders. A book flew from a pair of hands onto the floor. I stared ahead and plowed through. Behind me I could hear the man muttering *excuse me, excuse me*. Finally, as I ran out the front door into the brisk evening—now it was dark outside, the streetlamps lit and the fragrant smoke of food vendors thickening the air—I heard a shout.

Zong!

Zong, is that you?

I'm sure it's you, Yongzong!

I turned back.

It was him all right.

I gave him a look of utter bewilderment and stomped out into the dark.

HE WAS BO, Zhang Bo, big Bo from my high school class. He sat in the middle of the second row and farted during every test. We called him Bo Cai because his hair stuck up like a bushel of spinach. Now he was a middle-aged man, like me.

Bo wasn't a bully, but he could've been one. He was sturdy, solid, and he reminded me of the boys in xiaoxue I'd given my homework to copy so they wouldn't beat me up. He wasn't from Hangzhou but from some village in the mountains, where he'd grown up pushing plows and chopping firewood. He was a peasant boy and he looked it, brown and thick and brutish. And he had a personality that ran at you like a bull, charging into the classroom and commanding all attention. His steps seemed to shake the ground. His lowest decibel was a throaty shout.

From day one he was the king of the class, the one everyone saw and heard first. I wondered how he had gotten in. The Cultural Revolution was over, the high school had just reopened after ten years. The students in our class were supposed to be the brightest in the province.

During the first week we took preliminary tests in every subject. I knew what my father expected. Compared to most of the students, who had been recruited from all over Zhejiang, I had everything: the best primary schools in the city, an educated father who could tutor me, meat on the table and new clothes every year, and I never had to do anything in the house but study. I had come into the school with the highest entrance exam score in the entire class of new recruits.

I sat in the row behind Bo, one seat to the right, trying not to breathe in his warm farts, that sickly sweet smell I would later learn was from eating too many yams. I bent my head down and worked. I didn't let him distract me, not even when he turned in his test scroll a good fifteen minutes before time was up and sat back down in his seat, grinning like he'd won a prize. I had finished the test too, but had gone back to check over every problem, plugging my answers into the original equations to make sure they worked, redoing entire problems because even though I knew I was smart, I wasn't an arrogant jerk. I wouldn't let a careless mistake take me down.

The next morning a crowd gathered by the blackboard where the test results were posted. In the middle was Bo with his big head sticking up above the others, sitting on the teacher's desk and laughing with his mouth wide open. The other students stood around him, patting him on the back.

All the blood drained from my face. Bo saw me and looked over with a bemused grin. The other students stopped chatting and turned to stare.

You're Yongzong, right? he said.

I didn't respond.

Zong, comrade! Don't look so green.

He jumped off the desk and put his arm around my neck.

Hey, he said, grabbing my hand and raising it into the air, here's our Number One!

His followers cheered.

So I was Number One. Bo was Number Two. He'd scored just three points lower than me, and we were leagues ahead of everyone else. Number Three scored twelve points lower than Bo.

Bo might have been Number Two, but he was still king. He had the charisma, the big booming voice, the body that everyone feared. Because for some reason he respected me, we became friends. I was named class prefect, and the two of us ruled, I with the teacher's favor, he with the students' admiration.

Bo was the type of student who breezed through classes without trying. He did his homework in a flash and left it crumpled in the bottom of his backpack, or handed it around to other students to copy, never worrying about losing it or getting it smudged with greasy fingerprints. He lazed around campus, visiting people's dorms, playing cards and making jokes and kicking a soccer ball around the track. I never saw him study. Everything about him—his coarse looks, his bullish demeanor, his careless attitude—would have made anyone think he was dumb. But he was a genius. I studied furiously to maintain my position as Number One. I was terrified that one day Bo Cai would get it into his head to crack open a textbook and reveal to everyone how much smarter than me he really was. If that ever happened, I knew we could no longer be friends. Perhaps he knew it too.

THE SUMMER BEFORE our second high school year, I shot up like a sprout. I woke each morning taller than I had been the night before. White jagged lines appeared on the skin of my thighs, like a plastic bag pulled past its stretching point. One morning, as I got up to leave the breakfast table, I realized I was taller than my father.

For a moment my father and I stood frozen across the table from each other. My mother cleared away our bowls. From my new vantage, I could see that his hair was thinning. The smooth skin of his scalp glistened through sparse gray strands. I felt ashamed, as if I had taken something that was not mine. I slumped and looked down.

Stand up straight, boy! my father boomed.

He walked out of the room with the newspaper curled in his hand, swatted a fly on the counter, swept up the corpse in his fist, and threw it into the trash bin. I watched him, seeing for the first time what a small man he was.

Besides eating and sleeping, I studied. At the end of the next school year I would be taking the gaokao, the university entrance exam. My father made it clear to everyone in the house that I would not touch a broom or washcloth. I was to score high enough on the exam to attend Beijing University for civil engineering or physics, to prove my intellectual acumen. After graduating from Beida I would apply to be a party member and enter into public service, and rise through the ranks until I made Politburo and worked in Beijing.

My father was a mid-level city planner in the Hangzhou mayor's office. He had climbed to achieve this rank—he should have been proud, the son of a matchbox factory worker—but he continued to grovel in hopes of rising. Still, despite keeping his head low during the early years of the Cultural Revolution, despite the gifts and deference he gave his superiors, he remained stagnant.

In other words, he wanted me to achieve all he had not.

While I lived under his roof, my father's plan had been so much a part of the fabric of my existence that I could not question it. But living in the school dorms for a year had opened a door in my mind. That summer, as I listened to my father discuss my future as if I were a highly capable puppet, it occurred to me that, having worked so relentlessly to achieve my father's vision, I had also earned the right to deny it.

Perhaps a part of me never believed in my ability to be a politician. I was a follower by nature—if I ever did lead, it was by example, by adhering to the rules and succeeding by them. As class prefect I enforced the teacher's commands with diligence and gained respect through undeniable demonstrations of superiority. I thought about how naturally Bo Cai commanded attention. No one would say he was *trying* to lead. It was completely unselfconscious. He did not care about having followers, and so he got them.

The evening before my return to school my mother prepared a feast. Dajie, who now lived across town with her husband, came over to see me off. My uncle, aunt, and their two children were also invited. We pulled the kitchen table to the living room and brought out the round banquet top. I ate greedily, knowing that for six months I would have only cafeteria food. My father pushed the best plates of meat and fish toward me and poured beer into my bowl. He refilled it whenever it was empty.

I had drunk a little alcohol before, but never like this. My father was treating me like a man. Soon we were laughing and eating, talking over each other, finishing each other's sentences. I told anecdotes about school, about the dunces and the jokesters, about Bo Cai's exploits, all the while showing that I never let my arrogance get the better of me. Everyone serves Bo Cai, I said, and Bo Cai serves me. I drank a big gulp of beer and burped as I imagined a general in the army might. Good, my father said. His face was red with drink and he chuckled contentedly. He lifted up his bowl and waved it over the table.

Look, Yongzong, what a father provides for his son, he said. All with the hope that one day, his son will become a greater man than he.

My father nodded at his father and brother and took a drink.

Yes, that is every father's dream, for his son to surpass him.

I lifted my bowl and poured the remaining beer down my throat.

Ba, I said with a laugh, haven't I already surpassed you?

The table fell silent. My words rang in the room, my voice sounding louder than I'd intended. I looked across the table at my mother. She looked at her chopsticks. Dajie's husband, deep in conversation with my uncle, had stopped talking. Next to him, my grandfather continued to eat quietly, his eyes fixed on his bowl. For the first time, I noticed how his shrunken shoulders seemed always to curl inward, as if he were trying to make himself disappear.

My father set his empty bowl on the table and filled it to the brim. The beer gurgled and hissed. He poured it all into his mouth, his Adam's apple bobbing as he swallowed. He slammed the bowl on the table. He grasped my shoulder and turned me to face him. His eyes were red and sharp, boring into mine.

I made you, he said. Whoever you become, whatever big shot you turn out to be, you will always answer to me.

My mother cleared her throat. Dajie picked up a piece of meat and put it in her husband's bowl. Slowly, the meal resumed. My father laughed loudly with Dajie's husband about something I did not hear, my cousin whispered something in my grandfather's ear. Xiaojie went to the kitchen to cut some fruit, and my aunt followed to help.

I gulped down my rice, mouth dry as sand, and imagined standing up and striking my father dead.

WHEN I RETURNED to school I was the tallest in the class. Everyone had grown over the summer—suddenly we no longer looked like large children but like skinny, unsure adults—everyone but Bo. Bo was the same size. He still had a sturdy body, but now he stood a head shorter than me. Instead of getting bigger, he just looked more tired. From a certain angle, he almost looked like a comic book character, short and squat with a big square face. He'd grown into his adult body before the rest of us, and now we'd caught up.

Bo was no longer king—no one was king, we were too mature for that now. Of course he was still well liked. Perhaps because he now had to lift his head to look at me, I had the feeling he too saw me differently.

Or maybe it was that in the last year, I had come to see the Bo underneath Bo Cai. Bo woke at five thirty, a good hour before morning exercises, to jog laps around the track. Even in the winter he never missed a day. When I got to the exercise court at six thirty, pulling on my jacket and rubbing my eyes, moments after the wake-up call, he was always already there. He said that he was used to waking with the sun, but that didn't explain why he still rose early in the winter months, when it was dark even at breakfast. Often I overheard his dormmate joke about how Bo Cai didn't need to sleep like the rest of us mortals.

During breaks Bo Cai flitted around the various groups, joking and chatting with everyone, moving with such agility through his many friends that it was easy to lose track of him. Sometimes, in the middle of a soccer game or conversation, I would look around and notice that he had disappeared. Later I'd catch a glimpse of a lone figure with bushy hair sitting by the smelly pond at the far edge of campus. Once I walked over and saw that he was throwing pebbles across the surface and talking to no one at all. He was so lost in his own world that he did not notice me. He tossed a pebble in the air and caught it. Xiao yu, you're right, he was saying, I'll do it tomorrow. He sighed and tossed another pebble. What am I doing here? he said.

If you looked carefully, there was a moment in which Bo's face changed when he entered the company of people. His left eye twitched slightly and then he'd grin. His face wrinkled with those dimples that made him look so good-natured, but it also became flatter. It was as if he were wiping the thoughts from his brow, putting on his comic book face. But then he would laugh loudly and pound my back, his movements so natural they made me doubt what I'd seen. Mr. Serious, Bo called me, joking. Was there admiration in that nickname? Perhaps for Bo, serious was the most difficult way to be.

When we returned to campus after New Year's, the gaokao was on everyone's mind. Everyone except, it seemed, Bo Cai, who carried on messing around as usual. Finally I cornered him at his pond.

What if you tried just a little harder? I said.

He looked up in surprise: What do you mean?

I mean you had better learn from me and get serious. I know it all comes easy to you but the gaokao's no joke.

To my surprise, he began to study at my side. We worked through sample tests, memorized formulas, quizzed each other on coefficients and constants. I taught him my test-taking techniques: how to quickly note the most important details in a long problem; how to skip, mark, and return to the questions whose solutions did not instantly come; how to methodically check answers by putting results in and working through the solution backward. I don't know why I helped him—perhaps I wanted to prove myself superior while on equal footing, perhaps I'd grown to care about him. Whatever the reason, I genuinely wanted him to do well.

Studying with Bo, I was reminded of the sheer brilliance of his mind. My memory was stronger, better practiced, but he had an incredible intuition for patterns and underlying principles, so that more than once he would have forgotten the method we'd been taught but arrive quicker at the answer, re-creating from scratch the formula I had memorized. He grasped difficult concepts instantaneously, and while I was working through a solution with pen and paper he would race through many possible paths in his head to find the simplest and most elegant one. The only subjects in which I naturally exceeded him were the foreign languages. He seemed to be afraid of them, afraid of language in general. Even his Chinese was poor, he said, where he grew up everyone spoke the local dialect, including his teacher in primary school. He said I had a better memory, which was true. But good memory was just a marker of discipline. I told Bo all he needed to do was to train his mind. This did not come naturally to him. He struggled to slow it down and thus, he made many careless mistakes. Focus, Bo, I said, your brain is no worse than mine.

I did not understand why he continued to defer to me, why he repeatedly claimed he knew nothing. Only now, looking back, do I see what I should have seen then—the deep insecurity behind his careless veneer. No matter how well he performed, objectively, no matter how obvious his potential, he could not trick his mind into thinking he deserved perfection. So he continued to make mistakes.

I pushed him. He worked hard and improved. At the end of the term, I found that I remained in first place.

Had I been smarter than Bo Cai all along? Or was I learning more from him than he was from me? I pushed my own insecurities aside. Soon no one in the class was paying attention to rankings anymore—everyone was busy scrutinizing their own sheaves of practice problems. The gaokao was only one month away and the air on campus had stretched thin as a sheet. Though our official classes were over, we stayed in our classrooms from before light to after dark, quietly studying, breaking only for meals.

During this time anxious parents appeared daily at the school gates. They came from villages as far as Bo's, hours from Hangzhou, bearing homemade snacks or extra allowance money for better dishes in the cafeteria. My mother came almost every day. She begged me to return home to study, where she could feed me properly. I refused. Bo needs my help, I said. I shared the rich foods and expensive snacks she brought with my friend, and he accepted them, like he accepted my study companionship, without much fuss. No one from his family ever came, not even on the day of the test.

My mother scolded me: You're too good, like your father. He helped people step all over him and now he's old and bitter.

How could you compare me to him?

I didn't ask the obvious question, why my father, who cared the most about the test results, never once made an appearance. Was it possible he was ill? Was there something strange in my mother's voice, in the way she spoke of him? I began to sleep poorly. In the mornings I woke sweating, gasping for air, certain my father had died. At night, I dreamed that Teacher Ping walked over to my desk and led me by my elbow to the principal's office, where a man in a white suit whose face I could not see spoke to me in my mother's voice, which was soft and steady. Yongzong, it's finally over, my mother said, and I knew without asking that this meant my father was dead. Or I would see, in my dreams, my father's small body, doubled over the empty banquet table, coughing up blood until the whole thing was draped in brilliant red as if for a wedding feast. In the distance, firecrackers sounded with music and drums.

I asked my mother, How is Ba?

She said, As always.

ON THE DAY of the gaokao, I woke sobbing.

The sky was gray, it was not yet dawn, my dormmates were still asleep. My father was dead. This time I was sure. I whispered into my pillow: *My father is dead.* I could feel the truth of the words in my bones. I rose and walked out into the cool morning air. It was misty and the grounds were dark. I headed to the track, occasionally wiping the tears that were still streaming down my face. Halfway there I saw it was already occupied. Of course, Bo Cai was there. He was walking, not jogging, and I sped up to join him until I saw that beside him walked another student, a girl, someone I could not recognize from so far away. I turned the other way and headed down the long road leading to the campus gate.

As if to prove my dreams, I found my mother standing there. She pressed a jade pendant into my hand, a good luck charm. She took out a hand towel from her bag and wiped my face, patting my hair down as if I were a little boy. Your father would have come, she said, but he had to work early. I knew it was a lie. He was dead but she did not want to tell me, did not want to affect my performance on the test. They had done the same thing during my first term in high school, when my grandmother was dying, so that I could focus on my studies. I only found out she had passed away when I returned for summer and saw her portrait in the living room shrine. I clutched the pendant in my hand. It smelled like tears.

Through the first hours of the exam I sat sweating, unable to concentrate. My heart pounded so loudly I was sure the proctor would come over at any moment to remove me from the room. I focused on breathing—my breaths were shallow and loud—and forced my pen onto the exam scroll, writing slowly, keeping my head down, trying not to vomit. During the lunch break I ate nothing and spoke to no one. I paced in the corner, breathing.

Halfway through the afternoon mathematics exam, my nausea faded. In its place rose a light and yellow joy—what did it matter, who cared how I scored, who cared if I was number one or number three thousand and two, if I went to Beida or not? My father was the only one, and he was dead. On this wave of epiphany I plowed through the rest of the exam, hands shaking, muscles twitching. I wanted only to leap from my seat and run. By the end of the physics section, with forty minutes still left on the clock, I turned in the test, unable to sit still for a moment longer. I did not check my answers, though I knew I had rushed through many problems, had even guessed on a few, but I felt confident I had guessed correctly, even if I missed one or two—who cared, I would still do well enough. For the first time in my life I felt a power that was not practiced but intuitive. My mind was clearer than it had been in months, in years. I was driving in a dense forest and suddenly the trees were blown away, revealing nothing but horizon on all sides. I could see before me and behind me, into infinity, without my father I felt thrust into fullness. As I left the exam room I passed Bo, who gave me an incredulous look before turning back to his scroll.

At the end of the three days of testing, I called home. I was prepared for the news. I would not cry. I would accept the truth like the grown man I believed I'd become. I would forgive my mother for deceiving me. I dialed. The phone rang three times.

Who's calling?

I pressed my ear against the phone.

Who's this? the voice said again.

It was my father.

Who's this?

Finally I choked out: It's me. I just wanted to say the gaokao is done.

How did you do?

Okay.

Okay?

Fantastic.

Good.

THERE IS A photograph of my family from that time, taken before we sat down for that dinner the summer of my last year of high school. We are standing in the garden, lined up in front of the red gate of our home. My grandfather sits in the middle on a bamboo chair and his sons flank him on each side with their wives. The children stand in the back, all of us but my uncle's little daughter, who is in her mother's arms. The rest of us are grown, the same height or taller than the adults. My face appears in the space between my father's and my grandfather's, and it always shocks me, when I look at it now, how young and tender my features are, how clearly it is the face of a boy.

The class scores came out. I was Number Three. Bo was still Number Two. Number One had been taken by a girl named Su Lan.

I didn't know Su Lan. I couldn't even point out who she was. Our class of fifty-three students had sat together from morning to dusk for two years, and I could not summon her face when I saw her name.

The tiny dark one, Bo said, nodding toward the corner. Su Lan was sitting by herself with a small frown on her face. No one was congratulating her. No one was congratulating anyone. Groups of students whispered among themselves, glancing over at Su Lan and then at us.

Who the hell is she?

She's from around Dongyang, Bo said.

Where the hell is that?

Not so far from my home. She's been Number Three for a while.

For the last two years she had been climbing up the class list, Bo told me. She'd started at the very bottom. After the first test she had found Bo on the track before morning exercises and introduced herself, saying that they were laoxiang, from the same mountains east of Dongyang, and she hoped she could learn from him.

She was so ugly! he said.

She's still ugly, I said.

No one in the class had taken note of her. Bo had only noticed her because she was the one student who was even poorer than himself. Peasant boy recognized peasant girl. He could tell she had a good character, that she was determined and a hard worker. He occasionally offered her his homework to copy. Sometimes she took it, but instead of scribbling down the answers like everyone else she looked at the page very carefully, read over every line, then handed it back to him without writing down a word. By the middle of the last semester she was refusing his help.

Since the new semester had started, she had been hovering at Number Three, nudging up closer and closer to the two of us. I looked back at her. She was still sitting alone, looking straight ahead at nothing. Was it just me, or was her head raised a little too high, her spine a little too upright? Even this posturing did not help her become attractive or memorable. Her face, noticeably darker than those of the rest of the students, disappeared into her surroundings. Years later, when I would try to remember what she looked like then, I would only be able to call to mind a smudged brown spot.

The next week we filled out our university preference rosters. Su Lan's score qualified her for Beida and so did Bo's. Su Lan chose the most competitive course, pure physics, while Bo opted for nuclear physics. At that time, physics was the most desirable and difficult course, much like finance or economics today, because you could get a scholarship to go abroad. I had bombed the physics portion of the exam. Besides, Beida would not take me. The best program that would accept my test scores was the First Medical College of Shanghai.

Sitting by the pond after we turned in our rosters, I told Bo that I had planned it all. I had always wanted to be a doctor. I purposefully sabotaged the test because I knew my father would never allow me to pursue this path otherwise. The last thing I wanted, I said, was to do exactly what my father expected. I told Bo that the summer before high school, my grandmother had gotten very sick. Beside her sickbed, I cried that I would not go to school but rather stay by her side to nurse her. Silly boy, she'd said. Study hard and become a doctor to save me from dying in my next life. I told this story with such fervor that I began to believe it myself. It was true that I was close to my grandmother—mine was the last name she called out before she died, or so my mother later told me, as I wept before her portrait in the shrine. But even in the end, my grandmother had refused to summon me to her deathbed so as to not disturb my studying.

Did I convince Bo? Perhaps not. I had the feeling that he saw clearly the game I was playing with myself. Yet he did not think less of me for it. From the beginning, Bo Cai had never looked at me with judgment. Like a true friend, he now tried to love and understand me.

Was this the first time I invented something? I told myself it wasn't a total lie, because what made any lie possible was an emotion grounded in truth. Truthfully, I had wanted to defy my father. Truthfully, I convinced myself, I struggled with the lot I had been given: the burden of having more than those around me, of having more than I deserved. That was why I worked so hard; that was why I had once obsessed over checking and rechecking answers I knew were right: I wanted to toil, to earn with my own sweat whatever I got. Yes, eventually I came to believe my own lie: to be a doctor, to save other lives, that was the only way I could imagine living with myself, with my unearned existence.

So I went to Shanghai and Zhang Bo went to Beijing. When my father found out, he did not raise his voice. He looked at the paper, put it facedown on the table, and walked out of the room.

SHANGHAI SUITED ME. It was a city in which people looked at each other with scrutiny and judgment. There I was just another unknown entity, represented day to day by the cash in my hands. I retreated into the world of the medical university and found a happy solitude. The years passed evenly and swiftly, a thick moving liquid.

Twice I visited Bo in Beijing. The government buildings were intimidating and grandiose, scaled as if they had not been made for humans. Even Bo agreed there was something strange about the place, all those ancient temples and palaces dropped in the middle of anywhere, turning a seemingly normal street into someplace that was supposed to be special. The past was too intrusive. Bicycling down the wide avenues of the old city, with a view of the open sky such as I could find only on the Bund in Shanghai, I told myself that in Beijing I felt agoraphobic, I could not breathe.

My last year of medical college, I received a large yellow envelope in the mail, the sender a familiar name I couldn't place, the address in Hangzhou. It was February. I had just returned from Hangzhou, from my annual obligatory New Year's visit. I didn't like to go home, and though everyone was given two weeks off I never stayed more than a few days, compensating for my short stay with presents: Western medicines for my parents, clothes and perfumes from Nanjing Lu for my sisters, a toy truck for Dajie's son. The truth was I would have liked to remain in Shanghai for the entire holiday and watch the city empty as everyone went home to their families in the countryside. Even now my neighborhood was a ghost town, the dormitories hollowed out, the shops closed, the streets, for once, clear.

I tore open the envelope. It was an invitation to a five-year high school reunion. *Hangzhou First Secondary School*—twice I read the words, failing to understand. It had been years since I'd thought of that place, two or three since I'd last seen Bo. If I regretted losing touch with my best friend, I was buoyed by the feeling of life moving on, acquiring new images, names, resonances. In a few short months I would be starting a residency at Shanghai Oncology Hospital. The reunion was scheduled for late May. Returning so soon to Hangzhou was out of the question. Later that night, the building manager came up to say I had a phone call. It was Bo Cai.

Old friend, he said. We'll finally get to see how big your head's gotten after all these years.

My head? And what about your waist?

I was surprised by how pleased I was to hear his voice. We chatted, caught up. He had finished his degree and was starting a master's in applied nuclear physics at Beida. Life was good, evidenced by the fact he'd gotten even fatter, as I would see for myself in a few months.

You'll have to visit me in Shanghai on your way back, I said, I can't leave work.

Nonsense, he said, and when I did not respond immediately he continued:

Still afraid to face your father?

It was Bo's idea that I make the trip without informing my family. It would be possible, perhaps even simple. As long as I didn't go to my old neighborhood, how would anyone know? As he talked, something awakened inside me, a longing for company, and I remembered those years warmly, as my first years of freedom. I had made friends in Shanghai and was on good terms with my classmates, but the truth was, though I had seen him just twice since high school, Bo was one of the only people who knew some real part of me. I tucked the invitation into a textbook. A few weeks later, I bought a train ticket to Hangzhou.

ON THE TRAIN to Hangzhou I startled too easily. People jostled me unexpectedly and called out words that sounded like my name. I dozed, nearly jumping from my seat when the conductor, checking tickets, tapped my shoulder. I avoided looking out the window. I was afraid I would see my face in the glass and find my family name painted across it like a brand. By the time I stepped off the train I was soaked in sweat.

In the waiting room, standing before the exit, a hundred meters away, was my father.

He folded his newspaper and turned to face me.

I exhaled. It was just a man his age.

In fact, every man in the station looked like my father—I ducked from them all. I searched for a taxi. Again I heard my name, hurtling undeniably across the car lot, and this time I was sure: someone had recognized me.

At the front of the taxi line, Bo Cai dumped his bag into a car and waved me over. I looked around to see if anyone had heard him call me. Everyone went on as they were.

Look at you, Yongzong, what a wreck you are, Bo said, chuckling. He slapped my back: What, did you *run* here from Shanghai? I shrugged and let out a nervous giggle, which turned into full, rocking laughter, and proclaimed at the top of my lungs, What an *idiot* I am. I followed him into the car. The taxi sped through streets I had known since I was a child. I rolled the windows down, dug my face into the wind, and challenged bystanders to look at me twice. Perhaps this was the first time I realized how simple it was to act as if certain parts of the past did not exist.

HOW GENUINELY HAPPY I was that day to see who everyone had become. Scrappy Tudo stayed skinny but had grown tall and permed his hair so he looked like a cotton swab; pretty Jing was now chubby and matronly in her maroon suit-dress; Enkai had gotten more muscular; the beginnings of beer bellies were visible in Bo and Zheng; little Yu had gotten surgery on her eyelids and looked quite attractive in a pink dress. Unlike Bo, who greeted everyone as if they had just spoken the last week, I had trouble recognizing many faces. When they introduced themselves I responded with appropriate surprise. Everyone recognized me.

How could anyone forget you, Yongzong? Jing said. Besides, you look the same as ever—but even more serious.

We had a noisy lunch with plenty of beer and baijiu, barely eating, everyone busy toasting each other and getting drunk. After lunch we broke into groups and played silly games conceived by Bo and Jing, designed to help us reminisce about old times while catching up on the present. We all wrote down what we'd expected each person to become, back in high school. Jing collected all the papers, and as we went around the circle announcing what it was we were actually up to, she read out our projected futures. We were still drunk from lunch, munching on sunflower seeds, and laughed uproariously whatever the results. Sometimes our predictions were spot-on—nine of twelve said Yu would become a high school teacher and that was exactly what she was. Sometimes we were far off the mark: Enkai had not become a professional wrestler but had actually gone into business and recently acquired a line of women's lingerie. When it came my turn I knew what to expect. Chairman, CEO, astronaut.

I tricked you all, I said, spitting out the shell of a sunflower seed onto the table. I'm just a plain old doctor.

The table burst into laughing protests until Rui knocked for order. Just a plain old doctor! Enkai said. Modest as ever, Yongzong!

In the evening we feasted and drank on the northwestern banks of West Lake, far from where I'd lived as a child. Bo and I hung our arms over the edge of a stone bridge and talked as if we were old men. We spoke of the simple days of the past, when all that mattered was how we scored on some stupid test. Remember how much we cared? Bo said. You especially.

Now we had adult concerns. Money, family, our lives to make sense of. And of course, the fate of our dear country! Bo laughed.

He was thinking about going to work for the government after his graduate study. The ministry of defense was recruiting physicists and engineers. Being a scientist for the Party was equal parts politics and research. Politics is a pain, Bo said. You were smart to go down another path, to truly *serve the people*. He said this with great aplomb, waving his arm over the water. Reducing people to diseases comes naturally to me, I said. We finished our beers and got more. Abruptly Bo asked if I had a girlfriend. Hell, was I married? I hope not! I said. I had dated two girls in medical school, classmates, but was never more than fond of them. And Bo? I gave him a playful shake. He batted me away and then grew sullen.

He had been pursuing the same girl for years with no luck, he said. He couldn't get her out of his head, no matter how many times she rejected him. Who is she? I asked. What does it matter, Bo said, she's no one you know. I drank down half my beer and watched my friend looking pensively over the water. He shrugged and clinked my bottle and turned around to face our classmates. Would you ever date someone in our class? he said, chuckling. Yu looks pretty, doesn't she? For a few minutes we stood in silence admiring the girls.

Then Bo said, Hey, you know, not everyone is here. That girl who beat us isn't here.

For a moment his face darkened. Then he laughed and slapped me on the back. Remember that girl, Su Lan?

She probably thinks she's too good for us, I said. Forget her, she was so ugly anyways.

No, no. Bo shook his head with a drooping grin, tipping back the rest of his beer. I hear she's a beauty now.

LIYA

MY MOTHER WAS IN PERFECT health. Her heart, her lungs, her liver, her brain—all in excellent working condition. Except, the coroner said, that they weren't working; she was dead. He'd found no hidden medical conditions, no abnormal organs, no internal or external injuries, no toxins or unexpected chemicals in the system.

Strange, wasn't it, the coroner said, that a person could stop being alive, for no visible reason at all. Really strikes you with the fear of God.

God? I was furious. I was certain she had done it to herself, not killed herself, not anything so tragic, but somehow arranged it so she would cease to exist. After all, this was exactly how she would have wanted it: a surrender to nothing at all.

WE HAD SPOKEN on the phone a week before. I, the dutiful daughter, had called her once a week from the university town where I'd begun my adult life, just to say hello, I'm alive, I'm doing fine, and hear her say the same. She did not demand these calls from me, in fact I don't think she even desired them. She'd supported my decision to go very far away for school. I think she hoped I would go farther— cut her off entirely.

One night, when I was thirteen, or twelve, some terrible age, I ran away from home. It was summer, in a temperate place (Texas, perhaps, or Missouri), we had argued about something insignificant but seemingly momentous, and I, yelling insults, saying fuck shit fuck motherfucking damn goddamn fucking shit, all the ugly words I knew in all their ugly variations, whose sounds in my mouth made me feel bad in a good way, ran out the door and onto the street, hoping she would follow. She did not. When I got tired I lay down on the sidewalk, which was still warm. I had run far, I did not recognize where I was, I did not know how much time had passed. Still I expected her face to at any moment appear above mine, disrupting the view of the stars, apologetic, perhaps, or more likely, furious. She would take my hands and lift me, or she would yank me to my feet. Perhaps she would embrace me, perhaps she would hit me; either way she would admit I had caused her great pain. I fell asleep and when I woke I was the one in pain. The sky was gray and my hips and shoulders and back were stiff and screaming. Ants had crawled onto my hand and bit a fiery ring around my thumb. I got up and walked until I found my way home. My mother was sitting in the kitchen with a cup of hot water, bent over a piece of paper with a pencil, drawing a diagram for some new convoluted calculation she had dreamed up. She looked up and said with much disappointment, You're back, then returned to her diagram.

That was how it was: I wanted desperately to leave her and break her heart, but her heart would not be broken, so I came back, tried to make her love me, tried leaving again.

Now I couldn't break her heart if I wanted to. Instead, again, finally, she had broken mine.

THE WAY TO make her love me, I learned, or at least to make her talk animatedly and seem to enjoy my company, was to engage her in her work. It was not work that anyone was paying her to do. After enrolling in and dropping out of a number of universities (four? five?), she finally gave up trying to earn a PhD. Academia was too stiff, she said, too invested in its own accolades, too worshipful of tradition. Especially in science, which was supposed to be a revolutionary field, all ambition had been drained; the only new ideas that could be accepted were specialized to the point of losing significance. What she was offering would be a paradigm shift, it would require entire textbooks to be rewritten. They were not ready for it, they would see their mistake in ten, twenty, fifty years.

Of course she did not use such complicated words. Often when she tried to explain her feelings about a department she had just abandoned, she would stop talking mid-sentence and stare with ferocity at the wall, her mind continuing to roll silently around those thoughts language could not adequately express. It was in those silences that I read her criticism of academia. If I was feeling mean, I would give her imaginary voice a grandiose tone: she was too good instead of not good enough. But in truth she spoke plainly, not only without grandiosity but without bitterness, explaining not as a way of giving an excuse but simply as if trying to tell the truth. Whatever her flaws, my mother was never in the business of self-deception. She got a job as a technician for some computer chip company, really boring stuff, she said, and continued doing her research alone. She didn't need a title or an office, all she needed was paper and pencil and enough food in her stomach to keep working.

When we spoke on the phone, the week before she died, I'd asked as I always did, How's the research going? She said she'd made good progress. She sounded happy. It's nice and quiet, she said. I can finally think.

She was referring, of course, to my absence. This had been her answer ever since I left home, whereas before she complained about little things, this equation eluding her, this little problem presenting larger problems, circling back always to the issue of not being able to focus, of craving some clarity of mind.

It was a stranger who informed me of her death, a male voice on my phone belonging to a police officer in the cold seaside town where she'd recently moved. My first reaction was of disbelief. What! What! I shouted into the phone. Or perhaps I whispered it. The information was at once impossible and devastating and senseless; it was like returning home to find your dwelling place inexplicably filled to the brim with millions of sharp stones, like getting off a plane to Hawaii and finding yourself in Finland and suddenly under arrest, like discovering *The Matrix* or some other ludicrous work of fiction was a documentary film. It was like being told, Actually, you don't exist.

It became more like that.

CONSERVATION OF MASS and energy says that nothing truly disappears. I learned this early, in Vermont, in a town too small to have its own fire station. It was winter, so cold that the river froze over and even windless air bit through coats and sweaters and flesh, searing the bone. An old house down the street burst into flames, and I ran outside with my mother, who held me because I was frightened. I think she was frightened too. It was night. We walked closer to the fire and she told me not to be afraid. It's nothing to cry about, she said. A scientist looks at fire and sees not just destruction but change. Mass that seems to disappear is only transforming into energy, like the warmth of the fire, or something else with the power to create. That house? See how as the wood blackens and shrinks, the flame grows bigger and hotter? My mother spoke quickly, in Chinese, forgetting her own rules in order to calm me. I kept my body very still, trying to hold on to a feeling I couldn't understand. My heart had hands, the hands were reaching out for something my brain had already forgotten. The fire was growing so hot it was melting the snow. The next morning a ring of ice marked the burned black lot. There the snow had melted, then froze.

WHEN I WAS very little, my mother used to take me with her to work. Her work then was in the physics corridors of large universities, where there were laboratories full of small and large machines. She told me she was taking me to the university as if it were a special treat. She said because I was so guai, because I was so dongshi, favorable words denoting obedience and maturity in children, she would take me to a wonderful place where normally only adults could go.

I hadn't yet started school. Besides simple greetings I did not know any English. We went before anyone else had arrived and left late after dark. My mother put me in her office, which she shared with two other graduate students. Whenever they came in I slid off her lap into the space underneath her desk between her legs and the wall, and practiced being very still. It was one of the many games we'd invented together and I liked it very much. In the darkness I would pretend to be a rock in a garden, or a statue inside a museum, I would imagine all manner of people walking around me, observing, commenting on my beauty, on the special qualities that had earned me my place in the display. They would wonder what exactly I might be or mean. They would search on the walls for the name of my maker and read the name of my mother. All the while they would observe me as an inanimate object, not knowing that I was looking right back at them, observing them too.

I loved my mother so much during that time; if I'd had the language I would have called her the love of my life and no uttered words in all of time could have been more true. We must have spent nearly every minute of our lives together—I don't remember any babysitters—and in the hours we were apart, when she had to teach or attend a meeting, I missed her so much I felt as if an arm or a leg had been taken away—no, more, a heart or brain, some part of me that was undoubtedly the best of what I had to offer. But the separations were delicious in their own way, because they made our reunions all the more sweet. Upon my mother's return I was showered in praise and love. I was so good and brave, not crying or getting myself in trouble, successfully completing whatever game or task she'd assigned before leaving me alone. My mother picked me up and kissed my head and let me wrap my arms around her long neck. She called me guai. At night we went to sleep on the same twin mattress, her arm flung casually over my shoulder, my hand clutching a strand of her hair.

My mother kept me occupied in many ways while she worked. She gave me paper and pencil and let me draw, and when I learned to control the movements of my hands she wrote numbers and words in the margins and had me copy them, and after I got good at that I solved simple math problems and wrote little stories. In this way I learned how to read and write some Chinese.

My mother was not just trying to keep me out of the way, though writing those complicated words over and over was useful for keeping an obedient child busy. I believe she was genuinely interested in educating me. She was always teaching me things, answering any silly question with the truth. She pointed out little miracles I'd failed to notice—how a leaf fell to the ground, how certain things floated on water and certain things sank, how light bulbs turned on. I loved these lessons; I believed she was trying to help me become exactly like her by telling me everything she knew, and this pleased me immensely. I did not only want to be identical to my mother, I wanted to be absorbed into her entirely.

THE ONE-BEDROOM APARTMENT where my mother died was plain and bare. Sparsely and impersonally furnished, undecorated, it could have belonged to anyone. It was the first time I had seen it, in fact the policeman had had to give me the address, and when I walked into the room I had the feeling again I was inside some elaborate prank. If my mother had had a sense of play, perhaps I would even have suspected she was the one who'd arranged it—rented an empty apartment, staged her death—so as I walked around, opening cabinets, drawers, doors, I half expected her to jump out from some corner and laugh loudly in my face. In the white walls and the twin mattress on the bedroom floor, in the foldout table with a single chair, I read a challenge. I was furious, I wanted to undo her simplicity, her tracelessness, I accepted.

Most of my mother's personal items were meaningless: clothes, shoes, pens, stacks of papers written in mathematics and Chinese, languages she'd taught me once that I could no longer proficiently read. But there was one important discovery. Inside a shoebox stuffed with receipts, tax returns, and pay stubs, I found an envelope. Inside the envelope I found a letter in Chinese, typed underneath official letterhead, and a key.

It took me three hours to translate the letter; I had to look up every other word. I felt as if I were uncovering a part of my mind buried in shovelfuls of dust. Gasping, grateful, I searched for a handhold I knew was there. Eventually I pulled my first language out. It was this return that had brought the other things: early memories of my mother, the life my mother and I had lived in Chinese.

The letter's purpose was to congratulate my mother, a PhD student at Fudan University, on her housing assignment. At the bottom was an address in Shanghai.

MY MOTHER DID not like to talk about the past. But there are things you know without being told, the knowledge somehow baked into the making of you. I knew that we had lived in Shanghai before we lived here. I also had evidence: according to every piece of official paper and plastic I owned (Social Security card, driver's license, green card, eventually citizenship certificate, and soon passport), I had been born there, on the fourth day of June, in the year 1988. Shanghai was the correct answer to that question Americans liked so much to ask people who looked like me. But the truth was I didn't know a thing about Shanghai, which was as foreign to me as Timbuktu. When I conjured images of it I might as well have been imagining fairies, castles, unicorns—the myths I'd read in story-books as a child. Sometimes these images suited me, when, for instance, a person whose esteem I craved found my origins interesting or special. Most times they did not.

Briefly I considered my education—the redbrick university buildings, the lectures and seminars and term papers, the professors and acquaintances who mispronounced my name, the dormitory bed/desk/bookshelf I was paying for with the cashier job I had not informed of my absence—it was all there waiting to be picked back up again, and yet the thought of returning to do so was laughable, I could hardly convince myself that that life and that person living it still existed. I had gone to college almost solely to defy my mother, who to the end insisted on the uselessness of degree and pedigree—she'd once had the highest of them all, and look where they'd gotten her. Briefly I considered the thin scrim of what I'd managed to construct without my mother and watched its small remains wash away in the stream of every other significant thing I'd lost.

I booked a plane ticket to Shanghai.

It did not occur to me I was going back to my birthplace. It did not even occur to me that I was going to China, which to my mind was still nothing more than a colorful blob on a map. Certainly I had no expectation of discovering anything about myself. Rather, when I made the necessary arrangements, as I sat on the airplane looking over a sheet of clouds, I thought only that I was reversing something my mother had done, reconnecting a line she had cut. Only the thought of undoing her moved me.

MY EARLIEST MEMORY is of waking alone. The room was pitch-black; the bed was too cold. I felt for the edges of the mattress and found it empty. I cried out, jumped up, ran into the kitchen turning on the lights. The house was terrifying: night pushed on the windows, the vents breathed hot menace, the ceiling light bore down like a yellow eye. I ran outside, shoeless, in my underwear, to the front of the house, and did not see my mother's car in the driveway. I knocked on the front door where a bald man with an earring lived. He opened it and looked at me with surprise. He was wearing a blue robe, beneath which I could see his thin, hairy legs.

I sat on an armchair in his living room and tried to communicate my panic. He spoke and I did not understand him. I had not started school yet, I did not speak English, the few words I'd learned flew out of my head. *My mother, my mother*, I repeated, with the only other English word I could remember: *yes*. Your mother something? he asked. Your mother something else? And I answered, Yes, yes, my mother. He picked up the telephone and spoke, again I heard the word *mother*: I hoped he was telephoning my mother. We sat and waited in silence. I was staring out the window when the police cars turned into the driveway. There were two. Two big men, two sets of red and blue lights spinning. My mother's car came in behind them.

She parked and ran out, her face bright with fear, shouting at the policemen. When she saw me burst out of the neighbor's door her fear dissolved. She was relieved, and I ran to her, relieved too, I held her and let her hold me and was thrilled.

The policemen were not thrilled. They had not come to escort my mother home but to investigate her absence. They followed us inside and spoke to my mother in harsh tones, standing tall and large beside my mother, who suddenly looked very small. I felt my mother was in danger and I should protect her—I felt I should leap forward and push the policemen out. But something prevented me, a gray-black feeling, so instead I hid behind my mother's legs, my nose in the cup of her knee. I did not understand much. I remember one of the policemen, a tall blond man, saying *in America* followed by other words, while my mother struggled to explain herself. Or perhaps my memory supplied these words retrospectively. My mother had gone to the laboratory to finish some work, perhaps to check on some experiment she was running overnight on the big machine, she had been gone for less than an hour. Now she was being reprimanded for neglect, and later I was reprimanded, she said if I ever did a thing like that again I could be taken away from her, she could be put in jail, was that what I wanted?

I went back to sleep that night with ugly, afraid, ashamed feelings, which were gone by morning, burned away by a bright childhood sun. But the seed of shame remained. As I got older, as my mother and I grew apart, I would be visited from time to time by that gray-black failure. I would find myself crouching again behind my mother's legs, watching my opportunity to save her walk away.

I NEVER STOPPED loving my mother. Not exactly. A little pin fell out of the contraption of my love for her; bit by bit it fell apart, until one day I discovered she was my enemy. I never ceased to feel strongly—strongest—about her. Even long after the strength of emotion was no longer adoring, my mother retained an ability to extract, with a word, a glance, a simple tone of voice, the well of everything irrational inside me.

After the incident with the police, things between us changed. I started to go to school. My mother and I began to spend entire days apart. I could not stand being separated from her and at first resisted it with everything I had. But soon I saw that she could stand the separation, in fact she'd expected it and desired it. She turned after leaving me at the classroom door—I glimpsed her face and saw on it an expression of enormous relief.

I learned English at school. My mother encouraged me, she praised me, she loved it especially when I used words she didn't know, she said I sounded exactly like an American and gave me a smile that told me she was truly pleased. Because I loved it when my mother praised me, I quickly became very good at English, so good that I forgot Chinese. My mother did not care. She said learning Chinese was good for exercising the brain but otherwise it had no use. She made a new game: we would only speak in English, even with each other. When I realized what was happening, that with every new word of English I was becoming more and more unlike her, it was too late. I wanted to be exactly like my mother and she wanted me to be nothing like her. She was stronger; she prevailed.

One day I came home from school and found our few possessions packed in boxes. She told me to help her load the car and I did. We drove for days. She did not introduce the driving as a game. She did not talk to me. If I asked her something—where were we going, could we stop to pee, what was going to happen to the house—she responded with a nod or more often a shake of the head. When we unpacked in our new home she gave a speech in English about how

I had grown up, I was no longer a child, and so she would no longer hide from me the nature of things. And in fact, she presented our circumstance like the laws of nature: she had a new job, she had to work, I was old enough to take care of myself.

She pushed a bowl of instant noodles toward me and said, The thing about life is to endure it—my mother taught me this when I was much littler than you.

She blinked: her own words had surprised her. Much later I would wonder if she had ever said those words to me before, in any language. *My mother.* But at the time I was not yet ready to see her like that, as a person who, like me, had once needed a mother. She shook her head, clearing an unsightly vision from her inner eye, and continued: I didn't believe her then but now I do; you'll see later too.

For the first time, I found my mother unconvincing. It was as if she had shed a shimmering layer of skin. In English, she was flat and boring, and her words were inadequate, they did not soothe or charm me.

She saw that she had not convinced me and she didn't seem to mind.

We moved often after this. So often that in my memory the various homes pressed into each other—stubble green lawn, lakeside shack, bedroom with two twin mattresses on the floor, windowless living room, old television, broken rocking armchair pulled from the street, teal square dining table (paint peeling to reveal yellow foam), fallen log by the parking lot where once I found a five-dollar bill, low yellow kitchen lamp—and it became difficult, almost impossible, to separate out which part belonged to which place.

BRAZENLY, I BOOKED no hotel. The plane landed in Pudong airport at noon, and I hailed a taxi to take me directly to my destination, handing the driver a copy of the letter from Fudan University and a map with driving directions I'd printed from the Internet. He said something quickly. I thought I heard in it the word *no* but then he put his foot on the pedal and drove. It was only when we arrived that I began to understand what he had said, something perhaps like *It's not there* or *It no longer exists* or *You don't want to go there,* because the place at which he finally stopped was a dump. He pointed through a stone gate on whose arch three faded words had been carved and handed me back the Fudan letter, pointing to the middle of the second paragraph. By then I had memorized the contents of the letter; I saw that this was the *entrance to Bai De Li.* From there I was to *turn left and enter the fourth longtang,* after which my mother's building could be found near the end of the lane.

The neighborhood was deserted, and for good reason. Half of the buildings had been torn down; what formerly must have been a row of dwellings was now a row of holes, homes displaying their innards—beams, rubble, clods of exposed wire—empty spaces held between torn walls and floors, their jagged edges like claws, ripped while clinging to remain whole. In this disorder I could not help but see my mother's hand. It was as if her death had reached over the ocean, anticipating me, contriving to remove her traces before I arrived. I saw in the pulverized dust an analogue of what my mother had become, something that could be scooped into a plastic bag and carried on my back. I saw in the slabs of broken wood a suggestion of geometry—lines, rectangles, regular shapes, broken and reverted to their original material form.

I walked down the lane past the broken houses, toward the building at the end, and began to feel something like relief. I had accepted my mother's challenge, I had made it this far—how ready I was to surrender. I was exhausted; it seemed for days I had not slept; the destruction and chaos of my mother's last trace seemed, suddenly, exactly what I had been looking for.

At the end of the lane a chipped green plaque replicated the address on the letter. I pushed open the door next to the plaque, which required no key, and found myself in a dark room. It was some kind of shared kitchen, I realized, with five or six sets of stoves. A single bulb hung from the ceiling, for which I could find no switch. The walls and windows of the kitchen were blackened with oil and grime and the air was salty and stale, undercut with a bitter, medicinal smell. Past the kitchen the sun shone in through a narrow outdoor corridor, where there was a large stone sink on the ground and a set of stairs so steep I mistook it for a ladder. Beyond this corridor was only dust: besides the kitchen, every other room on the ground floor had been leveled.

According to the letter, my mother's room was on the second floor. I went back to the stairs. There was no railing, there never had been, it seemed. The steps were narrow, less than the width of my foot, the wood was old and black. I strapped my duffel across my chest and climbed up on all fours, ducking to avoid a beam as I turned a corner, looking down, carefully assessing the placement of my feet.

On the second floor I nearly screamed.

SOMEONE STOOD THERE, an inch from my face. A woman, I think. She was ancient. She hunched over a cane, her back bent sideways, her body a crumpled *S*. Her face too was crumpled, the most wrinkled face I had ever seen, her skin pale and thin, its creases radiating like a starburst from one eye, her mouth a thin opening at the meeting of two hollow cheeks. She had white hair and very black eyes.

She looked up at me, grimaced, and said my mother's name. I think, actually, she said: Su Lan, I told them you'd be back.

Later I would realize that my difficulty understanding her was related to my earlier difficulty understanding the cab driver—they were not speaking in Mandarin, the official Chinese I'd learned, but rather in Shanghainese. I gripped the key in my pocket and swallowed. I said in halting Mandarin: Is Su Lan's room here?

The ancient woman responded in Shanghainese. She said many things I did not understand. I heard repeated again and again my mother's name, the tone more agitated with each stroke. Perhaps she was rebuking me, perhaps she was asking me questions, finally I understood that when she said *Su Lan* she was addressing *me*. My chest hurt. I struggled to breathe. I tried to back away without falling off the landing—it was very small—finally I heard myself saying, forcefully: I'm not Su Lan, Su Lan's dead.

I pushed past the ancient woman to the door she had been blocking, which I was now sure was my mother's door—suddenly the peeling red papers glued on its face looked familiar, suddenly I remembered the way the light struck the wood. The key fit—the knob turned—

THE SHANGHAI APARTMENT was the opposite of my mother's final home. It was teeming, furnished, pristine—packed with items that revealed the personality of their owner. Was this owner really my mother? I did not recognize her in it at all. In the closet were feminine dresses, scarves, boots, heeled dress shoes. On the bookshelves were novels with my mother's name scrawled inside the cover. My mother, who had laughed at me for reading novels, and described the habit as evidence of a trivial mind. My mother, whose wardrobe consisted of white cotton shirts sold by the pack and loose-fitting pants. The bedsheets were covered with large red and pink embroidered flowers. The wardrobe doors were engraved with drawings of birds and trees. The room was decorated. Far from the functional, minimal spaces we had lived in in America, this room had been organized not just to be livable but to facilitate living; even the floor had been painted white to create the illusion of more space.

Modest as my many childhood homes had been, this one was even smaller: one long room, only slightly larger than my freshman dorm. It was separated in two by a bookshelf, with a bed and desk on one side, eating table and wardrobe on the other. Next to the door was a small refrigerator and across from that a bench. It was all so Chinese—I don't know how else to say it. The patterns on the bedspread, the style of furniture, the dimensions and lighting of the room, the neighbor who watched me silently from the door, so ancient she might have emerged from myth. Suddenly a vision of my mother appeared before me like the subject of some National Geographic or PBS documentary, I could hear the slow, benevolent commentary as the camera panned across the scene. And there I was, inside the scene, viewer and participant, exotic to myself. It was a strange and difficult vision, not incompatible with grief.

My head hurt. It raced. I discovered I had lost control of my mind, which was inventing impossible memories of childhood, constructing old scenes with new images: running down the cobbled alley, bathing on the concrete roof, watching my mother walk down the dark and narrow stairs, a radio crackling somewhere below.

I sat down at the small table and dropped my bags to the floor. Then I looked up and saw the portrait on the wall.

IT WAS A photograph of two people, a woman and a man. They stood together before a backdrop of pink blossoms, bodies nearly touching, his hand on her waist. She wore a white dress; its train fanned down a series of short marble steps. He wore a black and white suit. A pair of Greek columns flanked the couple, atop the columns plaster cupids balanced with arrows pointed and ready. It was a wedding portrait. The woman was my mother, made-up and dressed-up, a beautiful young bride.

The man was tall. Though he ceded the spotlight to the woman beside him, he was handsome too. I stood to look at his face: his wide lips, his square jaw, the high bridge of his nose—*my* wide lips, *my* square jaw, *my* high-bridged nose. People had always commented on how much I looked like my mother—now I saw in this man's face all the ways in me she had failed to make her mark.

I closed the door, shutting the ancient neighbor out, and turned the place upside down.

I HAD NEVER asked my mother about my father. She had not forbidden it; even if I'd had a general feeling that such questions were discouraged, I had no memory of my mother saying, *Be quiet, never speak of it again.* Had I been a coward? Indifferent, too absorbed in the petty present to care? Or perhaps I'd believed there'd be endless time for the confusions my knowledge might bring. However it came to pass, at a certain point it became too late to ask such questions—too late because it seemed I should already know their answers, and so an admission of ignorance would be an admission of great carelessness—and then (from shame? from sloth?) I turned *father* into a concept, an emptiness so abstract it was as good as dead.

I EMPTIED EVERY drawer—I opened every book. I found more of my mother's things—notebooks, pens, bowls, clothes—tossing them all aside until finally, I found my mother guilty:

Under the bed, a heavy dark thing. I crawled in and pulled out a wooden trunk. I dusted the clasps and eased it open. Inside: my father, my father, my father. His clothes—pants, shirts, jackets, shoes, two leather belts. A stethoscope, a lab coat, medical textbooks with his handwriting in the margins. More photographs—twenty—all of him and him alone.

My father was a person. He was flesh and blood, a man with hands and mouth and skin and hair; he walked, he smiled, he ate, once he coupled with my mother to make me.

I wanted to fight my mother. She had put the evidence of my father away, literally shoved it under the bed, then spirited me to the other side of the world, where she had raised me alone, making herself so substantial, so real, so overwhelming that she suffocated the need for another parent. I wanted to shout her down. I remembered the vicious way we'd fought, the cycle of our mutual care and contempt, how we would move to a new place, ushering in a period of lightness only to destroy it and start again. At first my mother would feel free; she worked well, laughed, lifted her eyebrows, gave a contained smile, and said her mind was clear. I made new friends and new interests and she liked learning about them, seemed to love me more, as if I too were a new daughter she was meeting for the first time. Then the lightness would wear down: my mother alluded to a bad day at work, to a combative colleague, or to a professor with whom she disagreed, her eyes were cast increasingly downward, more and more she ran her hands over her forehead, trying to wipe it clean. She spoke sharply to me, disapproving of any little thing I did or ignoring me altogether. I saw this and could not help but provoke her, and then we fought. With my growing vocabulary I found ever more eloquent ways to insult her, I said, *You have a morbid fear of history*, I used words like *consequence* and *responsibility* that neither of us really understood. I knew I had infuriated her properly when she broke out shouting in Chinese.

I never understood what she said in those moments. At the time I attributed it to my loss of my first language, but now I realized she had probably not spoken in the Mandarin she'd taught me, which was soft and melodic, but rather in some dialect—not Shanghainese, or I would have recognized it here, but the local dialect of wherever she'd been born. Her voice didn't just get loud. It assumed a nasal, forward quality that can only be described as violent. The sound was physical, meant to be used as a weapon, and though I could not understand what she was saying her voice itself hurt me, it slapped me across my face. I did not recognize my mother then, it was as if the sound had found another chamber of resonance, as if her body itself had changed to create it. This was the stranger I wanted to confront now.

She'd hated our fights. I could see her surprise and regret after we'd both calmed down. Afterward, the memory of a fight weighed on both of us, filling the empty spaces around us with ugliness. I sensed that she hated the person she became when I provoked her, that this person flew out of her without her permission or control; she wanted to be unflappable, simple, civilized. I was ashamed of being so bad that I made her act in this way. She was ashamed of me too, more ashamed than I was—she was ashamed for us both, and I felt at once furious and sorry that I had disappointed her by revealing her to herself. I knew then we would be leaving soon.

Leaving helped. In a new environment we were fresh and unburdened; we could live alongside each other in peace. Sometimes

I wondered if the only way my mother knew how to solve a problem was to abandon everything and start again. Once, she'd said: It makes the life of the heart more simple.

HER BODY UNDER the white sheet had been very small. In the morgue, I was afraid to lift the sheet. I was afraid I would find under it the shriveled body of some child-size mummy from a natural history museum, some primordial Eve. The face looked shrunken, but it was hers. I recognized the part in the hair, the strands of white and black curling over the crown of her skull. I recognized all the individual features of my mother's face: the arch of the eyebrows, the thin mouth, the soft plunging bridge of the nose. I understood that these features belonged to my mother and came together proportionally on a face the shape of hers. But I could not connect these certainties to my mother. Perhaps it was the lack of effort in the muscles, or the waxy paleness of the skin. The face did look like a stranger's.

I TRIED TO calm down, to return my breathing to normal. I neatly folded the men's clothing I'd torn from the trunk, stacking shirts and pants on the bed. I sorted through the remaining items. I had the feeling that I was standing on the edge of something. What else had my mother done to make my heart's life simple?

At the very bottom of the trunk was a dense stack of documents. I took out a bundle of letters—the rubber band binding them snapped. The script, cursive and tiny, was impossible for me to read, but I saw that the handwriting belonged to one person, and that the addresses on the envelopes were all the same. On each envelope I recognized my mother's name; on both sender and recipient addresses I was able to read the words: 北京. I remembered that my mother had gone to university in Beijing. Later I would open the letters and see that they were dated 1985 and 1986—years before I had been born. Later yet I would try to read them, moving through their contents word by word as I had the Fudan letter, searching for clues to confirm my suspicion that the writer—a man named Zhang Bo—was my father.

At that moment I still had discoveries to make. Underneath the letters was a green booklet the size of my palm, laminated in peeling plastic film. I opened it and found a small footprint stamped inside. It was a birth certificate. I read my mother's name after the entry saying *mother*. The entry for *father* was followed by a blank. But it was what had been written after *time* and *place* that made me stare, blinking, for a long time, uncomprehending. It said:

PLACE OF BIRTH Fuxing Hospital, Beijing
DATE OF BIRTH 4th day of June, 1989

I did not understand what I was seeing. I took out my crisp new American passport and compared:

The passport said Shanghai 1988.

The birth certificate said Beijing 1989.

I looked at the two documents many times, trying to make the words match. They refused. In the roil and shock of so many discoveries—my mother's death, her former life, the concrete existence of my father—I was left now with a feeling almost like a laugh. What in the world did this mean? Had my mother had another child, after me, in Beijing? No, I sat on the floor with my knees splayed to read the designs on the bottoms of my feet, which matched the baby stamp with spooky precision. I had needed no dictionary to translate the child's name. The words were familiar; the name was mine.

I HAD A strange sensation then, of being inside and outside my body at once, aware of sounds, feelings, smells, and tastes passing through me in a timeless fashion, lighting up parts of my memory so that I was suspended in a pool of emotions from disparate points in my past. Suddenly I was returned to a time in elementary school, fourth or perhaps fifth grade, when I was invited to go trick-or-treating for Halloween with some popular girls. I had not celebrated Halloween before and had only learned of trick-or-treating recently. Of course I wanted very much to go—I could not believe my luck at being invited at all—but I sensed it was the sort of thing that would upset my mother or make things difficult for her. This was a time when my love for my mother was being transformed into a kind of fear. Most of all I was afraid to ask her to buy me things. Halloween required a costume that could only be worn on one day of the year, and I knew the girls who had invited me would have beautiful costumes, nicer than the clothes I wore every day.

To my surprise my mother had brightened at the request. I know exactly what you'll be, she said, and she began to assemble my costume from old clothes. I didn't dare ask her what she was planning. I mentioned my friends were going as Disney princesses and they expected me to be Mulan. That's ridiculous, my mother said, you're going to be something much better. The night of Halloween she dressed me in black and put a homemade headband on my head. She had decorated the strap to look like a ruler and sewn on two horns shaped like thermometers. They looked like blue antlers.

You can tell your friends you're the devil, she said, and if they're mean to you, tell them to go to hell. Then she lowered her voice and spoke conspiratorially. She unfolded a piece of paper she had placed in the pocket of my shirt, on which she had drawn a picture of a partitioned box with little balls inside.

She had dressed me as Maxwell's demon, an imaginary creature conceived by the physicist who unified electricity and magnetism in the electromagnetic field. Maxwell's demon didn't have to do with electromagnetism, however; rather, this demon was the hypothetical being with the power to violate the second law of thermodynamics.

She pointed to the picture she had drawn and explained.

Imagine you have a box with two sides, divided by a wall with a small hole in its middle. One side is filled with a very hot gas, and the other is filled with a cold gas. After a certain amount of time, what will happen?

I thought and answered correctly: the two sides would become the same temperature, neither hot nor cold, both would be warm.

Exactly. This was the idea of entropy, the second law of thermodynamics, that the hot and cold would mix naturally with time, that everything moves toward an equilibrium. Now imagine that both sides are the same temperature, but on both sides there is a mixture of hot gases and cold gases. What happens as time passes?

Nothing, I said, and I was right.

Now imagine, my mother continued, a small creature like yourself sitting on top of this box. You are able to observe all the molecules inside moving, and to open or close a door, letting only the faster, hotter molecules through, so that as time passes, one side gets hotter and one side gets colder.

This creature was Maxwell's demon.

Of course, she went on to explain, it was simple to solve this paradox, Maxwell's demon changed the nature of the isolated system by joining it, and increased the entropy of the system by processing and storing the information gathered about the moving molecules. Gathering information too was a kind of irreversibility. But imagine if such a mechanism could be created, imagine if a true Maxwell's demon could be manufactured, it would give physicists the tools to manipulate and thus truly understand time.

You get to decide which way you want time to run, she said, pointing at my chest.

I thanked her for the costume and left.

For a few years we'd had a television in our living space. My mother had found it abandoned in the grocery store parking lot, rewired its insides to teach me about circuits and electric waves. What the grainy images taught me instead, while I was home alone after school, with the blinds down so nobody could see and tell social services, were the manifold things one could desire: toys, clothes, microwaveable snacks, toastable waffles and pizza pouches, cars, trucks, cars, clothes, a certain way a person should look. So the television had taught me shame. Standing in the free lunch line with fish sticks and soggy green beans and a paper carton of milk that made me ill, I envied the beautiful girls with silky blond and brown ponytails who sat together with their lunch boxes and brown paper bags, so happy. I had seen their yellow-haired mothers on television in pastel clothes, smiling as they packed lunches with Jif, Oreos, Lay's, Capri Sun, Chips Ahoy!

At the door of the new friend's house I took off the weird headband and pulled my hair into a high bun. I muttered to the television mother that I was Mulan. Poor thing! she said, she must have seen the tears I was blinking back. She led me to her room and rifled through her drawers, finally extracting a colorful silk scarf that she tied around my waist in an odd sash/skirt, and a paper folding fan the friend's older sister had gotten in Japan while studying abroad. My new costume did not look like Mulan's or even particularly Chinese, but everyone was satisfied, my face was the costume, it was enough.

But before this staged humiliation and triumph, before I left my house and knew to feel ashamed, there had been a moment when I stood in front of my mother and felt sheer power in my hands. My mother was looking at me as if I had actually transformed into her impossible thought experiment, as if I were indeed a creature of multitudes and mysteries, capable of overturning the laws of physics and making my own.

In Shanghai I looked at my documents. I looked at the strange gap in time and place and seemed to traverse this distance of years. Suddenly I felt as I had then, I felt my mother looking at me in hunger as I wore the costume of infinite power. For a moment everything almost made sense. I was exhausted, nodding off to sleep. I thought, yes, that's what my mother's done, she's dressed me as the demon again, she's dead so now she's chasing me around in time. Well, I would show her, I would turn around and catch her, make her reveal everything she'd hid.

I would find my father.

ZHU WEN

I'M HARD TO LOOK AT, I know. I have a face that makes people want to both stare and look away. Even when I was young, it was scrunched on one side, with one eye smaller than the other, peering out beneath its ugliness as if daring you to name the powers that made me and put me on this earth, defective as I am.

I have always been like this. My mother said ugliness was born inside of me, a cloud covering half the dark pupil of one eye, growing daily like the changing phase of moon. There was a surgery—successful, even now I have perfect vision—but a thick scar grew over the eyelid, and grew and grew. This was not enough for my body. When it was time for me to start walking, it became clear that my left leg was a bit shorter than my right. Learning to walk was painful, and I could only do so with this odd limp, swinging one leg out in a wide circle and jostling my hips up and down. Until I was old enough to justify it, I refused to use a cane.

Most people are like you: around me, they quicken their pace. The mean ones gape and kind ones stiffen their shoulders. There was a time, after my husband died, when I would grimace and stare them all down. Sometimes I lifted my cane and gave it a few swings, and when there were children nearby they scattered, little limbs flailing as they ran away. Once I made an infant boy burst into tears. I still enjoy it, being a terror. It's better than being pathetic. It almost resembles a reason to live.

WHO KNOWS WHAT would have happened to me without my mother's suffering, her prayers? She reminded me often of how she had labored to buy me divine favor. When she gave me her Guanyin statue to hide from the honglijun, she had clutched my wrists tight and whispered: Remember how the pusa helped you. Protect her as she has you.

If she were here today, she would point to the clear evidence: I am still here, I have outlived them all. Despite the way I was born my composition has proven robust. I rarely get ill, I have grown into a hardy person, hard to kill. Did I think all this came from nothing?

Every year when I was a child we made a trip to the city temple where my mother presented a good portion of our family's meager earnings to the monks in exchange for blessings and prayers. These blessings were conferred in the form of a yellow slip of paper, on which were written in calligraphy the amount of her offering and the things she had asked for. My mother protected and treasured this paper despite the fact that she could not read what it said. She could not read anything; like most women of her and my generation, she had not gone to school. I could read it, however—because I was too ugly to marry, I had been sent to school alongside my older brother. My parents thought I should be prepared to endure life alone. Every year, I would read among the things written on the slip of paper: A normal life for Zhu Wen. I think my mother truly believed that if only she was pious enough, the pusas would reach their hands into our lives and mold me into a different person.

Like most people, we had in our home a small shrine where we set things to burn or rot before symbols of our dead ancestors. In our shrine my mother kept also the statue of Guanyin and a paper cutout of a local god from her hometown. She lit a stick of incense for these inanimate things every day and offered to them our best fruits, and when we had them, pieces of meat and wine.

To this day when I think of my mother I see her mouth moving ceaselessly, chanting *amitofo amitofo* as she sweeps the floors, as she prepares our meals, as she brushes the gray dust of spent incense off the shrine into the upturned palm of her hand. And I cannot help but hear in her amitofos the hope for my normal life. Perhaps this was why I was so repulsed by her religiosity. I had gone to school, I had read books, learned mathematics and some basics of chemistry and physics—I had even read the Buddhist scriptures my mother kept boxed away from dust. I thought the holy writings were interesting, clever, sometimes even beautiful, but they also seemed clearly to be invented, invented and put into words by someone who was very smart and perhaps a little sly. The most convincing things they spoke of, which regarded the way we ought to move through life, seemed to have little to do with my mother's superstitions and the daily offerings of incense and expensive foods. Even at that age, I was interested in a reality dictated by logic and fact—by what I could see and prove. I think that was why, so many years later, I was so drawn to Su Lan. I saw in your mother a person I might have become if I had been born in different circumstances.

But in the world of her logic my mother could make convincing arguments. She would say that my life was the strongest proof of divinity there was. I had married—and her prayers were to be thanked for it.

WHEN I WAS eleven, my mother began to whisper with the neighbors about something that concerned me. I knew because of the way she avoided looking directly at me, glancing instead at my knees. Soon I heard it too. There was a rumor in the neighborhood about a boy a few longtangs down who had started to go blind. The condition was inexplicable: one day he woke and found a light had been blown out. Medical experts were consulted, remedies were tried, and not one could help; each day he saw less and less. Meanwhile, this boy, who had previously been bright, with a promising future ahead of him, was thrown into a kind of stupor. Since the beginning of his misfortune, he did nothing but lie in bed. We heard he was so terrified of the darkness he might encounter that he refused even to open his eyes.

He was a few years older than me. His family was better off—his parents were shopkeepers while mine worked at a cigarette factory—but, perhaps because their desperation was fresh, perhaps because of my mother's prayers, they agreed to meet us, and after the meeting a marriage was arranged. As I would come to learn intimately, the Taos were modest and good people, naturally gentle, who were not so wealthy as to be arrogant but had also for a number of generations skirted the kind of poverty that made you bitter and mean. Tao Kun's misfortune was the greatest they had suffered in living memory, and they were as grateful to have found us as we them.

I don't remember feeling one way or another about the engagement. My future as a wife or as a spinster had always been my parents' preoccupation, I had no say in the process or outcome and it did not seem like I should. At eleven years old, I could not imagine being married. When I thought of my future husband, I pictured only a dark shape lying despondent in bed, that image concocted from the little I'd heard. I considered this image with detached curiosity.

A few days after it was settled, I was sweeping the kitchen floor when my mother came in and started to comment on what I was doing, telling me to hold the broom like this, pointing out the spots I had missed, all the while standing with her arms crossed and looking at me with something sourer than distaste. It was a look I had seen often: regretful, squinting, straining to narrow her eyes or to observe me from a different angle, so that she might see someone different, and perhaps discover that I was in fact not so ugly after all. She could not help it and I did not blame her. But as I noticed this look and made sense of it, my mother said something along the lines of: You should learn to do housework the right way, we don't want the Taos to think they've made a mistake. That was when I realized that to marry meant to leave this house, where otherwise I might have stayed forever. I began to feel that marriage was a good thing. I looked forward to the day I would leave my mother's gaze.

TAO KUN WAS a shy man. It turned out that the rumor forming my sole image of him was false—it had been his grandmother who forced him to lie in bed, hoping that he was simply tired, using his eyes too much, that if he only rested them for long enough he might be cured. By the time we married, a few years later, any sign of depression surrounding his condition was gone. The man I met was openhearted and infuriatingly positive—my opposite, in other words.

I was fifteen, he nineteen. We understood: we had married to make life bearable for our families. On our wedding night we lay down beside one another and left a courteous space between our bodies. I turned my face to the wall; he turned his to the room. I breathed shallowly, sleeping with one foot in consciousness so I would not roll accidentally into his half of the bed. For months the only parts of us that touched were our hands: when I took his to lead him through a particularly narrow alley, when he forgot where he'd set a cup of tea, when I shifted a chair or table while cleaning and he could not find it.

In his company I soon learned not to fear being seen. I picked my nose, I let my face fall into grimace. I did not worry about the neatness of my hair, my clothes, my gait. It was a kind of relaxation, like being alone without the loneliness. I grew fond of this feeling, and of him.

When we did touch, my body responded involuntarily, producing shivers of feeling that were at once pleasant and unpleasant. Each time they shocked me so that I had to stop myself from snatching my hand back as if from a hot pan. Wickedly I craved this feeling. I began to misplace things on purpose: his walking stick, his teacup, his shoes. As I waited for him to discover the misplaced things, as I waited to touch him, I suffered a physical pain unlike any I had known before: it was an ache that could not be attributed to one joint or muscle but was felt throughout the body. One day I decided to call this pain love. I was very happy with this, happy to have found a name for something and happy with how lucky I was, to have fallen in love with the person I'd married.

Tao Kun was too good to suspect me in his growing mindlessness. He called me by my full name, not wife or woman, which made me feel like I was back in school—a wonderful feeling. Zhu Wen, he said, what would I do without you? When he said this it pleased me very much. At night, on my side of the bed, I fantasized in half-sleep about my husband reaching over, his hand falling on my elbow, my shoulder, my knee.

A FEW YEARS after we married, the Communists liberated Shanghai. The Taos, who were a little better off than most people in the longtang, made adjustments so they would not be denounced as bourgeoisie. Tao Kun's parents closed their shop, giving away the space and half of the living quarters above, along with everything inside: clothes, furniture, linens, food. The Taos kept the worst of everything for themselves. They crowded into the two darkest rooms in the back of the former living space. A stairway was hastily built by the back door; more stoves were installed in the kitchen so each of the new families could have their own place to cook. The room Tao Kun and I shared was divided into two: this one where I still live now, and the one that years later would become Su Lan's.

In this way my marriage into the family became an asset. The Taos had made themselves poor, and my ugliness and limp, next to Tao Kun's blindness, gave this identity an air of authenticity. No one could look at the family as it was and muster up any residual feelings of envy, and so we were left in peace.

Nonetheless, to prove the industriousness and humility of the Taos, or to assist in bringing in income now that the shop was gone, Tao Kun decided to find work. He had heard that in a hospital in a neighboring district, there were medical massage classes for the visually impaired, and he asked me to take him there to enroll. We met the elderly teacher, blind himself, who called their disability a gift. The hands of blind men, the teacher said, could feel illnesses that others could not see. I could tell that Tao Kun enjoyed the classes, enjoyed being among people like himself. It was in this time that he began to take special note of his hands and the sensations his skin imparted. And it was on an evening shortly after he began his classes that he asked if he could practice what he had learned on me.

I was washing rice for dinner. I said yes, too quietly for anyone but my husband to hear. I was glad he could not see me. At the question my body had tensed, betraying my desire.

The bed was low. After dinner I layered what blankets we still had to raise it up. I lay on my stomach and closed my eyes.

Many moments passed and he did not touch me. The pain in my chest grew and turned to shame. Had he changed his mind? I worried I had given myself away. He had sensed—I was sure, because as his teacher said, he had a special sense—my eagerness, the ugly desire of an ugly woman to be touched. He was embarrassed. He was repulsed. Despite being blind, Tao Kun was a handsome man, he had a nice face and a fine body, and he must have known this, and must have known too that I was not fit for him, could only be fit for him if he never fully knew what I was. He was just too kind to say it. I opened my eyes and sat up, suddenly relieved.

I saw him standing on the other side of the room, running his hands over the new wall.

I'm sorry, he said, I've suddenly forgotten where I am. Is this the west wall? Or the north?

I got up and took his hand, led him across the room. I mapped the room with words, moving his hands over the table, the chair, the curtain, letting him feel as I spoke. I sat on the bed and closed my eyes. This is my face, I said, and placed his palms on my cheeks. His fingers moved over my eyebrows and wrapped around my ears. His skin smelled like salt.

These are my shoulders, I said, and kept his hands there for a long time, they were so warm and large and comforting.

This is my chest, and I placed his hands on my breasts.

I lay down again on my stomach and gave him my hand.

He moved his hands up my arm until he found my shoulders. The span of his palms covered the span of my back. He moved them down my torso. He touched my back, my hips, my legs, my feet. He stopped and rubbed my soles, pressing his thumbs into the skin. He rolled the heels of his palms into my calves. He moved along the edge of the bed as his hands moved along my body, along my thighs, my buttocks, my back. My neck. My head. He threaded his fingers through my hair.

Could he tell, touching me, that I was deformed? Had they taught him at massage school what a body ought to feel like? Had he practiced on the bodies of beautiful women? And when he felt their slim waists and plump buttocks, when he rubbed their symmetrically shaped legs, did his hands recognize that they were beautiful?

His fingers and palms pressed into my body, rubbing away aches I had not known I carried—tension in my side and hips from walking in jolted steps, a knot in my neck from lowering my face—and as these aches disappeared the ache I called love replaced them. This time I could locate it in my thighs, between my legs. Blood pounded loudly in my ears. I took his hand and pulled him down.

I have never been interested in political matters. For a person like me, it does not matter who holds power—I will always remain outside the hierarchy, in that group of people everyone pities and secretly wishes did not exist because they would rather not bother with pity. So when wars are won or lost, when political movements succeed or fail, when great changes in government and power come about, I don't feel much measure of anything. The restlessness that overtakes the city, the illusion of time suspended that makes people like Su Lan's husband behave in strange and unexplainable ways, has no effect on me. The only exception is the liberation of Shanghai. My memory of dirty soldiers shouting down the boulevards in the spring of 1949 is happy; it is tangled with the memory of the first time my husband and I made love.

DEATH TOOK TAO KUN as blindness had: slowly, relentlessly, too early. He was fifty-three when a lump began to grow in his brain. As the tumor spread, he was forced to stop working; he could no longer control his hands. He spoke of the disease as an extension of the darkness that had taken his sight. Finally his optimism was conquered, and he turned into the man I had imagined before I met him, a shadow who did nothing but lie in bed. I reminded him that the doctors said they were two isolated, unrelated conditions. I fed and bathed him. When I was not maintaining his body I attempted to catch onto whatever remained of his mind, reading to him news-papers and books. I needed him to know to the end the difference between what was true and what was comforting.

NOW DEATH HAD taken your mother too. I believed you instantly, in fact you looked so much like her—the same crown of forehead, the same curve between chin and neck—that I had believed you were her: I believed you were her ghost. You spoke the words bluntly; without knowing who I was you hoped to wound me. Later I realized your childlike use of language was the result of living in America for so long. You had forgotten how to say any but the simplest things in Chinese.

You disappeared into your mother's room, where I heard you moving things around, opening doors, cabinets, drawers. I returned to my room and searched through my own things. In my desk drawer I found the one photograph of Su Lan I had. I blew off the dust and wiped it with my sleeve.

The photograph had been taken in Beijing's Yuanmingyuan when Su Lan was studying for her master's degree. In it, she stands in a mazelike hedge dotted with yellow flowers, wearing the same pale yellow dress she wore on the day we first met. She is not touching anything, and though she is completely alone, with nothing but shrubs beside her, she poses as if sharing the frame with someone else, her body deferent and her eyes retreating, as if hoping that the viewer's attention will land on the other person instead. I found the photograph in a bag of things Su Lan was planning to discard before she left. When she saw me looking at it, she plucked it out of my hand and stared.

This is why I hate photographs, she said before dropping it back into the garbage. They're so disappointing, they never show you as you think you are.

Later, I fished it out.

There had once been many photographs of her. She was very photogenic, she knew how to pose, how to look at the camera so her face was shown in its best light. Once upon a time her husband couldn't stop trying to capture her in film, and he had put his attempts up all over their room. But in the months before she left she had destroyed them all.

Now I glued the photograph of Su Lan in Yuanmingyuan to a piece of cardboard and took it to my altar. Between Guanyin and Tao I made a space and put Su Lan there. I lit three sticks of incense. Somewhere outside the neighborhood walls, a round of firecrackers went off. The first round was followed by another, then fireworks, and for a moment the sky behind the window glowed.

YOU DON'T HAVE Su Lan's face—not quite. Your eyes are sunk deeper into your brows, and they dart about without focus, wide— lost. Each time I look, I discover another difference: the square jaw, the thick, athletic legs, a rougher complexion, and a distinct way of holding yourself, with your neck sticking out slightly, like one of those animals that is always turning its head this way or that.

A few years ago I saw these attributes on the face of another ghost, one that came not too long after Tao Kun, but who stayed only shortly. He appeared after the new year. He stood in the alley-way underneath the window day after day in the same place, the ground beneath him littered with the blasted red scraps of firecrackers. He stared, silent and unmoving, at the red 拆 on the wall. Something about him looked familiar, but he wore a strange expression, one I had never seen on any living person's face. It was fixed yet far away, as if he could see through the wall. I sensed that he wanted to come up but something was stopping him. He only ever appeared for a moment—I would glance out the window and note his presence, turn away to do some things, and by the time I looked back he would be gone.

It wasn't until I went into Su Lan's room that I realized who he was. You see, I took the task your mother gave me seriously. Up to the day you appeared I went in there every so often to dust the furniture, open the windows, move things around so the air felt lived in. Each month I pay her rent alongside my own with the money she left for that purpose. The rent, which has not risen since she moved in, is laughably low—these days, less than a meal for two at the new restaurant down the street—and the amount she left could sustain it for an entire lifetime. For fifteen years I kept the room in a livable state, ready for the day Su Lan returned.

After the appearance of your father's ghost I decided to make some changes. Su Lan had left that man's traces everywhere, so thoroughly that the room seemed prepared not for her return but for his. His shirts, pants, and jackets hung in the wardrobe. His shoes were lined up on the floor. On the hook behind the door hung his white doctor's coat and stethoscope. Meanwhile she'd left few traces of herself; the clothes she had not taken with her or given away were packed in trunks and drawers, and her books were stacked underneath and behind his, hiding in shadow.

There was a trunk under the bed filled with cloth diapers and swaddling clothes, things you would certainly no longer need. I emptied it. I filled the trunk with everything that had belonged to

Su Lan's husband: clothes, medical textbooks, papers, a pen I had once seen him use. In the empty wardrobe I hung the dresses Su Lan had left behind. I rooted through her cabinets and drawers. In the bottom drawer of her desk was an envelope of photographs, twenty or so, all of the man I had seen outside. They looked like they had all been shot in the same day. I dug through the drawer, which was full of notebooks and papers. There were no more photographs, not one of Su Lan. But the search was worthwhile: in the back corner I found a bundle of letters bound tightly with string. I threw the photographs and letters in the trunk. I dropped the lid and it closed with a satisfying sound. I shoved it back deep beneath the bed.

You no longer needed your swaddling clothes; Su Lan no longer needed him. I was certain he had fallen out of her mind, had faded in her heart. In America Su Lan would be occupied by many important things, perhaps she'd found other lovers, perhaps she'd even remarried. I could hear her voice on the night before she left Shanghai: *I see them taking him, in order to drag me back.* I was simply enacting the natural work of time, and what Su Lan had confessed to doing that night. I was cleansing the future of the past.

I left just one thing: the wedding portrait. I had plucked it from the wall to press down the tangle of her husband's ties, but the wall was lighter in color where it had hung and the spot drew attention to the crooked nail that protruded from it. The white paint Su Lan had brushed on more than a decade ago looked yellow-gray and stained around the rectangle where the portrait had been, and I felt inexplicably sad looking at it, as if witnessing something that had happened to Su Lan herself.

I rehung the portrait.

It was enough—the next morning the ghost was gone and he never returned again.

YOUR MOTHER HAD not always wanted children. One day, when she was a child, she had learned that she'd been created inside her mother, and that this creation had been a decision—something that could have been prevented. On that day she had sworn that she would not make her mother's mistake.

She told me this once, when we were still strangers and she was trying too hard to become my friend. I thought she was this way with everyone; I found it incredibly irritating. Later she admitted she was trying to provoke me without explaining why, and in a backward way the admission made me like her. She said, If you think I'm trying to draw you out, you're right. She found reasons to admire me; among these—my independence, my stubbornness—was the fact that I had no children.

Children, she said, were a great responsibility. Contrary to what some people believed, children had nothing to do with the individual and everything to do with the species; they were a lie that biology created to make us feel immortal. Their true use was for labor: to sow the field, to bring in the harvest, to take the oxen out to graze. A person like her, who labored in the mind, had no need for them. Besides, she said, it was hard enough to make your own life what you wanted it to be. It was better—more honest, she said, to do as you have, to live fully in this life with no pretense.

I told her I'd hardly made such a dramatic decision.

She did not know, and I did not tell her, that it was not my choice. In fact I had been pregnant many times, and each time, I had hoped for a child.

The first time I had been very afraid. For a while I did not tell Tao Kun and denied it to myself. When he found the little bulge some weeks later, however, he did not react with horror or disgust. He was full of joy, and in his joy I allowed myself to believe I would bear our child. For three weeks I allowed myself to worry about my body's ability to carry this child, what the extra weight would do to my misaligned hips, if my legs would crack beneath me, the right calf curving out, the knee bending in. Sometimes I imagined that in the moment of birth, the child would squeeze through my pelvis and snap my distorted limbs into their proper places.

Tao Kun fretted over me, calling out to see if I needed anything so often I grew used to ignoring him. When we left the house he took my elbow instead of me taking his, and I wondered if he had ever needed me to guide him.

Our bliss was short. The baby came out of me in bloody clumps. I woke in pain; I rose and sat folded on the matong in the dark. My body ate into itself. I kept still, I breathed low. I did not want to wake Tao. Before daylight I emptied the chamber pot and rinsed it clean. I vomited in the alley. I bathed with a cold towel. The room still smelled acrid and bloody when I crawled back into the bed. That was the closest I'd ever felt to death. Later, we both agreed it was for the best. Did we really want to inflict our attributes onto a child?

FOR WEEKS BEFORE Su Lan revealed to me her condition, she seemed agitated, her feet tapping the floor, a flush rising quickly to her cheeks. She came into my room one evening before her husband was back from work, strangely giddy, and said, I think I'm pregnant, can you believe it?

She was wide-eyed, as if she herself could not. The back door opened and someone came up the steps. She pressed her finger to her lips and hurried out.

The next day she was more subdued. It was mid-afternoon and she had come home early from work. She had gone to the doctor's and confirmed it.

It's real, she said. Strangely, I'm not unhappy. I think—I'm quite sure—I woke up this morning and thought, if it's true, I'll keep it.

She spoke again about her fear of having children, the difficulty of raising them, broaching the same points she usually did, but whereas before she spoke quickly and passionately, now her brow was furrowed, her voice soft and light, and her opinions came out as questions and gestures rather than arguments. It was difficult, she said, not only because of the physical work it would entail, but because one wanted the child to be happy, which meant giving it a chance to make a life for itself. But there would always be the problem of history. How could you keep your history from infecting the child?

The child is innocent, Su Lan said. It should be born free. It will be difficult, she said again, it will be tempting to pass yourself on even though you know it's wrong. Already I've been tempted to make lines of causality to bind me to those I love.

You're a strange woman, I said, and I meant it.

Perhaps this was the first time I noticed that Su Lan spoke often about the past, about history, but always in these vague and abstract ways. She did not mention her childhood, her hometown, not even Beijing where she'd lived just half a year ago. I already knew by then that Su Lan had a great capacity for drawing pictures with words, filling in small details in the darkest corners. But this energy was directed willfully on the present and the future.

I watched her husband. The prospect of fatherhood could change men; some of them grew suddenly loving, treating the wives they'd once bullied as precious things, so that their women glowed, carrying their round bellies like queens. Shy men could become boastful and hold their chests high, letting their voices ring over the din, and slovenly men could grow responsible, and men who looked like boys matured overnight. Of course it went the other way too, pressure exacerbating vices, the prospect of one more mouth to feed making poor men petty and anxious and depressed.

Su Lan's husband stayed the same. So much so that I wondered if she had told him. I did not hear the subject in the courtyard gossip when the couple was at work. Su Lan continued to give me a conspiratorial look, one that said we were different together, which I had never understood before. Now I read in it the secret: she's pregnant, and nobody knows but me, and I don't know why that is.

Things went on as usual until she began to show.

PREGNANCY DID NOT suit Su Lan. The neighbors said she was letting herself go, she was getting ugly, and I saw that it was true. The bump ruined her figure. Her small body now looked short and squat. The child had sucked the blood from her lips and bloated her face, made her skin gray when she was tired, splotchy and red when excited, and covered her once-smooth cheeks with freckles and spots. Her hair dried to a brittle, dull floss. She was still attractive, but in a harsh, used sort of way. She smelled of sweat and rancid breath. She vomited frequently, sometimes more than once a day, reacting to the smell of simmering oil, which was impossible to avoid in the longtang.

She began to work at home, going into the university only to teach and attend meetings and occasionally run an experiment at the lab. She said she preferred this, that the sterile silence of the lab spooked her.

I thought she didn't like people seeing her weak. She shut the door when she was sick and hurried down the stairs to rinse the bucket immediately after. Returning with the clean bucket, she told me that she liked working in noisy conditions, liked hearing the conversations in the hallways and the vendors cycling past in the alley, the dogs barking and children crying and pots being dropped into sinks. When she was a university student, she said, she had studied in the most crowded public places—train stations, busy squares, restaurants and cafeterias. An unintended side effect of this practice was that her classmates and colleagues never saw her study, and thus considered her accomplishments the result of unnatural intellectual gifts. Even now having to mute outside noises helped her focus.

But she couldn't focus. She was listless, milling about the landing and terrace, walking back and forth without aim. As her belly grew she became afraid of going down the steep stairs but was also unable to sit still in her room.

I mentioned that her husband, a doctor, might have some medical advice. She denied that anything was wrong. I pointed to the changes in her complexion.

She said with a wicked smile, It's just my true self coming out.

SOME STRANGE SHIFT was taking place in the room next door. Su Lan began to embrace her role as wife and expectant mother. Her morning sickness had passed; she insisted now that pregnancy was a delicious feeling. She replaced her earlier reservations about motherhood with the idea of creating someone entirely new, the likes of whom she could not predict, and relished this idea. On more than one occasion she said with optimism, It makes the future new. I saw her surveying herself in the mirror.

Look, she said, beckoning me in. She turned sideways, and her belly was undeniable now, it defined her body's relationship with space.

I barely recognize myself, she said. Her body felt and looked strange to her. It was as if she had discovered for the first time her flesh, her blood, her bones, her organs, her skin, her saliva, all those thin membranes. Those elements that composed her body were changing, truly changing, transforming into something else, something that existed not just to perpetuate its own survival but to grow a separate body. It was change on a depth and scale that she'd been too dull to even imagine until it happened to her. Her new body, and inside it, another new body—two strangers, the result of this process. She said this as if it were the obvious solution to a question she'd been asking all her life.

To the problem of history she seemed too to have found an obvious solution. She said, as if stumbling upon a magnificent discovery: This child will be born in *Shanghai*. And wasn't this why she had married her husband after all? In order to create a new life inside his world?

For once, Su Lan did not feel trapped in her body but rather taken along with it as it transformed, making her into something strange and new. What creative feats the body was capable of, she said admiringly, how they surpassed the puny abilities of the mind. She stroked her belly and spoke to you tenderly, addressing you with delight: Who are you, little stranger?

Meanwhile, her husband changed too.

I never knew if she told him she was pregnant. Perhaps she had, like me, let her body do the telling. There was no quarrel, no smashing of plates on the ground. Not yet. It began, as most things do, without announcement. I saw more and more of Su Lan and less and less of her husband. He stayed later at work. He was on call. He started a research project and spent additional hours at the hospital enrolling patients in clinical trials. When he was home he was less social, greeting me only with an impassive nod.

When they first moved into the longtang, he had been unabashedly and passionately in love, letting everyone see it as if it were his first virtue. He had brightened when speaking about her, describing her as if a rare, most valuable jewel. I think he was by nature a quiet man who preferred to keep to himself, or perhaps a man with too much pride to speak freely. But at her side he'd light up and become gregarious, generous, almost carefree, laughing easily, asking after all those around him. Every few minutes he'd look at her and touch her wrist, or the small of her back, to make sure she was still there, still watching, as if his life found purpose only in her witness.

Now, through the wall between our rooms, I heard him speak more and more often in that tone used for complaining about insignificant things. The room was too small, they had too much furniture, the walls were too thin, the air was thick with dust. They both worked but he did not take over any more of the household chores. The rare times I saw the two of them together, in the evenings or on Sundays, he would be sitting with a paper or staring at the news on television, while she cleaned or cooked, sweating under the fatigue of her condition. He avoided looking at her; when he did look it was with contempt. Once, while Su Lan was sweeping the room, I saw her husband scanning her body up and down as if appraising it, his face blank with disgust. When he spoke, it was limited to the practical and mundane. He never raised his voice. He sounded tired, annoyed.

Retrospectively, it is too clear. If Su Lan had set her story going one way, this was where it pulled onto its own course, dragging me along with it. Perhaps if everything had turned out as Lan intended, I would have been left unimplicated, simply *drawn out* as she'd said, but as it was I found myself pulled in, the limbs of my life entangling with my accidental neighbor's future. Sometimes I wonder what I could have done differently, if perhaps I should have tried harder to extricate myself. But it all happened so quickly. It was only months later, when I was holding you, that it struck me like a light: Su Lan got pregnant, and her husband got mean.

IT WAS THE spring of 1989. The city's skin stretched too. In April a former government official died abruptly and the young people of Shanghai poured into the streets to mourn. The dead man had been very popular among the youth for his reformist policies but had some years ago been removed from power, and so his death carried great symbolic potential. I heard people marching past the longtang gate in waves, shouting about true patriotism and political reform. In the following days handwritten posters papered the walls of the alleys, before which groups of people I knew and people I'd never seen before gathered, reading over one another's shoulders with their hands clasped behind their backs. The quantity of posters increased and so did the quantity of people, who not only came to read but stayed to discuss and argue, and at times burst into spontaneous public speech, gesturing with their arms and pounding their fists. Torn and crumpled pamphlets filled the cracks in the cobblestone. Stray fallen petals, on their way to some makeshift public memorial for the deceased politician, gathered bruised and trampled in the gutters.

On my way back from the latrine a crumpled pamphlet stuck to the bottom of my cane. I unfolded it and read: tirades on government corruption and rising prices, demands for labor rights and increased salaries for intellectuals. Sprinkled between were repeated impassioned phrases wielding words such as *democracy* and *human rights* like righteous cudgels. In the newspapers I read about an ongoing student demonstration in Beijing at Tiananmen Square. I checked the publication date on the top corner. It seemed that these exact events had happened before, these same slogans chanted and these same patriotic songs sung in unison. I had read the same abstract arguments in pamphlets and big character posters, and perhaps it was this same deposed government official who had died and whose death transformed him into a martyred hero, propelling the parading of these same wreaths of flowers through the streets. In the *People's Daily* I read an editorial denouncing the demonstrations as incited by counterrevolutionary factions, and again it sounded very much like something I had read before.

In the streets the editorial was denounced with such fury it could have been mistaken for zeal. The television screens in the longtang windows flashed images of young men kneeling before the People's Hall with a scroll raised above their heads. Thousands of young people began to sleep in Tiananmen Square, some refusing to eat until the senior party leadership agreed to a list of demands. In the building the usual gossip—who was sneaking around with a mistress, which siblings were fighting over an inheritance—was replaced with rumors about government leaders, Li Peng's Hainan mansion or Zhao Ziyang's secret visit to the students on hunger strike. In front of the marketplace the old woman from Xinjiang who read faces for a dime began to sell cartoons of Deng Xiaoping in various poses of disgrace.

Su Lan had a hungry human inside of her. Her classes had emptied onto the street, and so she spent most days at home, scratching out calculations with her swollen feet elevated on the bed. The chanting and crowds did not bother her; she went on as if they were a part of normal life. I tried to do the same but could not help feeling agitated and embarrassed for reasons I did not fully understand. I was embarrassed for the protesters, who looked so young and sounded so naïve, but I was also embarrassed for myself. Each time this kind of thing happened, my alienation darkened; there was something in the collective mob of passion that challenged the tolerable solitude of living in my given body. Sometimes I felt as if I had been transported to a foreign land, thrown into the midst of many people speaking a language I could not understand.

Su Lan and I both avoided leaving the house, each of us with our own set of justifications. I told her I had been alive for long enough to see the order of things turn upside down once, and then again, and did not need to witness it yet another time, which wasn't untrue. But it was also true that even then I understood my behavior was not so unlike that of a child's, closing her eyes in hopes that what she doesn't want to see will simply disappear.

When I did venture outside for the necessary errands, battling through a crowd of shins with my cane, I would often look up to find myself face-to-face with Su Lan's husband. There he was, standing in a huddle, arguing with someone, nodding to an impromptu speech, once even gesticulating in the center of a circle at least twenty onlookers deep, his handsome face scrunched in scrutiny, the shadows under his eyes lengthening. I sat on the terrace and watched a procession going past the wall, fists and banners peeking over the roofs of the neighborhood, and thought I saw a man who looked very much like Su Lan's husband lifted above the crowd and carried along on its shoulders, waving a Chinese flag.

Many evenings he arrived home after the house had gone dark, banging his way up the stairs. Beyond the shared wall came the hissing of hard muffled speech. Interest in politics had changed his voice; it was now laden with the too-knowing tone of political science professors, laden too with the weight of the pamphleteers' words, *right* and *justice* and *wrong*. He accused Su Lan of not supporting her students like other university professors were doing, and asked why, if she disapproved or thought the students' tactics wrongheaded, she did not try to steer them the right way. He called her selfish and apathetic and unpatriotic. A few times Su Lan responded. Unlike her husband, she spoke without passion, and softly, so I could not make out what exactly she said. But her tone was firm and confident, and after she spoke there followed what sounded to me like a defeated silence. I fell asleep believing her husband had been proven intellectually inferior, and put back in his place.

The other residents of the house must have heard these conversations too. One day as I was coming back from the market I saw Ma Ahyi from the front unit holding Su Lan's elbow in the kitchen, her mouth an inch from my neighbor's ear. Sometimes you have to pretend to be stupid in front of your husband, I heard, sometimes you have to let him win. It's not attractive for a woman to be so strong. A truly clever woman, Ma Ahyi said, knows how to let a man think he's right even when he's agreeing that he's wrong. Especially—Ma Ahyi lowered her voice—when it comes to politics. If you ask me, I wouldn't even bother with it, let him have his opinions.

If Su Lan thought anything about this advice one way or the other, she didn't show it on her face. But she began to overcompensate for her husband's increased absences. She became too cheerful. She welcomed him home, a caricature of a perfect wife, with warm smiles and caresses and sweet sentences about absolutely nothing. She turned the television to the news for him but didn't discuss the contents. She made his favorite dishes—she tried. She was a disastrous cook, I discovered, she had no natural affinity for household tasks. I helped her in the kitchen; I taught her how to make some Shanghai dishes. If her husband was placated, I could not tell. I felt at once ashamed for and impressed by your mother, by how far she would go.

She became an insomniac. Often I woke before dawn and saw a bar of light beneath her door. From the terrace window I glimpsed her at the desk with her legs propped on the bed, working by lamplight beside her husband's sleeping form, and knew that she had not yet gone to sleep.

SU LAN'S HUSBAND was planning a trip to Beijing for a medical conference. The conference would require him to leave Shanghai for at least three days, though probably he'd be gone as long as a week. It was mid-May. The swallows were finishing their nest. Su Lan was unhappy, though the conference, scheduled months ago, had originally been her idea.

It's my fault, she admitted. It was she who had encouraged him to be more than just a physician, to try his hand at medical research, she who had stoked his scientific mind and creativity, who, when he at first resisted, goaded him by insulting his intelligence and courage, calling him a mere practitioner who was good for memorizing medical textbooks and nothing else. At an introductory dinner with his boss, the chair of the oncology department, she had declared her husband's ambition (as yet unknown to him) of going abroad to study new technologies and practices to bring back to China. She impressed the old doctor very much with her charm and intelligence. I didn't doubt it—she could put on her charm like an expensive coat. After this dinner the chair selected her husband to assist in a new study, concerning the efficacy of radiation versus chemotherapy on late-stage liver cancer, and this was why he had begun to work later, why he was so stressed and distracted of late. Su Lan hadn't minded—in fact, when it first began, she'd said he did it for her. He was talented at languages; with his English skills and a strong research background, they might one day have the chance to go abroad.

I should have heard it then, in Su Lan's praise of her husband's English, how desperately she wanted to leave China. Later, when she was gone, I would remember how she'd spoken of China in their political arguments like a place she had already left. There was something in her voice, bitter and quiet, similar to the low murmur that appeared in my own voice whenever I was forced to explain my limp. It was self-loathing, it was shame.

It was a big deal for someone so young to be invited to attend these conferences, Su Lan had said when her husband first received the invitation. They were usually reserved for hospital directors and the leading innovators in the field. At the time, her husband had been overwhelmed by the honor, and had spoken admiringly of how Su Lan inspired him to strive harder, how she pushed him to be more ambitious, how most of all she lit up his mind and made it more expansive and capable and hungry. He said he owed all his achievements to her.

Now she was eight months pregnant, her body exhausted and huge. She had stopped going in to the university altogether. At home she dozed with books open in her lap, snapped awake for moments to tap her pencil on blank sheets of paper. The early summer sun brought some heat to the longtang. Su Lan abandoned her wardrobe and wore the same loose housedress every day, walking around the filthy building barefoot. Her room was a mess, clothes and papers everywhere. Flies landed on her sweaty skin and she did not bother to swat them away.

She had changed, he had changed—the inspiration she'd kindled had become an excuse to stay away from her—and the environment had changed too, Beijing was a huge mess. She no longer wanted him to go.

Surprisingly, the conference hadn't been canceled or rescheduled or relocated despite the continuing protests in the capital. Su Lan suspected that in fact it had been, and her husband was pretending for an excuse to go to Beijing.

You know why he wants to go, she said. He wants to be in the action. He's feeling cooped up here playing my husband. He wants to play at making revolution instead.

The protests had become a fact of daily life. The students occupied Tiananmen Square as if they had been stationed there. I wondered why they kept at it, if it had become a habit or if they still believed in their causes. Perhaps things had gone on for so long that a stupid stubbornness had settled in—if these children backed down now, with nothing new to show for all their energy and protestations, they would reveal themselves as cowardly, or worse, hypocritical, and would have to contend with the fact of wasted time and passion.

Su Lan's husband packed for Beijing.

Did you know, Su Lan said, that he pursued me for years? I made an art of saying no.

She paced the length of my room. She spoke of her many other suitors. She had met her husband in high school. He had been a brilliant student, admired and loved by all, but she had thought him arrogant, self-absorbed, careless in his ambition.

I was right, she said, he is all those things. He's never questioned his ability to succeed, and this makes him easy to hate. There's something about hating someone so intensely that effortlessly turns into love.

Was this perverse?

I didn't know. Su Lan was in a strange, dazed state, without her usual focus, as if someone had spun her in circles.

My husband and I had met once before we married. We learned to live together, then time made us dependent on each other. Dependency turned into affection which turned into love. Perhaps there were times when I had resented his blindness, not because it made him less in any way, but because of what it said about me, because when people found out I was the wife of a blind man, it made sense to them. And when he was ill and dying, when I cleaned his shit and fed him porridge spoon by spoon, I had wished he would hurry up and die. But I had never seen him as a choice, so I did not consider these hatreds specific to him; rather, they were enveloped in that banal hatred of one's own life and therefore tolerated.

Su Lan raved on. He's become that arrogant boy again, she said. He's acting like he's seventeen, like he's one of those kids standing up in the square with megaphones shouting bullshit patriotic polemics. Have you seen these children? If you watch them for even a second you can see they just love the attention, they love hearing the sound of their own voices followed by thunderous clapping, they love hearing their words repeated and chanted by the mob, and that's my husband too. I can't believe it. I can't believe I'm in love with such a shallow man.

She swallowed and shook her head. She let out a slow breath. When she spoke next she seemed not to see me, though I was standing right there. She stared at me and forgot I was someone else.

Sometimes I ask myself why I married him. She shook her head. But the answer is clear in his face, in the way he walks and talks, the way he breathes. Whatever his flaws, he was always and will always be a person born as he was, on a ground that is solid and whole. I envy him so much for this quality. She touched her stomach: Perhaps our child will be like him. You see, ahpo, unlike my husband I am covered all over in cracks, they're so fine you can't see them unless you're looking. Remember the first time I came to the longtang?

You came to paint the room.

No, that was the second time.

Oh?

I'd visited a week or so before, with the Fudan housing director. He was very excited about this vacancy—there was a long waiting list, you see, and he had done quite a bit of digging and rearranging to find this room for us. It was only my third time in Shanghai. I was still so enthralled by the city, how you could feel the money in the air; even though the glory days were long gone and people lived modestly now, there was still the memory of wealth, of extravagance: just being in the city made me feel like I had that memory too. I remember when we got off the bus and turned into the longtang, the first thing I thought was, I'll live in a house made of *bricks*. I was like a girl in a wonderland, practically blind. It wasn't until I was standing in the room with the housing director that the spell broke. Somewhere along the way, while I was dreaming of my new life, his excitement had turned into embarrassment, and as we stood in the room he began to extol its virtues, but with a newly apologetic tone, muttering about how a fresh coat of paint would cover those cracks, which I hadn't even noticed, how a good cleaning and it'd be like new, how the neighborhood had a long history, was centrally located, in the heart of the old city, and with history came some charm. I blinked and began to see the place with his eyes—my husband's eyes. As we left, the director spoke endlessly of the waiting list, of newlyweds who'd had to dorm for months before a room opened up, of one couple who lived separately for two years waiting for the perfect placement, by which time the husband had started having an affair with her best friend. I got the message.

She looked out the window.

So your husband, I said, he's like that fresh coat of paint, but for you.

She blinked. She snapped out of herself. For less than a moment, before she forced a laugh and pulled on her charm, she looked horrified.

She threw up her hands and declared she had to get back to work.

The marriages of the past were better, I thought as she left my room. Modern courtship was silly, whimsical, almost certain to yield disappointment. It was simpler to treat a spouse as you did your own body: something given. If you were lucky you could learn to love it. If you could not, you lived with it.

THE WEEK BEFORE Su Lan's husband was scheduled to leave for Beijing, the couple argued many times a day. Su Lan no longer bothered to lower her voice. She spoke to match the unabashed timbre of the protests outside.

The news blasted from their television whenever her husband was at home. In Beijing there were developments within the movement. Li Peng had granted the student leaders a televised audience, which had resulted in absolutely nothing. The Russian leader Gorbachev's welcome ceremony was moved from the square to the runway of the airport where he arrived. Foreign journalists had descended upon the city for the historic diplomatic event. Martial law was declared. Zhao Ziyang spoke out in favor of the movement, and then he disappeared amid rumors that he would be deposed. With each development, whether a step forward or back, the protests seemed to grow, as if news itself had the power of biological contagion. Thousands of workers and young people streamed into Beijing from the countryside.

Democracy fever, Su Lan called it, *mingzhu bing*. She hated that her husband had caught it. She did not believe he actually understood the issues or even cared. She accused him of using political fervor as an excuse to look away from a weakness inside himself.

On the eve of his departure, I was sitting on the terrace catching the cool air when I heard my neighbor shouting *mingzhu* through the closed door. For a moment Su Lan's voice merged with the chanting on the streets, and it sounded like she was shouting out the window in solidarity. But her voice broke from the others: Tell me, she said, what do you know about *democracy*? Do you even know what the word means?

You're missing the point, her husband said. These are basic and fundamental ideas.

Basic and fundamental to what?

Human liberty!

And nothing less.

Su Lan's laugh was loud and full of disdain. I wonder, she continued, what this human liberty looks like. Can you draw me a picture? What color is it? How does it taste? How will life be different after all this parading in the streets? And if the Party steps down as you demand, what will you put up in its place? What are your policy proposals? Your electoral plans?

Her husband's response was drowned out by a surge of singing from outside. Then the crowd quieted, became almost silent, except for one voice that reverberated distantly, moving away, and Su Lan's voice emerged in the sudden still, sharp and shaking.

You know what you are? A phony intellectual. You've always been a phony, taking on ideas to feel important and intelligent without understanding their actual substance. Run off to Beijing, go attend to your *national affairs*, pretend it's harder to shout empty slogans about abstract concepts than to take individual responsibility for the result of your own actions—here came the sound of a wet slap, as she struck her stomach—but don't think I don't see right through you. Don't think everybody can't see right through you.

There was a crash. The sound of things falling, her husband's voice speaking, stern and passionless as the pair suddenly switched roles, and another crash, and the door flung open. Su Lan emerged, fists full of men's clothes, which she flung down the stairs, shouting *Fake, coward, go to Beijing and die there.* She returned to the landing with an armful of his shoes and books. They thudded down the stairs. The old walls shook. Her words became indistinct sounds, some language or dialect I could not understand, and her voice became sharp and substantial, so substantial it could plow a person down. I sat on the terrace without moving. I did not want to go inside. But someone had to hold Su Lan's arms to her sides; someone had to restrain her until she came back to herself.

Finally I grabbed my cane and stepped inside.

She stopped shouting. Her face gleamed, patchy and red. Her chest heaved above her belly and she clutched her lower back. She smiled, suddenly serene. In a voice that made me want to scrub my body with hot water and soap, she said:

I've disturbed you, ahpo. I'm afraid I didn't realize how late it was.

I went to my room. As I passed her open door, I saw that the floor of Su Lan's room was covered in black shards. The television was smashed on the ground, and littered amid the shards were the torn pages of what looked like an anatomy textbook, pages filled with images of the skinned human body, its ropes of muscle and bulging round eyes. Su Lan's husband sat at the table and stared blankly at the drawings as if they had always been there. The next morning, the mess was gone. Your mother acted as if nothing had happened. Two days later, when her husband left for Beijing, she carried her own suitcase down the stairs and went with him.

YOUR MOTHER SAID I looked like someone she'd always known. She said this quietly, the first time we met, as she was disappearing down the stairs. I never heard her repeat the sentiment, but it came back to me often, a refrain spoken in a small place in my mind. By the time she left I was sure this was in fact what she had murmured; I was sure because I finally understood what she meant.

Strange world. Unlike Su Lan, you *have* always known me, I am the second person you met, second to your mother, the second person most intimate with the fact of your fragile body. And yet you look at me like you never imagined I could exist.

I WAS SURPRISED to find her door open. It was the morning after you appeared, after a night of sounds behind a closed door. I had slept alone, fitfully, Tao Kun had not come, and when I went out onto the landing and saw the outline of your body through the door I nearly called out Su Lan's name again. You had changed your clothes and put on one of her dresses—the pale yellow one she was wearing in the picture on my altar—and you stood facing the wall bare-legged, without a coat or even a sweater, though it was still winter and the room, without sunlight or a gas stove, was more frigid than the outdoors.

You were looking at your parents' wedding portrait. At him, I saw. Not at her.

What had Su Lan told you about this man? It was possible, I suddenly realized, that she had said nothing.

On the table where Su Lan and her husband had taken their meals I saw something that had not been in this room before, which you must have brought, a small wooden box. I moved toward it. The wood was light and unpolished, as if it had just been cut. I opened the lid. Inside was a plastic bag of gray matter. I don't know what made my fingers reach into the bag and pinch. The contents were soft, almost silken, once you rubbed past the softness there were tiny granules—

I stepped back. The lid shut with a sharp *bang*. You turned and drove me out with your eyes.

My heart was racing. Suddenly I saw my deathbed: I had always imagined Su Lan there. What a discomfiting feeling to know for certain she would not be, a stone plummeting in my gut. Su Lan would not see me die, not because she had forgotten me, not because the return journey to Shanghai would be too long and expensive and arduous, not because I could not find a way to tell her, but because she had gone first, she now existed only as a bag of ashes inside a wooden box.

HOW?

I did want to ask you.

WHEN MY HUSBAND died I sat next to him and watched his body change. It relaxed then sagged then stiffened again, his skin shrinking, his eyelids pulling back. Blood drained from his cheeks and stained his palms, which lay flat against the bed. His skin turned pale and waxy and gray.

It seemed to me that Tao Kun had not died, but rather was slowly being replaced by his body, until he was nothing more than a thing. It was true that his body, losing him, was decaying. It smelled, and the smell surprised me, though I had been near dead bodies before, my mother's, my father's, Tao Kun's parents, many others specific and vague. It did not seem right that death should smell, because death was only passing into nothingness, and nothing should not smell like anything. Later I learned, from Su Lan or from her doctor husband, that in fact I had been correct. The odor emitted by the dead was caused by living microorganisms—think of them as tiny bugs, Su Lan had said—feasting on the abandoned body and turning it inside out. It was not death that stank but rather life continuing on over it, devouring it.

I had not attended to any of the rituals. I sat and watched my neighbors fuss. Someone called the coroner. Someone fetched Tao Kun's little sister, who cleaned the body and dressed it. Someone scolded me and dressed me in proper mourning clothes. Someone took my money and paid for the cremation. Someone gave me the box of ashes and said they were his bones. Bones? I had never thought of Tao Kun as having bones. They had been so well hidden inside him.

SU LAN'S FIRST days of motherhood were days of panic and deep exhaustion. It was not just you—it was not clearly you. The circumstances were extraordinary. She had gone to Beijing and witnessed horrible, frightening things, and in the middle of it, her husband, with whom she had not been on the best of terms, had disappeared, had possibly—probably—been killed. Who knew what circumstances like that could do to a person like her, whose mind was always pulling away to unimaginable places. And yet she was a mother, she had become a mother, and was faced now with the responsibility she'd previously sworn she did not want. You, her swollen breasts, her broken body. The reality of motherhood pulled her away from her mind.

She was a competent mother. She did everything necessary to keep you alive, and did it well, she fed you and held you and cleaned you. She performed these actions mechanically, with neither tenderness nor disgust. I sensed in her a certain gratitude; some part of her understood that the ceaseless movements of her hands, arms, legs, in picking you up and bouncing you, in nursing and cleaning you, in washing diapers and swaddling blankets, forced her mind to stay in a dull and inactive state, an inactivity which she must have understood was keeping her sane. When she did allow herself to think and feel, she returned to subjects that had consumed her in the beginning of pregnancy, the perils of raising a child. It was in these reveries that she sometimes mentioned her own mother and spoke, however fleetingly, of her past.

She had gone to Beijing University, Beida, one of the top universities in the country. It had been her first time in the capital, and the entire time she had felt as if she were enclosed inside another person's body. She'd walked across the green lawns of campus, around the paved pondside walkways, under the swooning branches of willows, not recognizing the way people looked at her or spoke to her, believing whenever she was addressed that the message was meant for someone else. Her own upbringing had been so far from the place she'd landed that she hadn't even known it was special; in high school, on the day university placements arrived, she had learned of the prestige of her placement by the hushed envious looks of the other students, who seemed to be seeing her for the first time. When she arrived in Beijing, and for months, even years after, she could not shake the feeling that she was there because someone had made a mistake.

She remembered a day in the fall of her first year, before she knew the way back from class to her dormitory, when she saw a young woman walking through the grounds surrounded by a large entourage. The woman was a fellow student, judging by the books in her hands and the youth of her face, but she distinguished herself somehow from the others, in the very way she walked and breathed. Su Lan asked a young man for directions; he noticed her gaze and said, That's right, that's such-and-such, and Su Lan nodded though she did not recognize the name. Some time later she came across the name again, in a newspaper or magazine, and learned that the girl was the daughter of a top party official. When she learned this, she became dizzy and disoriented, she felt a gut-dropping vertigo accompanied again by the certainty that she was in the wrong place. This dizziness would strike again and again, such as when she heard that Mao Zedong had studied at the university, that Lu Xun had taught there. Later, after she grew accustomed to the idea of sharing space with legends and myths, the dizziness came to her in her physics lectures, for instance when she learned the mathematics to manipulate electricity, or the principle that had made possible the atomic bomb, or when, lying awake at night, she memorized the infinite digits of the numerical constants that governed what we saw in the skies at night, that governed the warping of time and space. It seemed to her that the keys of truth and knowledge and perhaps even time had been thrown on the table before her, the gates flung open, granting her access to a world that was for most of her life so separate it might as well have belonged in the domain of gods.

Occasionally, of course, being at Beida had given her the confidence one might have expected, the feeling that she had earned her place, that she belonged among the special and the extraordinary. But this confidence was always fleeting, attached to a little success (a perfect test score, a word of praise from a difficult professor), and its glimmer faded as quickly and sharply as it had come. Furthermore, the reminder that she did not truly belong was present whenever she opened her mouth: she had not learned to speak proper putonghua until she left her hometown for high school, and for years she was unable to erase the remnants of her childhood dialect, the country accent, the illiterate phrases and idioms that had no written counterpart. When she first arrived in Beijing she had been ridiculed for failing to pronounce the difference between *su* and *shu* or *rou* and *lou*, and more than once she translated into Mandarin a saying in dialect so common she'd assumed it universal, only to be asked to repeat her words to bursts of derisive laughter. Though her excellent grades, and later, in her graduate studies, her excellent research results, confirmed on paper that she did deserve to be there, she was never fully convinced.

Ever since I left home, she said one day without introduction, gripping my wrist, I have felt this great—threat—hanging over me, looming, following me wherever I go, saying, *Any day, I will strike*, and now it has.

She had a fever as she often did in those days and was lying in bed. I was trying to take you from her so she could rest. Her voice was croaking, it sounded like she was trying to speak with hands around her throat.

Because I am not innocent, she continued. I have reaped the rewards and I have left everyone behind. I have been very lucky, and until now I have fooled everyone. My mother used to tell me I was nobody special, she used to say my bones could be broken like anyone else's, my skin could be cut and I would bleed too, and I left telling her she was wrong, I would prove her wrong.

She smiled sweetly then. She brought her hand up to my face and said, You're a mirror, aren't you? She touched my cheek; she darkened and said: Of course I've always known what I am.

She was confused. She shook her head as if to clear it. She returned to looking at you, petting your head. I picked you up and stood. I said, You'll get the child sick.

In her confusion I saw her words with frightening clarity.

From the very beginning Su Lan had seen herself in my disfigured face, had seen the truth of what she was in my lopsided body. You look like someone I've always known, she'd said that day, the day she painted the room white, and she had meant it. In her mind we belonged to the same class of people, but it was not as I'd secretly hoped, that somehow she'd glimpsed her beauty in me, that hers was the body in which my mind and self belonged. No, she saw herself as a disposable, hideous human. To the world Su Lan was beautiful but to herself she was a monster, and her greatest fear was that this monster would be revealed. So we did see each other in the same way, as projections of our true selves. But while she was my hope, I was her fear. This was why she had kept me close from the start, because she feared and suspected a time would come when I would be the only person left she could turn to. That time was now. She looked at my face and called me a mirror; she despised the reflection she saw. I swallowed. The taste was bitter and hard.

Go to sleep, I said. I moved my hands down her face, wiping the lids shut as to a corpse, and your mother, obedient, slept.

ALL THIS I could have told you, and more, if only you wanted to know the truth. When I think of Su Lan a well opens and one memory leads to another, one thought to many thoughts. After all she was the kind of person whose combination of personality and circumstance made you wonder what life was for, even if you were fundamentally uninterested in such questions. So ask me how she spoke when you caught her off guard, ask me how she walked down the stairs carrying a stack of books, how she fiddled with the dials on her watch, how she stood on the terrace looking over the roofs of the longtang, as if something immense and invisible were keeping her prisoner.

But you are not interested in the truth; you are interested in answers. I can see it in the way you move, as if your mother has hidden something, and you have a right to whatever it is. Perhaps you believe that solving the mystery of your father will fill the hole your mother left when she died. If this is a mistake, it is forgivable; grief, I know, can manifest in stupid ways. But I think it is a deeper quality of yours—one you have had since you were a child, one inherited from your father—this ability to turn your face away from one thing in order to obtain the other thing you want.

I remember watching you one morning while you were with your mother. You were leaving infancy then, becoming pretty, your expressions exhibiting more and more those characteristics that distinguished you from any other child, the ones that would eventually form your personality. Su Lan had sat you on her desk, next to a pile of textbooks. She had put you in a white and red dress and brushed your hair so it curled around your round face, and slid a shiny white headband on your head. She was applying makeup to your face, her back bent and her eyes inches from yours, her fingers smudging your cheeks and lips with rouge, drawing lines around your eyes, plucking your brows. You did not like these sensations and would not sit still. She grabbed your face and you began to sob and scream and rub your eyes with your hands, ruining what work she had done, so she had to start over; she wiped your face hard with a wet towel until it was red and clean. She spoke to you sternly and held your chin still and made you doll-like again. The whole time you screamed and fought. When she was done, she scooped you into her arms and kissed you and told you how sweet and pretty you were, how much she loved you.

Just like that you changed; it was like a switch had been flipped. She carried you down the stairs out the longtang onto the bus for the university. You beamed, any previous injury forgotten, hugging her neck like she was the love of your life. You never cried again when she dressed you. By the time the two of you left for

America, when you were not yet three, you had grown into such an obedient and conscientious child that you insisted on helping her with the luggage. You tried to roll a suitcase out the door and fell, nearly toppling with it down the stairs. Your mother gave you her purse, she looked you in the eyes and said that though this bag was little it was very important, perhaps the most important of all: she was trusting you to keep it safe. You nodded, serious. You clutched the purse to your chest, guarding it with the gravity of an adult, and walked down the alley toward the cab, following just one step behind Su Lan, walking too with attention and care, watching the rest of the luggage with vigilant eyes. It was only at the end of the longtang, when your mother said to say goodbye to ahpo, that you remembered me. Goodbye! you said, in English, with glee, and threw yourself into my arms, your familiar little weight, as if you were playing a game. My arms were not special, by then you must have known them much better than your mother's. You turned your head to make sure she was watching, and I couldn't blame you, I was watching her too. She said, I owe you too much, and looked away.

INSTEAD I SAID, in Mandarin, so you could understand:

The truth is, I didn't like your mother very much. I never trusted her.

Then you were gone. You stopped briefly in my room before fleeing down the rotting stairs, past the abandoned alleys, out the crumbling stone gate. Perhaps you had meant to say goodbye. But when you walked into my room and saw my altar—the white smoke, the candles flickering, my strange collection of gods—you marched to it with sudden certainty and picked up the photograph of your mother.

Underneath a black coat you were wearing the same pale yellow dress. Your shins showed, your feet disappeared into socks and boots.

Where did you get this?

Without waiting for a response you pointed to the portrait of Tao Kun.

Who's this?

You turned to the altar with a searing stare, looking at each item, roving over the table twice and then again, looking for something and not finding it there. You had taken some things from Su Lan's room—your bag was noticeably bulkier than it'd been when you arrived—and you began to empty it, searching for something. A few more of Su Lan's dresses, the box with her ashes, the photographs of your father, a Chinese-English dictionary. Finally you held up the bundle of letters I'd found in the desk drawer and thrown into the trunk. Searching the altar a final time, you said:

You knew my father too. He's alive, isn't he?

You brought the letters to your face. Read: *Zhang Bo, Beijing University.*

Is that him, is Zhang Bo my father?

I don't remember his name, I said.

It was the second thing I said to you in Mandarin. It was true.

Again you picked up the photograph of your mother, holding it like a mirror, then put it down rudely, as if discarding it, as if saying, you have it—this piece of trash.

You said, My mother never mentioned you, packed up your things, and left.

YONGZONG

RIFLE THROUGH MY WALLET AND search my house. Come into my bedroom and open my cabinet. Take this key. Unlock that drawer. Dump the contents on the floor and thumb through them all. Make sure you read my marriage certificate, my work license, my daughter's birth certificate. Look carefully at my ID.

That is my face, is it not?

Ask my wife. Ask my daughter.

They will say, Yongzong? I don't know anyone with that name.

I RECEIVED A postcard from Su Lan in June of 1985, two weeks after our five-year high school reunion. On the back was an aerial photo of Gugong, which I had bicycled past on my trips to see Bo but never actually entered. The postcard was sent to my address in Shanghai, tucked between the newspaper and a letter from the hospital. The script was small and neat. The note on the back was addressed *To my dear classmate*:

> *I regret that I was unable to attend the Hangzhou First Secondary School Class of 1980 reunion. I would have liked to be there, as I had looked forward to seeing you, and of course, beautiful Hangzhou, after all these years. Please visit me in Beijing if ever you have a chance.*

She signed it, *Your friend.*

I read the note again, flipped it over. Underneath her signature she had written her address, complete with room number.

When were we ever friends?

Su Lan. Her name was like a splinter, forgotten and flaring. I knew nothing about her. She had beaten me on the gaokao, she lived in Beijing, and was once ugly and poor but now, according to Bo, a beauty. How did Bo know? Had he been in touch with her?

I thought back to our conversation. I thought of the hesitant look in Bo's eyes when he finally brought up Su Lan, and how he had changed the subject, not wanting to speak more about the very thing he had led us to, as if embarrassed to be so blatantly showing his hand.

I read the postcard again. *I had looked forward to seeing you . . . after all these years.*

Was Su Lan in love with me?

Perhaps Su Lan had seen Bo in Beijing and asked about me. They were not in the same course, but they attended the same university and must have seen each other from time to time. Perhaps she had asked him to put in a good word, to plant a seed of interest. But once he executed the favor, he became embarrassed and abandoned the topic. Why had she not simply come to the reunion?

In two years of high school, she had never spoken to me. She couldn't have had very many friends. If she had really changed so much, as Bo said, then her presence at the reunion would have been an event. She would have been noticed, called out. Perhaps she did not want the attention. Perhaps she was shy.

It was all very odd.

I shook my head and opened the newspaper. It was impossible to guess her reasons for sending the postcard. But even as I tried to put her out of my mind, I could not stop imagining the quiet girl in the back row, admiring Number One from afar. How I must have looked to her, who had never left her village. Had she studied with such perseverance to get closer to me? I picked up the postcard again. This much was clear: I had forgotten about her, but she had not forgotten me. She was still thinking of me, had been looking forward to seeing me *after all these years*!

I assembled the pieces I had:

She was brilliant.

She was sneaky.

She was beautiful (Bo said).

She had no need to show off, as I did. In her place, I would have marched into the five-year reunion transformed, flashing my dazzling new self to everyone I had left behind. Perhaps she knew that her absence would speak more loudly than her presence.

And she had chosen me. She had seen something in me that she had not forgotten, after all these years. She had invited me to see her in Beijing.

I threw the mail on my bed and lay down. My lamp was dim. I reread the postcard and flipped through the paper. I opened the letter from the hospital and read it without registering the words. My fan whirred loudly. I read the hospital's letter again. There was a thoracic cancer lecture in Beijing. The department of radiation oncology at my hospital wished to send me as a delegate.

Please visit me in Beijing if ever you have a chance.

Followed by her address. Who did a thing like this? Who was so brazen?

I took out a blank piece of paper and began to write.

Dear Su Lan,

Thank you for ~~your~~ the postcard. ~~I was~~ We were sorry to miss you in Hangzhou. ~~Turns out~~ I will be in Beijing next month for a conference. ~~and since I'll be there anyways~~ I would ~~love~~ like to catch up.

~~Yours,~~

~~Your friend,~~

Your classmate,

Yongzong

I crumpled up the paper and threw it in the trash.

I would appear at her door, unannounced. I would barge into her world as she had into mine.

BEIJING WAS SWELTERING. In the wide avenues it was impossible to find refuge from the sun. I wandered through the city aimlessly for two days after my conference, sweating through all of my good shirts and failing to work up the courage to go see Su Lan.

I thought about ringing up Bo and telling him I was in town. Instead, I spent the days walking around the hutong by my hotel in Dongcheng. These old neighborhood lanes were not unlike the Hangzhou xiang where I'd grown up, and though I did not wish to return to my childhood, there was a liveliness and intimacy in the hutong that I suddenly missed, living for so many years in school dorms. I walked past gatherings of residents at doors and store-fronts, grandmas in their housedresses and grandpas in undershirts and boxers, children playing with a stray dog, neighbors gossiping, watching games of weiqi, and showing off new babies. I edged through a crowd that blocked the entire width of the lane and found myself nearly stepping onto the gnarly foot of an enormous snapping turtle. As I jumped back, the thing lifted its beaked mouth and swiped at me, and the old women standing nearby shrieked with laughter before turning back to their gossip. He'll feed four families, a woman next to me said, if we can find a big enough pot.

Each time I visited Beijing, I was surprised by how easily I could understand what the locals said. I had an aptitude for languages, but even so, it had taken me a good year to learn to speak Shanghainese like a local, and still I often gave myself away in an odd phrase here or there. In any other new city, I would not have so easily under-stood the old folks airing themselves in the street. But in Beijing, everyone spoke standard correct putonghua, which was Beijing's local dialect as well as the official language of the country, what we heard on the radio and learned in school. How much power these old grandmas had in comparison to my own grandmother, who would never have been able to communicate so clearly with a traveling scholar.

I reminded myself that I had not come to Beijing to walk around the hutong and eat liangpi, but to find out why Su Lan had sent me that postcard. The next day, the day before I was to return to Shanghai, I tucked the card in my pocket and got on the subway.

Beida was not so impressive. Certainly, imposing. Certainly, beautiful, with its wide sweeping lawns and classical buildings. I imagined being a student here—yes, perhaps this aura of prestige would have made me feel grand. But I could see my father standing watch at every corner, measuring me against his expectations. I was from Hangzhou, from Shanghai. Surely these parks were not as beautiful as Xihu; surely this academic architecture did not match the French Concession or the neoclassical buildings along the Bund? I walked without bothering with where I was going. I had been to the campus before, visiting Bo, but had never visited a female dorm, and I had not looked to see where Su Lan's address was on a map. Soon I grew tired. I had forgotten to eat. I was ravenous. I followed a canal onto a quiet street, walked on and on as if away from my father's preferred future, his thwarted pride, until suddenly I saw before me, as if surging out from my visions, a placard on a building:

Zhonghua Residential Apartments, Building 6.

Wasn't that where Su Lan lived?

I admit—I succumbed to a childish belief in signs.

I said to myself, as I often have since and sometimes still do, *When you are lost, go into life and let it take you.*

Perhaps this is foolish. But relinquishing agency to randomness has led me to my life today. And though I cannot say that I have no regrets, I am more or less happy, which is more than most people can say. So that morning in July, thirsty and hot, rabid with hunger, I interpreted my fortuitous arrival at Su Lan's residence as a message from the gods.

I took the postcard out of my pocket and checked the address. I was not wrong. I walked up to the gated door and rang the bell for number 47.

BO HAD NOT lied. Even my exaggerated imagination was a disservice to Su Lan. For I had only pictured the superficial elements of beauty—long hair, large eyes, small mouth, delicate skin—and though Su Lan possessed all this and more, a lovely face with fine, feminine features, and a small, graceful body, plump in just the right places, her beauty was much greater than their sum. In fact, if you looked closely, there was nothing particularly extraordinary about each individual feature. It was her aura, her totality, that was exquisite.

That day, when she finally appeared, she seemed to leave behind her a shimmering wake, as if each molecule were bursting into life, the very air around her teeming with the energy of invisible particles proliferating toward infinity. To say she took my breath away would be incorrect. Watching her inhabit space—beholding her—was like watching worlds unfold.

She arrived an hour after I rang her door. She wore a long pale yellow dress, high-heeled shoes, and large sunglasses, and cradled an enormous cloth bag filled with textbooks. She had not been at home when I rang. One of her roommates, a big-boned, big-faced, loud girl, had opened the door. The roommate was the type of girl one can easily see becoming a mother, yelling insults at her husband with two babes in arms. She was not unattractive, but rather, good-looking in a robust, healthy way—certainly, I immediately knew, not Su Lan.

I introduced myself. Before I could state my purpose the room-mate said, winking, Ask *me* to marry you—I'll say yes.

I stammered. She grinned at me with pity. Finally she said, Lanlan's out, she'll be back in an hour.

She gave me a look that said, I know exactly what you are, and closed the door. I walked down the stairs to wait. I thought of what to say to Su Lan when she arrived. *It's been a long time; I got your message; I'm not here to marry you. Have you eaten yet? I'm starving.*

In the end I said nothing. Simply stood and stared as she approached. She stopped in front of me and cocked her head, adjust-ing the bag in her arms. I was standing in front of the door, blocking her way. Still I said nothing. My hand was in my pocket, fingering the edge of her postcard. I suddenly felt very foolish.

Finally she said, Do I know you?

She laughed.

Yes, I know you. You're Number One.

I took her bag of books—if she was surprised she did not show it—happy for something to occupy my hands. I was in town for a lecture, I said, and hadn't she said to visit, and in any case I had wanted to see the Beida campus for some time so I thought why not and what did she call me, Number One?—I scoffed—we all know you're Number One now, just look at you—

I followed her up the stairs. A thin brown belt marked her waist, and I could see the faint line of her panties pressing through her skirt. I stared at her bare ankles against the red strap of her sandals. My voice trailed off. She laughed. She exclaimed how glad she was to see me, as if we were old friends. Her voice filled the stairwell, sweet and melodic, ringing with energy, it was saying how she never had visitors from home and today was perfect, she had finished her work early and just let her drop off the books in her room and we would head out right away.

WE STORMED BEIJING. Call me Lanlan, she said as we left, gripping my forearm. Lanlan had borrowed her roommate's camera. Before I could respond she snapped a picture of me, shouting, Evidence!

I told her it was my first time in Beijing. She did not blink, though much later I would discover that she had heard of my visits to Bo. Perhaps she forgot; perhaps she did not care—she treated me precisely as I presented myself. Not once did she question why I had come, or why I had not contacted my best friend, who also lived in the city. I took this as tacit acknowledgment of what we both understood: that her postcard had been a question, and my appearance the answer.

She was a tireless guide. You, Li Yongzong, she said, are my excuse to do every silly tourist thing I'm too embarrassed to do by myself. We went to Tiananmen and Gugong and Yiheyuan. We ran through the plazas and temples and gates and pagodas in order to see it all. That was another refrain she cried—You must see it all!—as if our failure to do so would result in a great catastrophe. I looked intently at the sights, feigning interest in order to not stare at her. Constantly I reminded myself—look away, look away.

When I slipped, I found Lanlan also looking at me. I should have been pleased. But her gaze made me uneasy. It did not seem to be a gaze of attention but of responsibility, and when I caught her off guard, I thought I saw her eyes boring into my face as if searching for something. In those moments, she shrugged, laughed, and lifted up her roommate's camera to snap a photo of me without warning.

I tried to take the camera from her, saying that I should be taking photos of her—she pursed her lips and shook her head.

She was most at ease when talking about our respective fields of study. Immediately I could tell that she was a passionate and brilliant scientist. She quickly grasped the fundamentals of my work, understanding instinctually the mechanics of the radiation technology we used for the treatment of cancers. She made guesses about how the machines functioned on an engineering level that I pretended to understand. She flattered me. Your work is human, she said when I gave a show of false modesty. Her least theoretical work, on the other hand, was research using subatomic particles, the platonic ideals of science. She said it with an air of dismissal.

I ventured: But surely there are practical applications of theoretical physics—computers, electricity, bombs.

Yes, she said, quietly, her eyes bright. And these particles are not only used for life and death. Under the right conditions, their effects on other materials are measurable, real. We are using them to interrogate the nature of *everything*.

We arrived at Yuanmingyuan at dusk. Lanlan had purposefully saved it for last. The old gardens were a close walk to Tsinghua, where we would dine in Lanlan's favorite roast duck restaurant, and where, kindly, she had arranged for a male friend to accommodate me for the night in his dormitory. I did not tell her that I already had a hotel—I did not think of any of it, my clothes, my luggage, my deposit, my train ticket for the next morning. The ruins of Yuanmingyuan, Lanlan said, were symbolic of more than just one civilization in decline, and most beautiful in the blood hues of sunset.

Something about Yuanmingyuan allowed Lanlan to take a breath. She slowed down, grew quiet. She became grounded, calm.

I myself did not think much of the place. There were gardens, footpaths, unremarkable greenery, and the crumbling stone bases of what might have once been glorious palaces but were now just large pieces of rock. After the pillage and fire a century and a half ago, the only pieces that remained were from the Western-style palaces, the bottoms of pillars and marble fountains. Intellectually, I understood the allure of these old ruins standing in the outskirts of the magnificent capital city, facing Tiananmen and Gugong and Yiheyuan, like acknowledgments of a grandeur that has since been surpassed. How ironic that the British and the French had razed our palaces to leave behind only the perfect monument of their own crumbling civilization, as all around it China surged forward into the future. Lanlan said this, and I nodded flatly. Only later would I learn, from Bo, that what Lanlan saw in Yuanmingyuan and what I could not see was precisely all that was not there: the shimmering structures of the magnificent palaces, water spraying from the fountain spouts, Manchurian emperors strolling in their silken gowns, ladies-in-waiting with their sheer summer sashes, the ghosts of the past filling every negative space.

We reached a white pavilion surrounded by a dark stone maze. The setting sun shone through the trees. Lanlan disappeared inside the maze without a word, as if chasing someone who had run inside. I followed her. Her head protruded just over the walls of the labyrinth, and though occasionally she turned to look back, I had the strange feeling that she did not see me. She continued ahead with curious determination. I wondered if this was some kind of test.

Finally I arrived at the end of the maze. Lan was standing at the point where it opened into a path toward the white pavilion. I stopped in front of her and smiled.

She handed me the camera.

Stand there, she said, and take a photo of me.

The sun's last rays were behind us, striking her face in orange light. She did not smile. She looked directly at the lens with a cold stare, and she was beautiful.

AS WE LEFT the park I asked her why she had chosen that spot out of all of the magnificent places we'd been for a photo. She didn't respond, and we continued to walk in silence away from the park toward the restaurant where we were to have dinner. Before we went in she stopped and took my arm.

For once I was alone, she said, her eyes glittering.

She closed her eyes and turned away as if afraid she had said too much. Then she continued toward the restaurant door, laughing.

When you're unsure of the real, she said, photographs are a way of making sure.

BO CALLED ME.

I have something to confess, he said.

I did not want to talk to Bo. It was almost midnight, I was exhausted, I wanted to sleep. But the night watchman had stood at my door expectantly. He'd come all the way up to the fifth floor to tell me of the call; he expected me to take it.

After I returned to Shanghai, to my patient load and a stack of mail, two envelopes of which were letters from my father I had not yet opened, I felt as if I had woken from a spell. I busied myself with returning to a normal state; I remembered the way I had behaved in Beijing and especially the things I had felt as an aberration of extraordinary stupidity.

I put Lan out of my head. The whole exchange mystified me. Now I feared that she had run into Bo and told him everything.

A confession! I said to Bo, trying to sound enthusiastic. Go on.

He paused.

I'm in love.

Yes, so you told me, on the banks of fair Xihu, I said.

I tried to tell you.

So what then? Does she love you back?

Perhaps.

He delivered this verdict as if it were a death sentence.

Congratulations, comrade!

What was Bo doing, calling me to chat about his love life in the middle of the night?

Look, Bo, I said when he didn't respond. That's fantastic. Good for you.

Bo, are you still there?

He was still there. I could hear his breathing.

Finally, he said, The girl is Su Lan. We've been involved for—for quite some time. I wanted to tell you at Xihu, but I thought you would laugh at me.

He took a deep breath.

Look, I don't know why I want your approval. I want you to meet her. She's changed. I mean it, I'm not just saying it so you won't laugh at me.

Go on, I said. I kept my voice even and slow.

Tell me everything.

DID I REMEMBER the girl he had mentioned at the lake? Lanlan, Lanlan, it was Lanlan. Lanlan, he called her, as if her name belonged to him alone.

He had run into Lanlan his first year of university, at an outing arranged by a mutual friend. Already she looked very different.

She had loosened her hair from her braid and let it grow long, with bangs that framed her face. She was dressed stylishly, not in those tubu she wore all through high school. Her lips were painted, her brows drawn. Bo had not recognized her until she came over to greet him.

Their hometowns were in the same cluster of mountain villages east of Dongyang, and so they began to take the train together to go home for the holidays, both traveling in the hard-seat section, where usually there were no seats at all. On the twenty-plus-hour rides, they played cards and ate sunflower seeds and talked about everything. It was on the train that Bo learned Lan had never had a father. Her family was her ancient grandmother and her aging mother. Their poverty was exacerbated by loneliness. She had no siblings, no aunts or uncles. The relatives on her father's side never spoke to her. Perhaps they blamed her mother for his death.

Something happened when they got on the train. It was as if they had shed their Beijing lives and left them hanging on hooks. In the city, they were both pretending not to be peasants. And yet after they stepped off the train in Yiwu, said goodbye, and boarded their respective buses, they began to pretend again, this time to be people who had never left. To their illiterate mothers they spoke tuhua, chatting in the village dialect about the crops and gossiping about people they'd forgotten. They pretended not to notice the dirt and the flies, the everywhere smell of sewage and manure, the cheap gaudy clothes of the villagers who were slightly better off. Since leaving for high school, those train rides between Beijing and Yiwu, sitting next to Lanlan, were the only time and place Bo felt like a full person, not bifurcated into his farm-boy self and his educated self. Lanlan alone could see all of him.

Bo could not know if she loved him back, but he was certain that she understood this feeling of bifurcation, that the train rides were for her too a place of wholeness. Affectionately, she called him Gege. She, an only child who never had a blood brother, who admitted to him that she had a hard time making close friends, spoke to him like he was family. No one looks out for me as you do, she'd said to him. He began to imagine that they were returning to the same place, that he was taking her home to present to his parents as his future bride.

When he sat down to write his first biaobai, declaring blankly the nature of his affections, he felt that he was simply giving words to what they both already knew. He wrote fluently, and by the time he put down the last word and signed his name, he had fallen even more deeply in love with Lanlan. He read over the letter. Suddenly it seemed woefully inadequate—he tore it up and started again.

She never responded. He continued to write her letters, not knowing what else to do. He hoped to show her that he could not be made ashamed of his love. He hoped to prove his sincerity, his seriousness. She stopped accepting his invitations to go out. When it came time to take the train home together for the new year, she wrote him a curt note saying that he should not buy her ticket—she would not be returning home that year as she had too much work in Beijing. Bo resigned himself to the fact that she did not love him. He continued to write her, as a friend, hoping that they could at least keep that. Then Jing contacted him, asking for his assistance planning the high school reunion. He threw himself into the silly logistics, trying to forget about Lanlan.

At the reunion, he wore a mask of joviality. He was certain that she had not come because she wanted to avoid seeing him. He tried to tell me, but he could not spit out the words.

But after the reunion things took a turn. When he returned to Beijing he discovered that she had written him. She called him her good friend. She regretted not making the reunion. They began to see each other again. She did not mention his love letters, but she was warm and available to see him. She called him Gege. She let him pay for things. Once he had taken her hand to cross the street and she had turned to him and smiled.

I'm going to ask her to marry me, he said. I can't wait anymore. Isn't it the right thing to do, if I want it so much? I want it desperately. What do you think?

MY MIND WAS spinning. What a story, I said, in order to say something.

I wanted to shout at Bo: *I* just visited Lanlan, *I* received her parting kiss on my cheek.

But if his story was true, then I had made a fool of myself.

Look, I can't tell you what to do, I said.

Did I have to tell him anything?

Of course I'd be happy to meet her, I said. I picked my next words carefully:

You know, she actually sent me a postcard after the reunion, inviting me to visit. It'll be a good excuse.

She sent you a postcard too?

What, did you get one?

Yes, after the reunion. That was the letter that made me hope again.

She probably sent one to the whole class, I said dismissively. As I said it, my confusion cleared: yes, of course, she had sent the exact same postcard to the entire class. I recalled the words in the letter as plainly as if staring at my own reflection in a mirror. How impersonal they had been! Besides my address, she had not even written my name! *To my dear classmate*. How could I have read it as a confession of love?

On the other end of the line, Bo berated himself, talking backward and forward, saying at one moment that Lan loved him and at another that of course I was right—

Think, Bo, I said, and the bitterness in my voice surprised me. What did she say on the postcard? I asked. To my dear classmate? Did she even address it to your name?

Bo let out a howl.

Look, Bo Cai. I'm sorry about all this but I have to go to sleep. I'll talk to you later.

I hung up the phone and leaned against the wall of the booth, breathing hard. Finally I walked back up the stairs to my room. The night watchman who'd roused me was dozing in his chair.

LATER THAT SAME week, I received a thick envelope in the mail from Lan. Inside were the photos she had taken of me, twenty in all. I searched for a note and found nothing. I rifled through the photos. She had not included the one I had taken of her.

What was she playing at? I fumed. And yet, even as it infuriated me, the idea that Lan *was* playing us impressed me, it made her even more desirable.

In her photos I looked dazed, aloof, grave. I'd had portraits taken before, but these were different. I had never understood before why people called me serious, why they assumed I possessed some inner integrity. Now I saw that I had the bearing of an intellectual, a face that looked thoughtful. I was pleased with how I had turned out under Lan's lens, pleased that she had taken these photos, developed them, and seen them.

Finally I turned to my father's letters. They were terse and thin, lacking details. They said my mother was sick. They said that if I wished to call myself a son I should come home. I crumpled the letters and threw them in the trash.

I looked through the photos again. I thought of Bo.

Everything made me seethe.

Dearest Lanlan,

How about a trip back to Hangzhou with me before the summer ends?

I've got two first-class train tickets on the fast train from Shanghai. There's also a ticket enclosed here for you to come to Shanghai. I'll meet you at the train station on Wednesday, two and a half weeks from today. I hope to see you there.

Yours,

Li Yongzong

I wrote the letter quickly, not thinking, not reading it over, and threw it into an envelope. I stuffed one of the pictures Lan had taken of me into the envelope as well—in it I stood with the crumbling columns of Yuanmingyuan behind me, looking introspective. I bought an overnight fast-train ticket from Beijing to Shanghai, sealed and sent the letter before I could rip it up.

TWO WEDNESDAYS LATER, I took the bus to the train station after work. There was traffic, and I arrived fifteen minutes after Lan's train was due.

The station teemed with travelers and vendors who swarmed to serve them. People crowded around the rickshaw taxis with bags, haggling, while others slurped bowls of noodles in street stalls or lifted their pants legs for a shoeshine. Feet and motorcycles and buses raised up dust, thickening the dusk. I made my way through the crowd, looking for Lan. I circled the station three times before I saw a young woman in a wide-rimmed hat sitting in the waiting area with her head lowered. She was wearing a black dress with little white flowers and red sandals—Lanlan's red sandals. As I approached I saw that she was reading.

I stood in front of her and coughed.

She looked up.

My mother once told me that Chairman Mao studied in loud public spaces, she said, closing the book. I have no idea if it's true, but I always thought it was a nice idea.

Yes, I said. I was smiling stupidly. I tried to look serious, as I had in those photos.

She showed me what she was reading. It was a scientific journal in English. Can you read it? she said.

Physical Review Letters, I wanted to say, but I could not get any words out of my mouth.

She stood up and touched my arm.

Are you hungry?

Yes, I said again, and followed her to a stall outside, where we joined the other weary travelers on the benches with bowls of steaming soup.

SU LAN BEHAVED so naturally that I began to wonder if there was something wrong with me. Was it not strange that I had appeared in her city and that she had appeared in mine, that we suddenly wandered about like a couple after seven years of knowing each other and not exchanging a word? Was it possible she was silently thinking what I was silently thinking?

She accompanied me back to my dorm, where we spent that night—she asleep in my bed, I awake on my roommate's bed—before leaving for Hangzhou. She did not mention Bo. When I finally asked her why she had come (a week later, on the way back), she pulled out her train ticket from Beijing to Shanghai and pointed at the price. Fifty yuan, she said. What a waste of money it would have been. That's it? I said. She turned back to her magazine.

On the train to Hangzhou, I apologized for not planning time to show her around Shanghai as she had done for me in Beijing. I said, perhaps too forcefully, You'll have to come another time.

The train ride was four hours. Lan had never ridden in the soft-seat section and asked to sit by the window. It was a good excuse for me to lean over her to point out a landmark or new development. We chatted about stupid things and played a few rounds of cards. When the food cart came, I asked Lan what she wanted and she shook her head.

Now I'll have to guess what you like, I said. See what you've done?

I bought more snacks than we could conceivably eat. She reached for the simplest, cheapest item, the bag of sunflower seeds.

She was impossible to read. She had brought with her a small bag holding one change of clothes and two books: the *Physical Review* and a Chinese-English dictionary. She seemed equally content talking to me or reading or sitting in silence. She did not ask about plans but seemed happy to follow where I led. Yet her passivity did not make her seem stupid or even passive. Rather, in her every gesture—even when she simply sat—I saw a quiet intentionality, as if she alone had found that elusive greater purpose for which we were all searching. I felt this acutely, the presence of some drive or meaning justifying her existence. It was at once comforting and unsettling.

How did I feel about her? Even now, it's hard to know exactly. I was energized, yes, but I was a vector with only direction and no substance. I wanted her to love me, but I couldn't tell you why, exactly. I drove ferociously toward my target, toward Lanlan. I went blindly, convincing myself of many things.

We caught up as if we were old friends. My work bored me, but to make myself interesting to her, I spoke about treatment advances in my field. I told her about the lecture I had attended in Beijing, the introduction of new cancer detection and treatment machines. Again she was fascinated by the idea of radiation treatment, that we could weaken or even destroy an illness inside a person without cutting open the exterior. How miraculous and counterintuitive science could be. This was what she was interested in too: how light, or particles that behaved like light, shot through our world, touching everything and changing its properties without our even noticing. You know, she laughed, in many ways physics has saved me. What do our petty pains matter in the face of—she paused—the laws of thermodynamics, say, or the law of gravity. She spoke so sincerely that she became almost vulnerable, like a child who must be protected from her curiosity.

As a theoretical physicist, working primarily with numbers and other invisible entities, she admired people like me, whose everyday work had a real impact on the lives around us. But she had chosen physics for its beauty and incomprehensibility, not because she wanted to change the world.

Or maybe I believe that thinking hard enough *can* change the world, she said. Again she laughed at herself.

She explained how recently she had developed a sort of scientific crush on massless particles.

Most people who have some understanding of modern physics think that relativity is the final word, the last frontier, Lan said.

But there is something about relativity—gravity and light, mass and speed at enormous scales—that is fundamentally more intuitive than quantum mechanics. Yes, our perception of mechanical laws, of space and time, is slightly off—more than slightly off when we are talking about the very large and the very fast. But with simple logical deduction, our perceptions can be shifted, and indeed, the human mind opens quite naturally toward those shifts. We are amazed, we are dazzled, we open our mouths in awe, but we are not dumbfounded. The behaviors of photons, electrons, and quarks, however—these particle waves, these vibrating infinitesimal particulars—

She paused. For a moment she had lost herself.

They defy any concept of sense, she finally said. Of reason *and* experience. And of course—they are too small to even *conceive*.

As we talked, an uncomfortable realization crept into me. Su Lan was a real scientist. I, on the other hand, was a mere practitioner. Even after I earned my degree, I would just be a competent person who did what he was told to do. I had no passion, only ability. Did Bo love his work? He must, I thought angrily. Here, so many years later, was the true reason I had given up those top spots to Zhang Bo and Su Lan. Because unlike Bo, unlike Lan, I was smart only to show that I was smart, not for a greater purpose, not to become something. I would never be like Lanlan, who fed off knowledge as if it were the only thing that could keep her alive.

In the last month, Lanlan had made a breakthrough in her research. Her face broke into childlike excitement as she spoke about a professor from an American university who would visit their department the following month on a scholarly exchange. The journal she had brought contained an article of his concerning high-speed ion reduction that used methodology she thought could be applied to her own research. She was determined to read it in spite of her lousy English, so that she could discuss it with him when he arrived.

Do you ever want to study in America? she asked.

I've never thought about it, I said honestly. But you have?

She shrugged. It was fine to keep doors open, she said. She commented on her poor English language skills again. I've been reading this for an entire day and I've only gotten through a page, she said.

At the time, I had thought of my aptitude for languages as an extension of my aptitude for anything that could be studied. Only much later, when I began to translate little things here and there for some easy income, did I realize that I felt comfortable inside foreign languages like I never had in medicine. Entering into a strange grammar, surrounded by strange sounds, my mind opened in ways that I could not conceive while living solely in Chinese. It was intensely intimate and freeing, this temporary escape, like walking into someone else's home and finding that everything has been made just for you. I offered to help Lan, and for the rest of the train ride we read the article together, I helping her with simple words and syntax, she explaining the physics. I nodded along, pretending to understand.

We arrived in Hangzhou in late afternoon. The platform was uncharacteristically empty and pink dust hung over the sky. I swept the unopened snacks into my bag, picked up Lan's satchel, and stepped into the aisle. On the platform I turned around and found Lan still standing by the train, staring at the place where we had been sitting. Our sunflower seed shells were piled on the table next to the window, and two young women edged sideways into our former seats, holding their bags out before them.

The train's whistle blew and it began to chug out of the station. I took Lan's hand and led her off the platform. I hailed a taxi and gave the driver my home address. I rolled down the windows.

Only then, with the car zooming toward the center of town, the dusty hot wind slapping our faces, exhaust billowing out behind us, did I find the voice to say what we were doing. Shouting over the engine and the wind, I said, My mother is sick. We are going to see her.

IN HIS LETTERS, my father had written simply that it was my mother's desire to see me. He had put it specifically in those terms. My mother desired to see me and he was writing for her, as a gesture of husbandly duty. The second letter had been identical to the first, except that instead of my name, it was addressed to *her negligent son*.

The truth was I did not think about my mother often. She quietly kept the peace, moving between my father and me, making it possible for us to coexist, giving us both her care and attention without taking sides. Today, looking back at the young man I was with the eyes of a father, I can see so clearly his foolishness, how lazily he conceived of his mother's existence. When he considered her, he considered only a vessel for his and his father's wills. He didn't see how well she knew them both. She'd made her presence so inert that it was like that of air, so when he was forced to turn his gaze toward her, he struggled to see anything.

The taxi slowed. I recognized the stores lining the sides of the main street, the restaurant at the corner of our xiang. I told the taxi to stop at the side of the road. Down the narrow lane jammed with parked bicycles and cars was the door to my parents' house.

We walked past the open dish room at the back of the restaurant. Gray water poured onto the cracked pavement; dish suds mixed with oil. At the corner, trash spilled out of a dumpster, watermelon peels scored with bite marks protruding from red plastic bags. I suddenly felt embarrassed. In childhood, my home had seemed large and opulent.

I'm afraid it's not much, I said to Su Lan.

She looked, as always, as if she were taking everything in, even the sparrows pecking at rice grains on the curb.

Don't apologize, she said.

No, I just mean—

Your eyes have gotten bigger, that's all.

I nodded, my face turned hot.

Well, here it is.

I banged on the metal door. There were shouts and footsteps and the door swung open. My mother gasped and took me in both arms. I stood stiffly and tried to remember if she usually embraced me. I stepped back to take a good look at her, as if with my medical degree I should have been able to see what was wrong. But she just looked tired. She nudged her head and said, Yongzong, who is your friend?

I followed my mother's gaze and saw Lanlan, standing behind me, her beauty like sunlight one could swim in, and I was surprised. I had not forgotten she was there, but I had forgotten how beautiful she would look to my mother.

I said, Ma, this is Su Lan, my fiancée.

THAT EVENING, MY mother's illness was not mentioned. My mother moved about as she always did, cooking and cleaning and being hospitable. She had felt that something special would happen today, she said; that morning she had purchased a big fish at the market. She called my father and told him to pick up some spiced beef on the way home. At dinner I looked between my father and my mother. Had they agreed not to speak to me of it? Was it possible that my father was lying, using his woman's life to manipulate me?

Su Lan did not deny our engagement.

My mother was exuberant.

How hard it was for me to really see her. Her hair had gone entirely gray and her body was thin and small. But the version of her I had known as a child surged over these superficial elements. It was only when I noticed the sagging skin around her eyes that I realized: to a stranger on the street—to Lanlan—my mother must have looked old.

We ate. Su Lan complimented my mother's cooking. I bragged about Su Lan.

Su Lan is a Beida graduate, I said. My father glanced up.

She's a master's student there now, I continued. She's going to America to study with a famous physics professor.

America? my father said. Your English must be very good.

Not as good as Yongzong's, she said.

A pity, he said, America wouldn't want Yongzong.

Yongzong's field is growing very quickly, she said. He was smart in picking his specialty.

Please, I picked randomly, I said.

It's good to have a doctor in the family, Lanlan said, especially one working in Shanghai, with important connections, like Yongzong.

My mother coughed. For a moment no one spoke. I swallowed but before I could say anything, my mother said, Where is your family from, Su Lan?

Shanghai, Lan said. My father owns a line of designer shoe shops on Nanjing Lu.

She gave me a look that said: I can tell better lies about myself, if that's what you want to do.

THE NEXT MORNING, after my father left for work, I took Lanlan to Xihu. I asked my mother to come but she said, No, no, you love-birds go alone. My father had arranged dinner at a new restaurant down the street, she needed to invite my sisters and tell them I was home.

I led Lan down the roads I'd walked with my sisters when I was a boy. I told stories and remarked on the little things that had changed. I was lighthearted. Overnight, my lie had cemented into reality. It felt right. Without asking, she had become my girlfriend. Now she was my fiancée! I thought of Bo, and for the first time since he'd inserted himself into our narrative I felt calm, even happy.

We neared West Lake. Before us emerged the stone paths lined with willows, behind which the serene water stretched clear to the horizon. For the first time in years, I thought of my hometown warmly. The ancient poems were right: how beautiful Hangzhou and Xihu were! I said to Lan, Now you know everything about me. When will you show me your shoe factory in Shanghai?

Lan did not laugh. She said, Your mother has stomach cancer.

She continued to walk, looking straight ahead.

They found it five months ago, she said. For a long time your mother did not wish to be treated. But she's finally changed her mind. She'll have the operation in a few weeks.

How do you know all this? I said.

You should arrange something at your hospital. Have them do the operation there.

Who told you?

Didn't you notice how she ate nothing but rice and soup at dinner? Didn't you see her slip out halfway through the meal to take medication?

I had not noticed. I had thought I was watching my mother carefully.

Su Lan pointed her finger at my chest.

There's no room in there for anyone but you, she said. What makes you think I'll marry you? What makes you think I want to be associated with you at all? The thought of it makes me sick.

SU LAN HAD woken early that morning, as was her habit since childhood, and found my mother in the kitchen, rolling pork and pumpkin maibing, my favorite breakfast. Without a word she began to help. In the kitchen, my mother noticed what I might have seen in school, if I had paid any attention: Lan's natural industriousness, how she immediately assessed a situation and made herself useful. My mother admired Lan's skill handling the dough, pulling the logs apart then rolling them into small balls, stuffing each with meat and pumpkin before rolling them flat. Lan brushed aside the praise, saying she was a terrible cook. But her mother had made pancakes like these too, she had learned how to stretch the dough thin.

While they cooked, the sun rose and gray light pressed through the kitchen window. Your mother must be so pleased to have a daughter like you, my mother said. Again Lan shook her head: I'm not a very good daughter. Children are bad at appreciating their own parents, she added. She complimented my mother on the assiduous care with which she kept the house, on the quality of the meat and vegetables she'd bought, on how well she took care of my father and me. As the first maibing fried in the wok, sizzling and steaming, Lan asked my mother how many they should make. How many would I eat, how many would my father eat? Lan herself would have just one. And you, qinjiapo? To which my mother replied, I don't like such rich foods.

Lan said nothing, and for a moment the two women listened to the oil crackling in the pot.

Then Lanlan touched my mother's wrist and called her *Ma*, as if we were really engaged. Ma, she said, are you well? You did not eat much last night.

Su Lan had a way of making you want to tell her everything. She was not only disarming—she asked as if she understood you perfectly, as if, once you opened the doors, she would be able to walk into your soul, treading gently, and know you only as you knew yourself.

My mother told Lanlan she was ready to die. The pains had started over a year ago, she said. She'd assumed that it was simply age. It was reasonable that an old woman like her, with three children all grown up, should not be eating so much meat and fish, such rich foods covered in savory sauces and oils. But eventually the pain grew so unbearable that she could no longer hide it from her husband. Often, she had to sit down abruptly; many nights it kept her awake until dawn. Half of the meals she swallowed to appease her husband she later vomited up. Finally, she had gone to see a doctor and found the cancer, vigorous from being ignored for so long. She hoped the doctors could help with the pain. She did not want to become an invalid in her last years of life. She wanted to die quietly, without bothering her family.

Yongzong is busy, my mother told Lanlan. He has his studies and his work; he doesn't need to worry about me. She had begged my father not to tell me; she only wished that I would come home more often; she wanted to see me a few more times before she died. Not knowing that Lan had heard nothing about my relationship with my father, she confessed that she also hoped to see us reconcile.

Here, my mother began to cry, and crying, her desires—those tempered yet unrelenting desires—broke through the surface. She looked to Su Lan, for a moment, like a girl.

My mother gathered herself, checked the time, wiped her face. At least he's come and brought me this gift, she said. Now I can die, knowing he is engaged to you. And Su Lan reassured her with the words that every mother wishes to hear:

Yes, I love him, I will take care of him forever, I promise. But you mustn't die. Look at you, you are still so young, so full of life.

By the time my father and I came down for breakfast they had both rearranged their masks.

I DID NOT lie to your mother for you, Lan said to me on the train ride back. I lied for her.

Again we sat next to each other. But we did not touch, not even our knees. She stared out of the window and told me these things, as if speaking to the passing fields.

So you don't love me? I asked.

Her laugh was like a bark. Do you love me? she said.

Yes. I tried to take her hand. She jerked it away.

You men are all the same, she said. All you know is take, take, take. You, your father, all of you. You think you are better than your father but you're just like him, you're worse. You think you love someone, but you only love yourself. You want a mirror, not a woman, any woman who marries you will be worse off than your mother.

I wanted to protest but Lan was not finished.

I've only met one decent man in my life, she said—your friend, Zhang Bo. He's the only one who's ever treated me with any respect. You don't deserve to wash his feet.

Bo Cai? I stood up and began to shout. Don't tell me you're in love with Bo Cai. You came all this way to tell me you love some- one else? I called her a liar, a cheat, a whore.

That was when she laughed, as if delirious, as if drunk, and held up the train ticket to my face: Do you know who I am, Li Yongzong? Do you know me at all? Shaking the ticket, she said, Fifty yuan! What a waste of money!

In Shanghai, she grabbed her bag out of my hands and stomped off the platform. I ran after her, remorseful, thinking that my mother was right. Before I left, my mother had gripped my hands and said so only I could hear: I don't know what you did to deserve that girl, but don't you ever lose her.

I reached for Su Lan's arm and tried to take her bag from her.

Please, I said.

Don't you dare speak to me again, Li Yongzong, she said, and then she disappeared down the street.

MANY THINGS HAPPENED in the following year. I returned to work. I lost myself in clinic, in the advancement of my career. I did as Lan suggested: I brought my mother to Shanghai to be treated. But it was too late, the cancer had spread to her lungs, her liver, her spleen. Little of my mother remained her own. I visited Hangzhou many times, my father and I pretended to reconcile, my mother died wretchedly in July of 1986. I arrived home only in time to smell with clinical recognition the first rotting odors of her corpse.

In this time, I went to Beijing twice for work. I did not seek out Bo or Lan. I reached out to other high school acquaintances and friends of friends. It was not uncommon to hear gossip about Su Lan within the high school group. Everyone had heard about her transformation. She was a heartbreaker, people said. She was endlessly pursued. Men arrived at her door like dogs, throwing down gifts that she threw back at their feet. Some proposed to her on first sight. As far as anyone had heard, she had not dated a single one. There were rumors that she was engaged to the son of a top party official, but no one had any proof. There were rumors that she loved women, that she lived a secret underlife, that her heart had been replaced with rubber after a childhood accident and she was actually a highly functional machine. I laughed and said, Who would've thought? I didn't ask about Bo, not because I wanted to protect him, but because I was afraid of giving myself away.

I dated here and there; I did not care for anyone. I was surprised how easy it was to convince girls to sleep with me, now that birth control was free and widely promoted as part of the one-child policy. I was a good catch, I reaffirmed with each conquest. I dated girls who were prettier, more fashionable than Su Lan. Pretty waitresses, pretty shopkeepers, pretty strangers I approached in cafés and restaurants. I even slept with a model for a month. I stayed away from educated girls.

Meanwhile I spoke less and less to my father. He did not ask about my life, my work, or the marriage I had once announced. My mother had asked for Lanlan a few times before she died, but I told her my fiancée was busy, Beijing was too far away. To make up for the lack of visits I wrote letters to my mother from Su Lan, copied by my roommate so they would not appear in my handwriting. These letters assured my mother that Lan was fine, that once she finished her master's she would be looking at doctorates and teaching positions in Shanghai, perhaps at Fudan University. I gave Su Lan sentiments I was too cowardly to own. I remembered the way she had spoken about my mother on the train, with a tenderness and knowledge that shamed me. *You have given too much all your life,* I wrote. *Now you must take all you can.* My mother kept the letters in a silk pouch and read them when she was alone, opening the pouch only after my father and I left the room. I pretended to assume their contents merely casual. *How I wish I could have had the chance to know you before now—to have truly known you as a mother,* I wrote. Did Lanlan mention the purse I bought her? I asked.

I hoped that my mother would write back to imaginary Lan. Instead, she gave me presents to pass on to her: a jade bracelet, an embroidered vest, a silk scarf. As she got sicker the gifts grew stranger: a handkerchief wrapped around a small stone, a ragged old blanket with a pattern of stitched persimmons, a wrinkled photograph of herself as a young woman. I tucked them all inside a drawer I never opened. Just seeing the closed drawer was enough to hollow me and make me numb.

From my father I never heard a word about my supposed fiancée. When my mother was still alive, we spoke of her health and treatment. He deferred to me in all health-related matters.

I expected my father would blame me when the treatments failed, but he did not. After my mother died, he became helpless. It was not just that he could do nothing for himself. He seemed not to know what to do, and spent hours standing with his hands in mid-air, looking for something to clutch. My sisters alternated visiting his house to cook and clean until I hired him a maid. They encouraged me to marry soon and buy a house, then bring him to live with me. But I hated my father's uselessness even more than I had hated his tyranny. I returned to work in Shanghai, busying myself during the day and getting drunk at night, calling up the girls I had met. The girls started to make more demands. They wanted gifts, jewelry, proof of my devotion. I promised them all I would marry them. How easily that word came out of my mouth now, *marriage.* I lost them one by one.

Then, in May of 1987, two years after the high school reunion, I got a letter in the mail.

It was a plain envelope, without a return address. The handwriting looked familiar. It was unsigned. There was no letterhead, no greeting. Rather than a note, I found a list of numbered items. It started:

1. Li Yongzong, you win.

1. Li Yongzong, you win.
2. Congratulations. I know winning is what Yongzong likes best.
3. I must have known from the day I met you.
4. You were small, but you had that ferocious look.
5. I thought: maybe this boy can teach me something.
6. I thought: with his look in my eyes, maybe I could become someone.
7. You had that big-city carelessness, that certainty you would succeed.
8. I began to care for you, to desire your success, as one desires good things for those he loves.
9. Still I did not trust you completely.
10. After the gaokao, I thought I had misjudged you.
11. Perhaps I have misjudged you again—perhaps you are still my brother.
12. Still I cannot help but think that even if we had ended in this same place, we might have gotten here differently.
13. For example, you might have told me the truth.
14. When I confided to you that I was in love, you encouraged me.
15. Finally I asked her to marry me.
16. Her answer: I am engaged to Li Yongzong.

I FELT AS if I had been doused with cold water. I blinked and reread the letter.

Finally I asked her to marry me.
Her answer: I am engaged to Li Yongzong.

I had been wrong about everything, I had been hiding from and chasing the wrong things, my energy had been flying down all the wrong roads.

I still had a chance with Su Lan.

Bo was lost forever. A friend, a true friend, once.

But I still had a chance with Su Lan. She was not engaged to Bo, she was not so disgusted with me that she could not say my name. I had given up too easily. She had been waiting for me to try harder.

I called Bo.

He came to the phone and so I spoke, hoping that he was listening. I started: I am not engaged to Su Lan. But yes, I have been a shit friend. I told him everything—almost everything. I told him that we had fallen into the same trap. I shifted the order of events to exonerate myself. I had gotten that same postcard, I too had thought it a confession of love. Even before he told me about his love I had courted her. I had already planned to take her back to Hangzhou, where my mother was sick, dying, expecting to meet my girlfriend. At the end of this trip I proposed to her but she rejected me. By the time I knew about Bo and her, I had already been tossed aside—I was too heartbroken, too ashamed, to admit what had passed between us. But now—now there was nothing. I hadn't spoken to her in over two years. This much was true.

Forgive me, I said. After many minutes of the two of us breathing into our receivers, I heard a click, and the dial tone.

I bought a train ticket to Beijing. I would leave the following Friday evening. I would go from the train station directly to Su Lan.

IT WAS AN excuse, Su Lan said. It meant nothing, now go.

She tried to close the door. I held it open with my foot.

You ruined our friendship, I accused. You must have a better explanation.

I didn't do anything, she said.

You didn't do anything. You didn't lead us on. You didn't realize we both loved you.

It seemed to me that Lanlan had changed. Grown wiser, less transparent. What had been a searching curiosity in her eyes was now calculating, shrewd. The look suited her. It made her more fiercely beautiful, her lips pale, her eyes bright, her skin white and cold.

You don't deserve to be Zhang Bo's friend, she said.

But you'd rather be engaged to me than to him.

Go. Leave me alone.

I just want to hold you to your word.

So leave.

The three most important people in my life think we're engaged: Zhang Bo, my father, my mother.

I had not meant to speak of my mother as if she were still alive. Su Lan must have noticed a change in my face. Her pressure against the door softened. She looked into my eyes fully before narrowing hers.

It was a game you invented! she said.

She pressed on the door again.

Go, or I will call the police.

I relented. The door slammed and I started down the hall. I had expected this. I had another visit to make before the day was over. When I turned for the stairs I heard the door open again. Lan called out:

How is your mother? Is she well?

Without turning my head I shouted, She's dead.

BO GLARED BUT let me inside. His roommates were out at dinner. I sat next to him as he watched the evening news and ate leftovers. He did not offer me any food. The news update ended. The television began to broadcast the weather forecast in all the major cities. We stared at the placid blue screen and listened to the lady announcer's voice skipping with false urgency over bland music. It was raining in Sichuan, high twenties in Hainan. Bo flipped through channels, then turned off the TV.

Do you want to know the truth? he said, not getting up from his chair. He put his empty bowl on the floor.

I loved her even in high school, he said.

I had no idea, I said.

We were friends back then too, but nobody noticed. Not even you.

I never saw you with her.

You never saw her at all.

Fair.

We stared at the blank television screen.

In high school I got up hours before morning exercises and jogged around the track, he said. I was always trying to tire my body out. Many of those mornings, Lanlan joined me.

He added after a moment, She has no trouble falling asleep, but often she wakes early from bad dreams.

Most of the time, they did not even speak. But somehow she could tell he was lonely despite his gregarious personality.

I loved her before anyone else did, Bo said, before anyone even knew she existed. I am the only person who knows who she truly is, the only one who saw her beauty before she went and made herself into this beautiful thing.

That was what he'd told her when he begged her to marry him. She did not have to deny who she was with him.

Su Lan had pleaded obliviousness. His love letters had been full of politics, current events, Bo's most recent thoughts on the state of national affairs. She had read them as intellectual inquiries, correspondence between two active minds. She became icy. She said without hesitation that there was no way she could marry him, as she was already engaged.

Bo did not believe her. He did not give up. He demanded evidence. Finally she said she was engaged to me.

It's a lie, I said. Cautiously, I repeated my story, painting Su Lan the villain, emphasizing the naïvety and sincerity of my own feelings for her. We're both victims, I said. Bo looked weary. I picked up his empty dinner bowl and put it in the sink. I waited for him to respond. Finally I said I'd better go. I'll leave you to rest, I said, and turned to leave.

As I was turning the knob, he blurted out, I know why she said you. He stared ahead, not looking at me.

It's obvious, isn't it? The truth is, Yongzong, I only believed her because her engagement to you was my greatest insecurity.

What do you have to be insecure about? I asked, baffled, wholly sincere for the first time that night.

Just look at the two of us, side by side. Li Yongzong: handsome, refined, intelligent, rich. Zhang Bo: the civilized farm boy. Just look at this face.

He grimaced and bared his teeth.

Who would you choose?

I HAVE ALWAYS known how my character is flawed. I cannot see people. I can look hard, I can register and even understand a person's existence. But to see that person objectively, as she really is—

I could never see Lanlan, or Bo Cai, or anyone who mattered, without the screen of who they were to me, and perhaps more important, how they made me look. To others, to myself. Su Lan was and is still right. There is too much of me in everything I do, and this *I* infects every part of my being, down to the very way my eyes perceive.

That week in May of 1987, as I returned daily to Lan's door, begging her hand in marriage, a shell seemed to harden around her skin. She rebuffed me again and again, and with each rejection she appeared more and more desirable. Each second I was away, I was sure that someone more worthy would take her. Years later, when clear skies in Beijing became rare, I would remember how the weather that week was beautiful, blue cloudless horizon and a breeze that smelled like mountains. Students lazed outdoors and bicyclists filled the streets. Lan shined with an almost alien glow. Her skin was pale, her cheeks were pink with impatience. I had to have her.

Daily I returned to her door, and daily I was ignored. I waited for her to break. I wandered the empty capital at night, unable to sleep.

On the fifth day, as I sat by the wall in her hallway, Su Lan's roommate left the apartment. She walked past me and said, Hey, handsome fellow, give up already and marry me.

I ignored her and leaned my head against the wall.

She knelt in front of me and pinched my cheek.

Look at those shadows under your eyes, she said. You look more like a heartbroken poet every day.

I batted her hand away. She got up, laughed, and skipped down the hall singing a Deng Lijun song.

Was that how I looked to Su Lan, like a lovelorn poet? I remained sitting there after her roommate left, hitting my head on the wall. Su Lan had told me once that according to quantum mechanics, there existed a small possibility that solid matter could penetrate solid matter. Technically, if I sat there and hit my head against her wall *forever*, eventually, I would fall through.

I had dozed off when Su Lan opened the door. She knocked on the wall to wake me up, and then, as if I had just arrived, invited me in.

I got up, I brushed off my pants. I entered and stood with my hands in my pockets. She plugged in a hot plate and put on a pot of tea.

Her dorm was small and simple, with a bunk bed and a small table with two chairs like any other university dorm. Someone (her roommate, I assumed) had unabashedly put up a giant poster of the Taiwanese rock star Hou Dejian on the back of the door. Between the windows was a magazine cutout of the Chinese women's volley-ball team with Lang Ping front and center. There were stacks of books on the floor.

Su Lan sat on the window ledge and looked at me. Zhang Bo is too good for me, she said. Zhang Bo deserves a nice, normal woman, a woman who will take care of him and his mother and father. Not a woman like me, who is constantly running away.

I did not say anything. She continued:

You know why I went along with your stupid engagement? I knew that your mother would be dead before she discovered the truth.

She paused and walked around the room, taking out paper cups, pinching in leaves of tea, restacking her books without purpose.

You see, that's the kind of woman I am.

Then she stepped in front of me, her mouth a hand's length from mine.

Maybe I'm the kind of woman who deserves to be with dirt like you.

I could barely hear what she was saying. My sleepless self was surging awake, the hairs on my skin shaking, alive, sure that I was on the brink of life as only the very lucky few could live it.

IN THE WEEKS that followed, I opened my mother's drawer and gave her presents to Lan, one by one. Lan accepted them without comment, and I didn't see them again, she never wore or used or displayed them. Finally there was only one item left, a gold necklace with lovebirds engraved on the pendant. My father had given it to my mother when they got engaged.

My mother wanted you to wear this at our wedding, I said. I held out the necklace to Lan and watched it glitter in the light. I took a breath and continued: I want you to wear it too. I know I've said it before but let me say it again, properly, I want to marry you. I want it so much.

Su Lan was silent and still, her face thoughtful. I reached to clasp the necklace around her neck. She stepped back.

I don't want it, she said. Stop giving me these things. I can't handle it. I can't—betraying my own mother is already too much, I can't betray yours too. You have to know this, I don't want a wedding, I don't want your family to meet my family, I don't want children. I don't ever want to become a mother, I can't bear the possibility that any person might feel about me the way I feel about my mother.

She shook out her shoulders, sharpened her face.

I'll marry you, she said, but these are my terms.

She looked at me with composure, almost bravado, as if prodding me to protest. But I was in oblivion. Everything that had come from her mouth before the words *I'll marry you* dissolved in the morning air. I stuffed the necklace in my pocket and forgot about it. Who cared about a wedding, families meeting? And children? They had not even crossed my mind. What I wanted was the woman in front of me and whatever unimaginable, brilliant life she was barreling into.

I took her in my arms, I said, Of course, anything for you.

During that time, I did not question Lanlan's motives or doubts. I loved the mystery of her decisions—how she seemed to operate on a logic entirely her own, one as firm and true as the laws of physics she studied and tried to decode. Why had she gone along with me to see my parents? Why had she led Bo on? Why had she chosen me? None of it mattered. I still could not believe *that* she had chosen me, that I, Li Yongzong, had won her, that after everything, she was falling in love with *me*. That, that, that. Lanlan's most distinctive, seductive quality was her ability to make you forget every question. Her presence was so exhilarating—sound, smell, taste, disturbance of air of her—that she erased the need for history. She erased even the need for the present. Her beauty was a promise, and so when you were with her it was the future that lit up, materializing endless possibilities and roads, like the network of neurons and synapses in some god's brain.

Only much later would I realize how deliberately Lanlan had worked all her life to destroy every trace of her past. She'd studied the way Beijingers dressed and cut their hair and walked. She'd plucked her eyebrows and saved her scholarship money to buy expensive lipstick and skin creams. That was why she'd led so many men on, so she could continue to receive their gifts of nice clothing, continue to supplement her food income with meals at Beijing's best restaurants. Later I would watch her replicate this assimilation in Shanghai. After the outburst about our mothers, she never spoke again of her family. I didn't mention what I had heard of them from Bo, sensing that she preferred my ignorance. When she saw the rising of a question about her past in my eyes, she cut it off, saying, You, of all people, should understand.

She knew I had not spoken to my father in years.

Once, I had countered: Even so, you have met my family. Sometimes I speak of my childhood without noticing or thinking of it. But your omission is so complete—it feels pathological.

For a long time Lanlan looked at me, her eyes burning. It was the first time in our courtship that I thought she might cry. I thought I had finally cracked her open, and at that moment, when I was still falling in love with her, or perhaps more accurately, still trying to make her fall in love with me—at that moment my heart rejoiced, ready to meet her tenderness.

Finally she spoke.

The people I knew as a child have an incredible ability to wallow in their sufferings, she said. They rehash little injustices that build up to a lifetime of irredeemable wrongs—they exploit the past to show how they have unflinchingly swallowed bitter fruit, they suffer silently until they vomit it all in a wave of sudden unburdening. I don't want to participate in this ritual. It's disgusting.

Later, when Su Lan was my wife, I would often be reminded of the crouching insecurity I had occasionally glimpsed in Bo. It was all rather simple, now that I think of it, the simple insecurity of being born poor. Today, it is clear this was the real reason she chose me over Bo: she was too recognizable to him. It did not matter that he alone, precisely because he had seen every part of her, could truly know her and thus truly love her. She did not want to be known, or perhaps, even, to be loved. She wanted more than anything to amputate that past from her self, to be accepted as the person she'd created, for her lover not to love her, but to make her someone new.

I visited Beijing; she visited Shanghai. She completed her master's and started her doctorate at Fudan University. With her infallible charm, she convinced the people in her danwei's housing department to move us up the waitlist, and got us a couple's housing assignment that had just opened up in the city center. We moved out of our shared dorms into a room in the old city. It was small and dirty but at least we didn't have to live with roommates like some other newlyweds we knew. We forgot about Bo. By the following autumn, just four months after Lanlan invited me inside her dorm, we had filed for our marriage papers. There was no ceremony. We went to the municipal offices and completed the required physical examinations and paperwork. Afterward, we took wedding photos at a studio and had steaks at a Western restaurant by the Bund. We carried our few possessions into our new home. Lanlan lit up and I flew around her, exhilarated, like a moth charging toward the brightest of flames.

THE OTHER DAY, I was staring out of my office window when I thought I saw Lanlan walking down the street. It was mid-afternoon. I was translating a popular detective novel by an Englishman that would soon be made into a movie. I tapped my pen on the windowsill and looked at the young woman as she rounded the corner. She wore a simple black coat and walked with her head down. I could not see her face clearly, but for a moment I was struck with a feeling of recognition so strong that I almost ran outside. It was only after the woman disappeared that I realized Lanlan must have aged by now, that she, like Zhang Bo, like me, would be old.

Was that you? I realize I don't even know if you are a boy or a girl—a man or a woman, perhaps, by now—if you are dead or alive. I look at the year and subtract: if you were born and survived, you would be seventeen years old, just old enough to pass for your mother, if you had been a girl.

I am not cruel. I do think of you sometimes—often. I haven't forgotten that I made a child with Su Lan, even if when I think of her, the image that comes to mind is always from a time before the idea of you existed. When I try to remember what she looked like during the months she was pregnant, I am met with a black fog of shapes and sounds. My mind leaves the small room where we lived, leaves that stinking alleyway, so old and poor, which she treated like some kind of palace, and memories of the outside world—the city, the protests, the energy, the colors and noises of the streets—rush in.

SOME YEARS AGO, I encountered again the image of my second face. I was not Li Yongzong anymore. I was married again. My wife, six months pregnant, was going through old drawers and cabinets, cleaning out our apartment in preparation for the arrival of our child, when she came across a faded and expired government identification card—the very first document that bore the name I use now. My name.

She held it up with a perplexed smile.

You looked so different when you were younger, she said, turning the scratched plastic to the light.

When I saw what it was I snatched it from her, replacing as quick as I could my expression of terror with one of embarrassed surprise. Is that so? My thumb pressed into the face, a smudging motion remembered instinctively. I peered at it in mock inspection. That's funny, I said. I think I look exactly the same. I laughed. I guess that's just getting older, I said.

I wasn't lying. Later that night, after my wife had fallen into deep sleep, I retrieved the card from the trash and looked at the photograph by lamplight. Indeed, when I imagined my face, this was the one I saw: it looked more like me than my own reflection in the mirror. I remembered the first time I had seen it, bloodied and pressed against asphalt, attached to a body that was already going cold. Even then I had recognized it as my own. I stood over the image of my dead self, rotting on the ground, and felt the heat of blood in my hands, the slick of sweat down my back—every sensation of life—as an incredible gift. A few steps away a wallet lay open, its contents strewn: cash, coins, a newspaper clipping, this card I now held in my hand.

I dropped it back into the trash. Pushed it in deep. I tied up the plastic bag and took it down to the dumpster.

For the next few days I observed my wife. Did she seem colder, wary? I thought I saw her watching me from the corner of an eye. I felt a familiar mounting anxiety: the walls of a shared home closing in, the swelling of a new life preparing to enter an already shrinking space. I told my wife I had to travel for work. I packed a small bag. I left.

I found myself in Shanghai. For years I had not set foot in my former city. I wandered the streets with the same aimless desire that had once driven me to Beijing University's campus, to Su Lan's student dormitory. Before I knew it I was standing outside the building where we had lived. I didn't know what I wanted, if I hoped to see Su Lan and confront her, if I needed her blessing or her curse.

I went to the building many times that week, never going inside. I stood underneath our former window, blinking—I could not see clearly—it took only a few minutes for me to lose courage. When the fog finally cleared, on my fourth or fifth visit, I looked around the old longtang and saw that it was even smaller than I'd remembered. In fact the whole neighborhood had been deemed such an eyesore that it was marked for demolition. Many buildings had already been torn down. It was clear that Su Lan no longer lived here, that no one lived here. Each morning, in this alleyway that once had been clogged with residents, I was the only person in sight. The demolition symbol on the wall of the building, painted in crude red, was a plain sign of my stupidity. Of course Su Lan had moved on. She had always been better than me; who was I to think I could have anything to settle with a person like her, who had certainly found her way to much better and brighter things, who was probably in America, rich and successful, whose name if I opened *Physical Review Letters* today I would undoubtedly find. Perhaps one day I would see her face again, but it would be in the newspaper, as she accepted some international prize or achieved some other entrance into collective historical memory. I heard a noise in the building. It seemed to come from the second floor, from behind the dark window of our old room. I ran from the neighborhood. I returned to my wife in Beijing.

LESS THAN A year after Su Lan and I married, she got pregnant. Around that time, I was growing increasingly bored with medicine. I had gotten to a point where I was a fine doctor, but it also meant the work was repetitive and easy. More and more I felt like an assembly line worker in a machine. Su Lan had suggested that I try medical research, and I followed her suggestion. At first it was exciting to learn new techniques, the rules and logic of clinical trials. I felt the joys I always felt when faced with something new and strange, with discovering I could understand it. It was like learning a new language, you plunged in and searched for patterns, a neat structure from which all else could easily be deduced. In medical research the pattern had to do with zooming out, then in, then out again. First you established a treatment problem in global terms, quantifying it (the number of people affected by such-and-such disease), then honed in on your specific interest, invented a rigorous way to test various treatments, gathered data, and from that data, drew lines from the minute and specialized numbers to the large issue from which you began.

More exciting than learning research techniques, however, was coming home and discussing what I had learned with Lanlan. She listened attentively, she got excited with me, she asked questions that illuminated approaches I had not seen, which helped me to advance with more speed and virtuosity. My superiors praised me, my wife was proud of me. I started to feel not just like a technician but like a scientist, someone like Su Lan, who was making a difference in her field.

The feeling did not last long. This has always been my problem: once I get the gist of something, I get bored, I move on. During the gaokao I'd lost the discipline to keep at a subject until I achieved perfection, regardless of how much it interested me. Soon Su Lan's interrogations began to irritate me. It became clear that she was more passionate than I was about my own research; our discussions sparked new ideas in her mind even as they remained dull to me. I began to feel—correctly, I still believe—that if Su Lan were to decide to drop physics and become a doctor she would soon outstrip me. She had more interesting questions. She was able to turn simple formulations in a way that revealed their complexity, to come up with hypothetical scenarios that pushed the boundaries of the structures we'd set. When she repeated back to me things I'd said, her paraphrases were more elegant, more succinct, and I wondered why I had blabbered on for so long when I could have just said that. In the shadow of her mind I again felt the uselessness of my pursuit: I was not a scientist, like her, I could never have her passion, her creativity, her sharpness and intuition. I withdrew, I stopped talking to her about work, I began to spend more time outside the house, inventing excuses. Often I simply went alone to a café or bookstore to read. Only once or twice did I end up in bed with another woman, and when it happened, I was surprised by how easy it was, how interchangeable these bodies were with the body of my extraordinary wife.

It was in the midst of this restlessness that the student democracy movement began. On the streets I heard impassioned speeches, beautiful and moving phrases, words put together for the purpose of motivating people to act. In the newspapers I read furious debates. My consciousness lit up. I felt like I had when I was courting Su Lan, like my life, finally, had reached its place of yearning. The debates about the fate of the nation were more immediate and urgent than Su Lan's physics; they were grander and more ambitious than my clinical trials, and the language that fueled them seemed inexhaustible; you could see their patterns yet be reignited again and again. Some of the protesters felt that China was on the brink of death, they protested with the desperation of believing that something great they loved was dying, weeping so with patriotism that it did look like grief. I argued against them; I thought the nation was coming alive, that all these people in the streets were not the last gasp of a dying order but rather the birth of something wonderful and new. My passion, I believed then, was patriotic and optimistic—I believed in a better future for us all.

Su Lan did not even believe in the idea of China. Not, at least, as anything more than accumulated coincidence and geography. She distrusted any notions of collectivity. She refused to engage with the protests, and I discovered that when it came to politics she responded with the same shallow dismissiveness of my relationship with science. She glanced at the political and philosophical essays and articles I was reading and summarized them crudely (so the students believe that money will solve everything; the government believes instead in power), simplifying them to the point of missing all their nuance and meaning. At last I had found a subject for which my mind was better built. This recognition drove me in deeper.

If you had asked me which one of us would have become involved in a grassroots movement, I would have said Su Lan. I was more selfish, more petty, more narrowly focused on my own comfortable life. She was the one with lofty concerns. But my instinct was wrong. Su Lan was focused on such large things—the laws that governed universes—that human behavior, even on this grand, social scale, could not move her, could not but appear trivial. This was her flaw, her strength. She was obsessed with extremes, with the very small and the very large—her mind had no room for what was in between.

We had many arguments during this time. The walls of our room were shabby and thin, and so most of our exchanges were conducted in hushed tones, short phrases whispered in the evening, lobbed across the dinner table like little darts. I can't remember most of what we said, but one fight remains with me vividly. When I think of it, I begin to understand why I have made my life as ordinary as it is today.

Su Lan was pregnant. For once she let herself shout, and I began to shout too, both of us forgetting that we lived in a cramped building with dozens of other families. We said things out loud that should have been kept silent. With each word we sought injury and pain. The room disintegrated under their force; picture frames began to fall off the walls, books tumbled off the shelves, plates crashed from the cupboards. Su Lan stood in the midst of it, her face red, her fist clenched, her body huge and unrecognizable. I had the impression her body was bursting out of her, and suddenly everything went silent around me, though I could see she was still yelling. She was breaking, the edges of her, and through the cracks I saw something terrible, it was dark and powerful and churning, and I recognized with frightening clarity that everything I knew about Su Lan—her excellence, her beauty, her composure—was actually an attempt to control this thing.

I realized that I did not know her, and did not want to.

I LEFT SU LAN while she w   he was in the grip of an exhaustion so deep it made he   hand was covered in sweat. It had exerted so much pressu   on to mine, it had lost the shape of a hand. At that moment, under the temporary relief of medication, her muscles had loosened. By instinct, I shook my wrist free. I stood up, stretched my legs, and looked around the room, seeing it for the first time as if I were a bystander, as if I had already stepped out.

We were in Beijing, in a hospital. The walls were gray with soot, and the thin white sheets covering the empty beds had been eaten through in many places by rats or moths. Though certainly clean, sterile, the tiled floor was stained with age. I remember thinking with disgust that this was a hospital in our nation's capital, the best that any of us could do. Finally my eyes fell on Su Lan, who lay on the farthest bed from the door, flanked by IV poles. Her mouth was open, drooling. She looked, with that enormous belly, like a stranger.

After eight and a half months of pregnancy, I still couldn't understand. She had not wanted a child. She had not wanted to leave behind any part of her biology, to perpetuate herself into the future. A perfect life, she'd said, is lived, and then it disappears. For eight months I had looked at her, blinking, unable to believe that a transformation so irreversible was happening.

I did not think. I found my legs moving—not running, not propelling me out of the room as had been my impulse for many months—but walking steadily, calmly, as if nothing of note were occurring, as if I had somewhere to be but not urgently—

I walked between the two rows of empty beds and turned out of the room, down the dimly lit hospital hall. I could hear my steps echoing loudly, filling the hall with clamor. I walked out of the front door, across the concrete lot, and through the gate.

It was dusk. The sky was smoky and pink, and I could feel night running toward me. When we arrived at the hospital, the streets had been full of protesters, and I had been impatient with the knowledge that I could not join them. My desire to be closer to the heart of the movement was why we had overstayed in Beijing. The capital was chaos, was contradiction, was pure energy that roiled the streets; I stepped onto the avenue and it was like stepping into my mind, every unspoken desire and fury manifesting in living, breathing form.

The streets were as crowded as they had been when we arrived. But the protestors were no longer chanting or holding up signs. Now they were frantic, running down Fuxingmenwai Avenue holding large objects—wheels, wooden chairs, metal bicycle racks torn from the pavement—I followed to a bridge where a barricade grew. I pushed into the throng and met my restlessness. I confronted it, acted beside it, without needing to understand what it was.

Minutes, hours passed. How much time exactly I can't say. All I know is that the sky grew dark then light. I walked through and among people, becoming a part of the organism that moved them. Perhaps I carried things, perhaps I ran. I remember hearing my voice in the night as a disembodied shout, loud and ferocious. I don't know what I said. My mind was a buzzing blankness. Even when shots tore the air and the living fled, I continued to wander. It was not that I did not feel fear. Fear did not strike as I'd imagined. It did not make me hide or run or curl into myself but rather filled me with clarity. The night was serene and dark, and I was floating on a white ocean whose depths I knew were turbulent and full, and yet from where I lay I could see only water meeting sky. I recalled the day of the gaokao so many years ago, the exhilaration of believing my father dead. Around me, all was dying, but death pulsed with possibility. Now I understood: the earth could turn itself inside out, buildings could sink into the ground, men could grow wings, and none of it mattered—I was free.

LAST YEAR WE sent our daughter to a prestigious boarding school where she would learn to read and write and solve mathematics problems with the children of our country's leaders. The apartment quieted. My wife and I fell into a pattern of easy coexistence, friends who spoke to each other mostly about practical matters: the price of groceries, what was on TV, the electricity bill. Simple things— eating, shitting, sleeping—pushed life from one day into the next. I had too much time. I began to wake in the nights, intensely hungry. I got out of bed and sat under the yellow light of the kitchen, eating bread or leftover rice or whatever food we had, chewing slowly, listening to the grinding of my teeth.

One night, I heard a low tone somewhere inside the flat, like the drone of a cello sustained underneath a flying fugue. I walked through the living room, the bathroom, my daughter's empty bed-room, and finally to my own bedroom, where my wife was asleep. I could not locate the source of the sound, but it grew louder and more insistent as I searched. I picked up objects and put them to my ear. They were silent. I looked at my wife's body. She snored and turned on her side. I left the bedroom and then the flat. I went down the stairs into the courtyard, where the flickering streetlamp outside the door made the parked and hooded motorcycles look like animals sleeping in the night.

Still the tone grew louder. I walked and walked, and it continued to pursue me. The sound was inhuman. It did not vibrate and it did not breathe, and yet it had a fullness that made me think it was not merely mechanical. I walked briskly down streets that looked unfamiliar. The streets were lined with buildings, and I thought about going inside to escape the noise, but when I turned to enter I saw that none of the buildings had doors.

After walking for a long time, turning down dark, high-walled alleys, I finally came upon an old house that looked familiar. The lights were on inside and the windows glowed invitingly. I was relieved to see a door. I pushed it open and shouted a greeting, but no one responded. I went inside. A lit hallway led up a stairwell to a landing where another door stood in a rectangle of light. I opened this door too and stepped in. Finally, the noise had ceased. I breathed deeply, happy to find a quiet place where I might get a bit of rest.

The room was small and had been sectioned off into living and sleeping areas by a half-open curtain. A light bulb hung from the ceiling. I lay down on the bed and closed my eyes. The bed was hard, the blanket stiff, but it was nevertheless comforting, in the way that familiar things can be. That was when I realized—I had slept in this bed before. I sat up. I walked around the room, picking things up and putting them down. I tried to read the spines of the books on the shelves, but I could not focus the words. Still I seemed to know where everything belonged. I opened the wardrobe on the far side of the room and saw there, in the door, a person looking back at me.

It was my reflection. For many moments I did not recognize it. The mirror was thin and stained and my body was flimsy in it. I looked through the clothes in the wardrobe and discovered that they were mine. I circled the room again. I had sat in this chair, I had eaten at this table. I had paced across these floorboards listening to the neighbor's radio. It was the room I had once shared with Lanlan. And there was our wedding portrait on the wall.

Lanlan looked young, like a girl. One day, sooner than I could imagine, my daughter would be that age. And I? In the photograph where I should have been I found instead Zhang Bo.

Zhang Bo, also known as Bo Cai, also known as Number Two. His face was handsome. A sort of goodness shone through it, making his rough features pleasing, even gentle, to the eye. I took the frame off the wall and held it in both hands, shaking it until I awoke, sweating, standing at my window in Beijing, clutching the branches of my wife's kumquat tree.

LIYA

WHEN I MET MY FATHER, I imagined, the body would respond. The senses would open, the lungs would gulp deep air. The body would feel an attraction to the one that preceded it, and move involuntarily, as a river toward an ocean.

I imagined I would desire him.

I was on a train to Beijing. It was a slow train; it had dented containers and jamming windows, it matched my imagination of trains in developing Asia. When I'd arrived at the station in Shanghai, I'd had two options: the new high-speed, leaving in an hour and arriving five later, or the one I was on, leaving right away with a journey three times the length.

I could not stand to be in Shanghai a moment longer.

I did not really want to be in Beijing either.

I wanted to be nowhere, to be trapped en route, forever if I could manage it. Transit was a space free of decisions: a relief. I looked out the window at the paved roads and traffic lights falling slowly away, and was thankful for this hard plastic cushion, peeling at the edges, for the stiff springs pressing into my legs. I listened to the metal churn of the wheels. Here, I could pretend that time was suspended, and the future, always imminent, might never fully arrive.

The landscape turned gray and white. I passed muddy fields dotted with long domes of stretched plastic sheets. I passed flat huts with black shingled roofs that rose from the earth like low hills. I passed frozen ponds and patches of unmelted snow. I thought:

How thoroughly my mother has succeeded in hollowing me out.

I HAD ALWAYS wanted to be a person who was from somewhere. Three short months ago, I had wanted it desperately. *Where are you from* was the sort of question you were required to answer not just because it was supposed to say something about you, but because it was supposed to be easy. Starting college, meeting classmates, roommates, and potential friends, thrilled for my chance, finally, to define myself independently of my mother, I'd replied: I was born in Shanghai. It had seemed the simplest way to convey a complicated truth. It had always felt like a lie.

Now I had the true answer to that question. According to my birth certificate, I was from Beijing.

I didn't want to be from Beijing. I no longer wanted to be from anywhere. My desire for roots had been more than a desire for belonging. I had seen what people who were from places were like, how they glittered with solidity and substance, and I had wanted to be filled with that substance too. Now I was afraid. Like any foreigner's my knowledge of Beijing consisted mostly of stock images—the Great Wall, Tiananmen Square, Mao waving serenely over a rapturous crowd—I was afraid of arriving in Beijing and encountering the real counterparts of these images. I didn't want to discover that they were different from the stock images, or the same, to discover anything about them; most of all I was afraid of feeling as I had when I'd first entered the Shanghai apartment, of seeing myself inside some television or movie scene, flattened, defined by the borders of the camera's eye.

My mother had told me, and the United States government, that I was a year older than I really was. June 4, 1989, was my true date of birth. I turned the date over in my mind. It had a familiar quality, like I had seen or heard it before, identified it as special somehow, but its significance eluded me. Perhaps the familiarity pointed to my preconscious knowledge of its truth. It made sense: I was always the smallest kid in class, I had gotten my period so late.

I pressed my forehead into the cold windowpane. I stared at the reflections of my eyes. I tried to understand why my mother would have told this lie.

An obvious answer was childcare. When I looked back at my up-bringing, it was painfully clear that so much of what I had once thought special about my mother had simply been created by necessity: our closeness, our games, the hours spent at her place of work. It would have helped her tremendously if I could grow up faster, start school a year earlier. It was possible, I imagined, that she'd made a mistake while filling out one of a hundred immigration papers, and, seeing how the mistake was advantageous, let it stand.

Perhaps one mistake had led to another. Perhaps some govern-ment bureaucrat had heard her Chinese accent and written Beijing without thinking twice. Or perhaps her memory of Beijing was tainted somehow. Perhaps Beijing had something to do with my father. Yes: this suspicion was why I was headed there.

Perhaps, perhaps. My mind cycled through these possibilities, one leading only again to another, none of them satisfying, until finally, spent with unknowing, I fell asleep.

BEIJING WAS COLD. I stood in front of a twelve-story building, shiv-ering. It was midnight or later. When my train pulled into the station I hadn't been ready to arrive, so I'd kept moving. I walked, kept walking, six miles in the dark, until I arrived here.

The building was nothing remarkable: a concrete high-rise apartment composed of identical rectangular units. It had twelve floors and fourteen windows on each floor, one stairwell up the middle. On the long train ride I had seen similar buildings at the edges of other cities. A building such as this could be found anywhere in China, and probably in other economically developing countries too.

Nothing remarkable about the building, no, except that its address appeared on many letters written to my mother. One hundred letters, to be exact, written between the years 1985 and 1987 and postmarked exactly seven days apart. They had been bound by a rubber band, untouched for so many years it snapped immediately when pulled. The man who wrote them was named Zhang Bo. The contents were mundane. The style was direct and dry:

A recent editorial in the People's Daily *presents illuminating statistics on inflation.*

In the last week the particle accelerator broke twice.

The exam was difficult, as expected. The results are announced in May.

They were love letters. They had to be, because of their frequency and consistency, because Zhang Bo was my father. Fourteen of the hundred used the word 爱 (ai, love). Though usually 爱 was not used in a romantic context, one letter made the romantic intent clear.

It was dated the third of February 1987. It was the final letter in the pile, and the only one that overtly expressed a desire:

I want to make some things clear. I intend to make you my wife. It is undeniable that we are well matched. I think you will agree.

This letter was not one of the fourteen that included the word 爱.

The stairwell lights were off, the windows were dark. It was too late to go knocking on anyone's door.

I left, walked until I saw the lit-up sign of a hostel, and got myself a single room. At the foot of the hard bed a radiator pumped out waves of singed heat. I wrapped the blankets around my shoulders, shivering, and dozed until afternoon.

THE NEXT DAY I returned to the building. It was late evening and a few window lights still blazed bright. I was not alone on the street. I watched the people appearing from and disappearing into the stairwell, staring hard, trying to discern their qualities. A couple walked past me, talking animatedly, and ascended hand in hand. Their steps echoed and quieted. Three people came down, separately, then two together, followed by two more going up. I told myself to follow but could not motivate my legs to move. I stood and watched the window lights go out one by one. I stood until the pool of lamplight around me disappeared with a click.

The next morning I put the final letter in my backpack. In the tiny hostel room, which was just big enough to fit one twin bed, which had a slanted ceiling so I couldn't stand up straight without hitting my head, I rearranged my few belongings and rearranged them again, delaying my departure. By the time I convinced my body to face the city the pimpled receptionist was drowsy from lunch. The noodle shops and cafeterias were empty, tables littered with used napkins and piles of bones. I roused the owner to take my order. I ate, I paid. Darkness set early.

I walked small roads until I reached Beijing University. On the map it looked close, just four or five blocks, but these blocks were eternity. The sidewalks were slick with ice. The main avenue, a river wide, could be crossed only via a raised bridge. Outside the university walls I turned down the block lined with barren young trees, into a courtyard behind the road, and not letting myself pause for breath or hesitation, walked to the stairs of the building I had stood outside for two nights without entering, whose address appeared on the letter inside my bag, along with a room number: 303. The stairwell was weakly lit and grimy and smelled like dust and piss. From above, voices echoed—teenagers discussing something trivial with casual animation. At each floor peeling posters papered the entrance to the main hall. Flaked paint dusted the corners of the landings. On the third floor I stopped and turned down the hall.

NINETEEN EIGHTY-SEVEN? THE young man said. He was thin and tall and stood in the doorway looking at me with his head cocked to one side.

This is a student dorm, he explained.

Indeed—behind the door of room 303 were three sets of bunk beds with metal frames, lining parallel walls of the narrow room. Books and clothes and shoes and empty takeout containers lay about with a carelessness I recognized from my own brief collegiate life. Between the beds a group of five or six boys huddled around a small wooden table, where two of them were playing chess. The chubby one in a red shirt made a move and sat back, looking over at the door.

No wonder this building is falling apart, he said, it's older than I am.

His opponent, who had a long skinny face and rectangular glasses, called out to the one at the door.

Feng, don't be rude. Invite the lady in.

Inside, clothes were swept to the foot of a bed and I was motioned to sit.

Who did you say you were looking for again? one of the game watchers said.

Glasses made a move and a commotion erupted.

His queen!

Too late now—

Will you all shut up and just watch?

You idiot—

I'm looking for a man named Zhang Bo, I said.

Hey, Jian, you know anyone named Zhang Bo?

Let me think—Zhang Bo, Zhang Bo—isn't that tall guy in our class with the fancy computer called Zhang something?

That's Zhang Bei, you idiot—

He was a student here in the nuclear physics department, I said.

Red Shirt lifted his arm to make a move and for a moment everyone quieted. He dropped his arm without touching a piece. A groan of exasperation followed.

Guo, you're in the physics department—know a Zhang Bo?

Nope, Glasses said, can't think of a single classmate named Zhang.

Nineteen eighty-seven! said Feng, the boy who opened the door. He was a student here in 1987! Do any of you have ears?

That's before I was born, another boy said, as if that settled the matter.

Me too, I said.

Zhang Bo, Zhang Bo, Glasses was repeating, as he hunched over the chessboard, eyeing the pieces. The name does sound familiar.

He'd be—the boy named Feng said—something like forty years old, forty-five?

An old man—

Your dad's age—

Red Shirt made a move. Glasses picked up his queen and placed it down firmly two squares to the left. Checkmate, he said, and stood up. He stepped away from the table, where the other boys were bent over the board talking over each other, gesticulating, where Red Shirt sat with his brow furrowed.

Zhang Bo, Glasses said to me. Do you mean Professor Zhang? I've got electromagnetic theory with Professor Zhang tomorrow morning. I think he went to Beida for his bachelor's. Maybe it's him.

A collective shout of discontent rose from the chess watchers. Glasses looked back, ready to reenter the mix and claim his victory. Before he went, he instructed me to meet him the next day at ten. He would take me to the university to meet Professor Zhang.

IS THAT HIM? Glasses, whose name was something-Guo, whispered in my ear. We sat in the back of a large lecture hall, watching a small man write equations on a chalkboard.

I should have been in my own classes. Suddenly I was reminded that I had been a student, with a life, with a direction in my life (I was moving into the future). In fact I'd forgotten that time had continued to pass in the world I left behind. The future had vanished after my mother died. I had entered another world where time moved in a circle and the participant could enter wherever she liked.

The last time I'd checked my email, a few days before coming to China, my inbox had been swelling with concerned and increasingly stern emails from advisers, professors, university administrators. There was an email from my roommate saying that some people from the college had come to empty out my things. I responded to nothing. Everything about that world felt ridiculous. Despite the evidence I could not imagine it continuing on, could not imagine students walking over the green lawns to their classes, eating meals in the cafeteria, groping one another at parties, falling asleep in the library, all while I traveled to the apartment where my mother had died and then to the cold room where they'd kept her corpse. What had been the point of that world? Of living in it? Who had I been, that girl so eager to leave her mother?

The man standing at the front of the lecture hall wrote and spoke. His voice was all sound. Numbers and symbols appeared on the blackboard. He turned around. I leaned forward, looking into his face.

Is that him?

I hadn't signed up for physics classes in my university. I had convinced myself that truth was more than invisible particles interacting as my mother believed, that being alive was more than a meeting of matter, electricity, and force. I had convinced myself that my mother's way of seeing the world (grounded in objectivity, evidence, material fact) was simplistic and crude. Once I had told my mother what I thought in these exact words. She'd looked at me with amusement and said, You're stupid after all.

Is that him? the boy named Guo asked again. I don't know if I answered yes or no.

THE LECTURE ENDED and Professor Zhang gathered his things. A student approached the lectern, followed by another. I stepped into the shadows and waited for them to leave. Finally the hall was empty. He walked out alone, nose buried in a stack of papers. I followed. He went down the hall, up the stairs, down the hall again. He reached for the handle of what appeared to be an office door. I called out:

Professor, I—

He was not my father. I thought he was not in the lecture hall, and now, as I moved closer, I was sure.

He wore a collared white shirt and brown pants, and round metal glasses that made his eyes look small. In the lecture hall, I had leaned forward, trying to read his face, and they'd glinted off the ceiling light and made me blink. His hair was half white but thick and unruly like a teenage boy's, his face unshaven, the kind of man who did not care how he was found.

He turned and saw me.

Did his eyes widen?

He opened his mouth—then stopped whatever it was in his throat.

You are . . . ? he said instead.

I know who you are, I said.

What I meant was, I know who you are not.

It wasn't that I felt nothing looking at Professor Zhang. Certainly I did feel something. I'd like to call it disappointment, but it was more like relief.

Professor Zhang was not good-looking, but he was not ugly either. His face had a pleasant quality, the kind that came from smiling often, from giving people the benefit of the doubt. He laughed but not in a mean or condescending way. He folded his papers under his arm and turned fully to face me.

Are you in my class?

Professor, I began again.

But I could not continue. I stood there searching for some sign of shock or curiosity in his eyes. I pulled the letter from my bag and handed it to him.

He crinkled his eyebrows, almost tenderly, and took it.

His expression did not change. He did not look surprised, which meant either that he had seen the letter before or that he had not. Or perhaps, despite his kind-looking face, he was a shrewd manipulator of emotion and hid himself well. I'd always hated it when people equated niceness with innocence, though of course I did it myself. Professor Zhang could look like a nice man, but that didn't mean he was dumb.

Many minutes passed, and Professor Zhang did not say a thing. Other professor-aged men walked past and went into rooms along the hall. A few students strolled by, chatting excitedly, gesticulating with their arms. Was he waiting for me to speak, to explain? Was he remembering?

I looked at the plaque on the door behind him. It said *Zhang Bo, Nuclear Physics*. The door was made of polished brown wood, its handle painted gold.

Were you in love with her? I blurted.

He looked up.

He sighed.

Come on in, he said, and pushed open the door.

HIS OFFICE WAS cluttered with newspapers and books and smelled like day-old oil. Behind his wooden desk a large window was decorated with a drooping plant. Professor Zhang gestured toward two chairs by the door flanking a small table with a ceramic ashtray. He asked if I wanted tea. He pinched leaves into a thin plastic cup, filled it with hot water from a thermos on the floor, and brought it over by its rim. He did not have tea himself; he gulped down a cup of plain hot water and sat with his hands clasped loosely. Among the papers and notes and diagrams, a photograph of a boy toddler in yellow shoes was pinned to a board on the wall.

Professor Zhang said, We were good friends.

He said, You look like him.

He said, They were a good-looking couple.

He said all this as if in a business meeting, blandly pleasant and without discernible emotion. He looked up at me and his face sagged.

You look like her too.

He continued:

They were both my good friends. We were all classmates.

He shook his head as if clearing it. He said, What do you want from me?

I didn't respond. He looked at the letter in his hand.

Your mother and I were laoxiang, our hometowns just half a day's walk away, then we both went to university here, at Beida. She was a brilliant woman. I was stupid, a kid. All I knew then was that I was old enough to start trying to find a wife, and there she was. It didn't mean anything.

He handed the letter back, folded into thirds, and smiled—a real smile, pressing in all the wrinkles in his cheeks.

So, is it true? he said, hunching his shoulders, leaning in, looking at once eager and afraid. Are they back?

They?

The pronoun struck from behind. I repeated the word and again it ambushed me. Suddenly I understood that this man knew nothing. This man knew even less than I.

Your mother and father, he said. Did they come back to China? I thought—some time ago I thought I saw . . .

Perhaps he saw my panic. Perhaps I was starting to get up, my hands shaking, my mouth opening and closing. The voice that came out was one that hardly realized it was speaking.

I was hoping you could tell me, it was saying, about my father. I was hoping you would—

His confusion made me angry. It made me hate him. It made me want to push my chair to the floor and spit in the grass-green tea he'd poured me.

I said: Yes. Yes, they're back.

YES, THEY ARE back.

They have come to Beijing this month. They are—going into business.

Professor Zhang blinked and ran his fingers under his eyes. I looked straight at him. His weakness egged me on:

They are working on—on a new technology with a Chinese venture capitalist, a machine that combines both their fields of expertise, physics and medicine (as I said it, I realized it was true, my father had been a doctor, in the trunk with his photographs there had been a doctor's coat and stethoscope, many medical textbooks). It—I paused, reaching for some obscure fact, some glob of scientific nonsense—the technology aims to use Cherenkov light to treat late-stage tumors noninvasively.

Professor Zhang murmured, Lanlan was always interested in optics.

Mom's a tenacious woman, I continued. I said *Mom* in English and the rest of the sentence in Chinese, I said it like I was from Hong Kong and had gone to international school, like some hip cosmopolitan mongrel.

These investments are hard to land, but she gave such convincing pitches that the investors were lining up to give her money. Of course it doesn't hurt that Daddy's an expert in cancer treatment.

They're very rich, I said, emphasizing my new pronoun.

I looked disdainfully around the office, at the drooping plant, at his simple clothes, at the thin plastic cup in my hand, hoping to illustrate to Professor Zhang his relative poverty. Cruelty was so easy, it was exhilarating. I tossed the letter with the marriage proposal on the table next to the ashtray and widened my eyes.

We were going through some old junk, since we're selling the apartment in Shanghai. That's how I found this.

Long moments passed, listening to the sound of breath. My tea turned light brown, the leaves unfurled and sunk to the bottom.

I haven't thought about them in so long, Professor Zhang said at last. So they're happy? Happy and healthy? I'm glad. I'm so glad.

We continued to talk; the professor asked questions about my mother's life and I supplied answers. I became an expert at inventing, I filled in the negative image of my mother's life, perhaps as I'd always imagined it might have gone, if she had been a different person, less stubborn, more ambitious for worldly things, if she had wanted anything instead of wanting nothing. If—I had the thought and pushed it away—if she hadn't had me, or had someone else to help her raise me, or if I'd been a better daughter, more self-sufficient, more supportive, more like an adult. In this alternate life my mother quickly finished her PhD and obtained a professorship at an American university, then quit academia for industry because it paid better and gave her freer rein. I went on to describe my father, *Daddy*, as I called him; I spoke of his medical practice and all the patients he'd saved. I talked for so long that Professor Zhang forgot lunch and had to run to catch his afternoon class. After he left, apologizing, thanking me hastily for the visit, I stood dumbfounded in the hall, staring at his name on the door. When I finally left the university I was exhausted. It was evening. My heels dragged on the pavement and I stumbled over nothing. Somehow I reached my hostel.

MY FATHER'S A well-known doctor in America, I said to Professor Zhang. He is—I tried to remember and translate the titles of the medical textbooks from the Shanghai trunk—a radiologist. His specialty is—liver cancer. It's a very big problem in China.

I asked: And your wife, Professor Zhang, what does she do?

Somehow, I was back in the professor's office, drinking hot tea from a plastic cup. It was evening, the sky was purple, Professor Zhang should have been leaving work to have dinner with his family. I hadn't planned to come here, but when I woke, full of energy, I started to walk and found myself at the university just as the sun was setting. I hadn't expected him to be in his office but he was. He had looked confused when he opened the door but now seemed genuinely pleased.

My wife is a high school physics teacher, Professor Zhang says. We're sure our son is going to run straight away from physics when he grows up.

His son was nine years old, in the third grade, a loud, energetic boy with enthusiasm for trucks and cars and impatience for home-work. He was small for his age. Professor Zhang looked forward to the boy growing up; he hoped his excess energy would be channeled into getting taller.

You should come sometime for dinner, meet my family, he said. I'm a decent cook.

He didn't ask me why I'd come back to his office. He didn't mention the letter or the visit the day before. He treated me like an old friend he was glad to see, requiring no explanation at all.

We talked about what I was studying in college (history?), if I had a boyfriend (no), how I kept up my Chinese after spending most of my life abroad (I had a good memory for languages—this was true, after a week in China the language was emerging as if from hibernation, each day it grew in strength). He asked if I liked

China (sure), and we talked about food, of all things, whether I ate rice at home (yes), whether I preferred rice or noodles or bread (all).

How incredible Lanlan's life has been, he said suddenly, bursting out, his face breaking into an expression so intense it almost looked like pain. How far she has come! She must be so happy. I'm so happy, for her.

Do you know what she has been through? he continued. Do you know what she was up against? I'm sure your parents have told you, but still I find it remarkable. Every day I'm amazed by what a long path upward my own life has taken, and she—she started lower and has climbed higher.

His story sounded familiar. Professor Zhang's parents were farmers in a village in Zhejiang. As a child he dreamed of having enough money to eat rice every day. He could never have imagined living in the capital city, working at a desk, getting paid for performing engaging work of the mind instead of tiring out his muscles with hard labor, having enough money to buy silly, unnecessary things like a car or a TV. Once when he was a boy he had been beaten for eating a piece of pork smaller than his thumb—it had been in a dish meant for guests. Now he didn't even like to eat meat anymore, he'd eaten so much since.

And Lanlan has gone farther than I have! he said again. To America and back again, and not just wealthy but influential.

He smiled, then his eyes floated to his hands.

But as I'm sure you know, your mother is a rare kind of person. She never lacked for dreams. She never imagined herself as a peasant. I'm sure she dreamed of leaving the mountains even when she had no idea there was a world beyond them. I never knew anyone with a bigger ambition than her, and a stronger will to make that ambition true.

Oh, I am so happy for her, he said again. She got everything she wanted.

What did my mother want?

I didn't ask this question out loud.

I noticed how Professor Zhang, like the old woman in Shanghai, seemed to have forgotten about my father.

And my father, I said. He's very ambitious too.

I said it as a statement, but added a slight lift to the end, so if Professor Zhang wanted to take it as a question, he could.

The professor blinked, looking at my face. He frowned, looked contrite, frowned again.

Yes, he said with softness, yes, I suppose he is.

PROFESSOR ZHANG WAS the second oldest in his family, he told me at our next meeting. He had one older sister and two little brothers. When he was a boy he wore his older sister's secondhand clothes. For years I went to school wearing a dress with flowers printed on it, he said, and cloth buttons up the side.

So the professor and my mother both wore dresses! Another common experience, I said. He laughed generously.

Two times could be an accident, three was a pattern. Something about my third visit to Professor Zhang's office made the meeting familiar, an expected appointment. Again he did not question me. I stopped questioning myself as well. He talked to me about his childhood as if we were old friends reminiscing.

Since your mother didn't have brothers or sisters, he said, she had to wear her mother's old clothes, which were her grandmother's old clothes. Lanlan hated wearing dead people's clothes, it made her feel like she couldn't breathe. I guess that's why she became so obsessed with fashion.

He spoke of winter in the countryside, how in the snowy fields he wore thin cloth pants and a cotton coat, and for months it was so, so cold. One of his most vivid memories of early childhood was of warming his feet on a hot coal stove. As he sat there he nodded off to sleep, and his feet slipped and dropped onto the coals. He woke up shouting, the soles of his feet seared, hissing with burn. There was no medicine, no money for creams or balms, so to disinfect the burn his mother dunked his feet inside the bucket where they pissed.

He told me of how the skin on his face blistered when he was an infant, because his mother went out to the fields to work with him strapped on her back, and the hot mountain sun burned it raw.

He kept speaking as if pulling something out from inside himself. I drank it in.

His grandmother had an old ox that he took up the mountain when he was a boy. It had blue eyes and was so thin you could see the rungs of its ribs. Most mornings he walked for at least an hour before finding a spot with enough grass for the ox to graze. Before he let it eat, he scanned the area for wild edible plants he could pick for the family. Once the ox wandered into a neighbor's plot of potatoes and when he tried to pull it out it picked him up with its horns and threw him in the rice paddy. When he was eight that old ox died of hunger. For the next five months his family had meat— first eating the organs and the heart, salting the slabs of ribs so they would keep. They boiled the same bones over and over for soup and sucked out the marrow, scraping the hollow insides clean.

The day the ox died, his mother beat him so hard he couldn't sleep. She often beat him, but this time, when her fists got tired, she didn't stop. She picked up a long piece of firewood and broke it on his bare back. The next day his older sister helped him pick out the splinters, and he still remembers—there were fifty-two.

As a child you don't understand how poverty can make a person mean, he said. You don't understand how terrifying being a parent is, how powerless you feel. It sounds obvious, but now that I'm a father I understand. When little Zhang gets even a small cold I start to feel like a failure. It's hard to manage these feelings. My mother didn't hate me, even if I felt like she did at the time. She was frustrated with the world and her inability to give me a secure place in it.

He paused.

I tried to tell Lanlan that, he said. I told her, Now that you've gotten this far, let old pains go. But she was never good at that. Nothing could just be an unfortunate circumstance—everything had to have a meaning. This attitude of hers used to frustrate me to no end.

I nodded. I saw an opening, and measured my next move carefully.

Professor Zhang continued: Now I understand that this stubbornness was what made her mind so special, and what made her such a good physicist. Every discordant note in the universe had to have a meaningful, fruitful reason, whether personal or physical, and she wouldn't give up until she got to the bottom of it.

I'm getting so sentimental, he said apologetically. My wife and I agree not to talk to our son about the old days, you know. Or each other, for that matter. Some parents are always berating their children with comparisons of how much they suffered, but we just want our son to enjoy his life and have a happy childhood. Anyways, enough about me! Tell me about you. Are you moving to China with your parents?

I waved away the question. I don't mind, I said. My parents don't talk to me about the past either, it's nice to hear about it from you.

I took a drink of tea.

What about my father? What was his childhood like?

Professor Zhang shrugged. No idea, he said. He paused. He had a very different upbringing from your mother and me. He grew up in the city, in Hangzhou. If you're curious you should ask him—he'll be able to tell you much better himself.

ALONE IN MY hostel, I sank into my lies. I imagined I was in one room of a nice big house, that Mom and Daddy were downstairs. I imagined them speaking to each other, in English and in Chinese, switching between the two seamlessly, scheming their future, collaborating on a work project, discussing financial and property investments, discussing the summer home they'd keep in America after moving back to China, all sorts of conversations I had not known existed until I went to college and met rich people. Then they were gone—out shopping, perhaps. The house was empty. I found myself in small spaces, the undersides of beds, the corners of closets. My hands dug in these corners and grew tired, my fingernails packed and sore with dirt. I found evidence that they had been here—hairs in the carpet, nail clippings on the floor—but the image of what I was really looking for receded, faded to black, and it was my fault, I was too exhausted, I could not keep my eyes open, I wanted only to sleep.

I woke to a nagging feeling. Lying to the professor was too easy. Easier than trying to understand how my mother had changed so much. How strange that the mother I'd invented, who was nothing like the mother I'd really had, somehow matched his memory of her. Perhaps my lie was an act of mercy. The professor would be shocked to hear the truth. It was inconceivable that I stop him and say, actually, the woman my mother became shrank inside a room and disappeared. She didn't care about clothes and she didn't want anything. To an outsider she appeared plain at best, pathetic at worst. No one would have described her as a person who never lacked for dreams.

It was easier to imagine the mother I didn't have than to remember the one I'd had. With every day, with each new revelation, with each new image of the places she had been and the people she knew, remembering became more confusing.

PROFESSOR ZHANG SAID my mother was born in a house with a floor made of mud. The first time he saw her, he recognized immediately that she had suffered and learned to hide that suffering under an expression of stupidity. She came dressed in the coarsest country cloth, and you could see the bones of her face through her skin. Her skin had that peasant look; it was brown and splotchy from the sun. It looked perpetually dirty, dirty from dirt that couldn't be washed away.

We were all poor and hungry then, but Lanlan was a little older than the rest of us. Just a year, but even that was enough to make a difference. She was born in the last of the famine years, and so she felt its last repercussions.

A year older? I said. I thought you were all classmates?

Yes, we were. He leaned forward. She dropped out of school for a year. Did she never tell you? Oh, but it's such a good story! He was excited, like a child preparing to present his favorite toy. It did not surprise him that I didn't know.

It wasn't uncommon for kids to drop out of school then, he said, especially in the countryside, and especially for someone like your mother, who didn't have a big family. Lanlan's grandmother had gotten ill, and around the same time her mother got injured in the field. So Lanlan stayed home to take care of her waipo and help her mother—your waipo—with chores and cooking and maintaining the small plot of land that fed them. When the injury healed, your waipo didn't let her go back to school. She had no brothers, I think her father died when she was young, so there were never enough hands in her family for all the work. For years I urged her to forgive your waipo—anyone else in that situation would have done the same.

Having no education herself, all your waipo knew was that your mother's going to school meant one more person to feed who wasn't helping to generate food. But in a strange twist of fate, that year helped your mother. Listen to this, Professor Zhang said, taking on his professorly persona. Lanlan dropped out of school in 1976, the year Chairman Mao died. The next year, in 1977, Deng Xiaoping reinstated the gaokao, the national higher education exam, along with secondary school entrance exams. Many of the top secondary schools, which had been depleted during the Cultural Revolution, opened their doors to merit scholarship students based on the test results. If your mother had stayed in school the year before, she would have continued on to the village secondary school. She might have ended up a factory worker at best.

I know your mother resented your waipo for taking her out of school, but maybe she should have thanked her, he said, adding, Maybe she has. Of course it was still incredible that after a year working the fields, she was able not only to convince the teachers to let her take the test but to get the highest score in the county.

That was how Professor Zhang had made it into the Hangzhou school too, with the highest score the next county over. But he'd had many siblings, younger brothers, and his father could read and thus had some sense of what an education could do for a person. Professor Zhang had always been encouraged to study, had seen his education, correctly, as a way out of the hard life. He still couldn't imagine how my mother had pulled it off.

He called her a remarkable woman, and more and more these seemed like the right words to describe her, even though he spoke from misinformation. He told me about my mother's transformation in just two years (high school was only two years then, he explained, because after the Cultural Revolution there were not enough teachers and students to go around). He could not stop talking about her. He seemed to need to do it.

We both grew fatter the first year of gaozhong, he said. Your mother had an allowance with her scholarship. It must have been the first time she could choose at every meal what she wanted to eat. She always picked the simplest thing—rice, vegetables, one egg—and by the end of the year she had saved up enough money from her food allowance to buy a piece of nice cloth, which she stitched herself into a dress.

From the start, my mother was intent on becoming someone new—this will was her defining feature, and to this day when Professor Zhang met someone with a similar fire he couldn't help but think of her. She might have tested into the school with the highest scores in her county, but in their scholarship class she was at the very bottom, dead last place. There were certain mathematical concepts that everyone was expected to have mastered by middle school that she'd not seen before. She had a natural talent with numbers and abstraction, so once she reviewed the concepts she caught up, but she always struggled with Chinese. There were words she had never learned, and her country accent was terrible. She studied when others were sleeping. She woke up every morning at five to practice proper pronunciation of putonghua with Professor Zhang while taking laps around the track. For a long time she continued to pretend to be stupid. She didn't care about making friends. By the end of two years she had made it to the very top of the class, and had changed the look of stupidity on her face to one of defiance.

I think she became what she wanted, Professor Zhang said.

Which is?

A rich person. He laughed. But I mean, a real rich person, a rich person through and through.

You would think, he said, that a poor person would carry a habit of frugality. I certainly did. Even now when I have enough money to buy a nicer house for my family, I think, what will we use it for? This is fine, this is more than enough. Part of me is always count-ing, adding up prices and bills, making sure there's enough left to survive if—I don't even know if what.

But the minute your mother started to make money, Professor Zhang continued, she changed her habits. She bought nice clothes and cosmetics, eventually she even began to eat extravagantly. She wasn't rolling in cash, but it was more money than she had ever seen, and she did not hoard it. She sent a portion to your grand-mother and then spent the rest of her paycheck before the month was up. And she had plenty of suitors, who bought her gifts of food and clothes.

In Professor Zhang's office, my parents were happy, wealthy, full of life. They wore Swiss watches and Chanel perfume and rode around the city in cars with tinted windows and chauffeurs. They laughed loudly and had big appetites.

Professor Zhang got up and poured himself some water, nodding and looking out the window.

He said, I guess Yongzong was right after all.

I sat up. What did you say?

I guess your father was right about her after all. He paused, then continued: Your mother changed so much in university, after she came to Beijing. Your father said her transformation was remarkable not because of how much she'd changed, but because it was less like a change than a return to a natural state. Her true self has emerged, your father said. At the time I thought I knew her better.

I was trying to listen. Trying to listen as I searched my pockets for a piece of paper. Finally my fingers closed around something. I pulled out the receipt for my train ticket to Beijing and held it out to him.

I asked, Can you write something for me?

I said, without hesitation, without making it a big deal: I've been relearning Chinese since I got here—it's a steep curve. Now that I'll be living in China, I'm trying to become more Chinese.

I paused, continued: Still, even though I know how a lot of words sound, I don't know how to write them.

This, at least, was true.

Sure, Professor Zhang said, looking a little confused. What words do you want me to write?

I tried to keep my voice even. I said, My father's name, Yongzong.

I WALKED—RAN—back to my hostel with the marked train ticket in my hand. Gripped between the fingers, already bending, the paper revealed its vulnerability, how easily it could be torn or blown away. It didn't matter. I had already memorized the shape of the words.

李永踪.

In the hostel room I looked at the paper again.

Li. Yong. Zong. Professor Zhang had explained the meaning of each word without raising his eyebrows. Or perhaps he had—at that point I no longer cared about the illusion—his or mine. 李 (li), he said, a common Chinese family name, referring to a plum or plum tree. I nodded (of course! this was my name too). 永 (yong), as in 永远 (yongyuan), as in forever, eternal. He wrote the word slowly so I could see the proper order of strokes. The teakettle boiled and he stood to retrieve the hot water. He sat down again and eagerly picked up the pen.

踪 (zong), as in 踪迹 (zongji), as in footprint, or imprint. He paused, staring at the page. A solid name, he said. I guess his parents wanted his life to make a lasting mark.

Underneath the professor's neat script I copied my father's name until my hands memorized the motions.

李永踪
李永踪
李永踪
李永踪
李永踪
李永踪

Zong, I thought, as in 失踪 (shizong). As in lost, as in missing.

IN THE UNIVERSE, there exist objects that cannot be seen or have not been seen—black holes, undiscovered planets, massive presences of gravity that assure us of their existence simply by the way they affect the behavior of nearby lesser objects. This, according to my mother, was the measure of an object: something that exerts substantial influence over others in its field, drawing continually toward itself, even if ever so slightly. In some ways, this evidence of effect is more necessary than sight. An image alone could be merely a hologram, a vision. No, scientifically speaking, seeing or not seeing is not equivalent to making be or not be. Rather, it is the inevitable attraction and movement of that which surrounds a mass that secures its position among real things.

FOR A LONG time—days, I think—I didn't leave the room. I sat there copying my father's name on the hostel notepad until I ran out of pages. At some point a bird outside my window began to sing a pattern of three notes in an infinite loop. Short short long, short short long, short short long. I took out the envelope with my father's photographs and arranged them on the bed. Twenty fathers looked back at me. I turned them over and wrote his name on the back of each.

Finally I forced my body out of bed. I pulled on socks, sweater, coat. I closed my Chinese-English dictionary and threw it in my bag. I scooped up the photographs and threw them in my bag. I left before I could wonder where I would go.

At Professor Zhang's former dormitory, I found something-Guo, the chess player who had taken me to the professor's class. He came to the door pinching his nose with a tissue. His roommates were out at dinner and karaoke—it was a Saturday night—but he was home sick with a cold. His head felt like a swamp. I invited myself in. I sat at the table, where the chessboard was out, the pieces everywhere, as if in the middle of a game. He sat across from me and moved them absentmindedly to their starting positions.

So was it him? he asked. I nodded, yes.

Really!

He leaned back, clearly pleased with himself. He fiddled with the pieces, moving a pawn out, then back, then out again.

Who is he to you? he asked.

I shrugged. Someone who knew my mother.

Are you visiting Beijing with your mother?

I hugged my bag to my stomach. My mother was, as always now, inside it.

I pushed a pawn out. Your move.

He moved his knight and folded his arms.

As we played, something-Guo warning me now and then to look again, instructing me to take back moves (I was not good at chess, I knew only the rules, nothing of strategy), I told him everything. Well, not everything—never everything—I could not explain about my mother. But I told him things I had never shared with anyone else, sentences I was afraid to say out loud. I've never met my father. I didn't even know his name. I still don't know if he's alive or dead, if he knows I exist. My mother won't tell me anything. In Chinese, I realized, verbs don't change based on past or present tense. Instead you added a marker to the sentence indicating when an action occurred relative to the moment of speech, and this indication was more akin to an indication of space than of time. So instead of before and after, things happened in front of you and behind you, up the stream and down the stream. My mother won't, I repeated, using none of these markers. I felt good, using this ambiguous present tense.

Something-Guo won and we started again.

And now, I said, I have his name. Professor Zhang gave me his name.

Watch your knight, he said.

I stared at the board and said my father's name out loud. Was this the first time I had said it to someone who was not Professor Zhang? I said it again. It was a gush of weight from the chest. I felt satiated and hungrier at once.

Something-Guo was silent. I continued to look for the mistake in my last move. I don't see it, I said.

You're exposing your queen.

I moved my knight back and shifted my queen to the right.

Good move, he said, then took my knight.

Hey!

Okay, okay, he said, and returned it to the board. Look, you never should have moved it here in the first place. It allows me to make one move that forces you to choose between your knight and your queen. Besides, it's not doing anything useful for you.

How do you know what's useful?

That's hard, he said. What were you thinking when you moved it?

I don't know, I wanted to advance.

That makes sense. But this direction is better.

He moved the pieces backward two steps and advanced my knight in the opposite direction.

See, now you're pressing me to move my bishop while also opening up your own bishop for more lines of attack.

He sneezed and got up for another tissue.

We played the game through, walking back steps, stopping at each one so something-Guo could explain why he chose to move as he did.

How do you plan your attacks? I asked.

Look at the board, see if there are any openings. Pick an area to target where it looks like my opponent is weak, adjust as the game goes on.

Where am I weak now?

Left corner.

I moved my bishop into the left corner.

Good move, he said.

How would you go about finding a person? I said.

He paused.

No idea, he said. I'm sorry.

He retreated.

My life is pretty boring, he said.

My life feels pretty boring to me too, I said.

I thought of Professor Zhang's explanation for why he and his wife didn't talk to their son about the past. There was so much nostalgia in novels and on television about the old hard times, Professor Zhang said, but you know what I think? I think hardship is just boring. There's nothing interesting or instructive about poverty—it's just hard, everywhere, and that's it.

What would you do? I asked something-Guo. If you were me.

Move your queen here, something-Guo said. He pointed to a square.

Look, I honestly don't know, he said. Maybe I'd hire a detective? Go to the police? That's what they do in TV shows, right?

The police? For a moment I almost protested: but I don't want to get my mother in trouble. I moved my queen to something-Guo's spot.

Right, I said.

I'D SEEN THEM, I realized as I left something-Guo's building. Men and women (mostly men) in light green or blue uniforms and black flat hats, stationed here and there throughout the city. At the entrance of the small road leading to the building, one of them sat in a box, dozing, his hair pressed against the glass. I had no reference for police in this country, and had barely registered their presence. I didn't know if they carried guns or batons, if they rode in cars or motorcycles, if their siren lights were red or blue or both. I didn't know if they were scary or nice, what they'd see when they looked at me. I glanced at the man sleeping in the box. A newspaper lay open on his lap. His face, in rest, looked bored.

I turned onto the main street off something-Guo's dormitory and found the sidewalk blocked by a huddle of bodies shouting. The shouting came from three people, two men and one woman who pointed fingers and gesticulated with their arms. The rest were spectators, talking mostly to each other and only occasionally throwing in a loud remark. In the middle of the crowd a motorcycle lay on the ground half off the sidewalk, one of its side mirrors smashed.

The shouting was of an animal intensity—faces red, mouths puckered, veins bulging from stretched necks. Because this was Beijing, it was in Mandarin, but this was not the gentle and melodic Mandarin of TV and radio announcers. The pitch of language was violent. A trio of young women (university students, by the tone and cadence of their voices) walked past quickly, clutching each other's elbows, saying, *Ignore them ignore them ignore them.* I slowed my step. A policewoman arrived on the scene (on a motorcycle, no flashing lights but announced by a modest siren). The policewoman took out a notepad and the three shouters turned to direct their arguments at her, not lowering their voices or restraining their arms, yelling over each other.

I crossed to the other side of the road and walked back to the subway, where at the entrance two police in green uniforms stood beside various security devices, instructing passengers to submit their belongings for inspection. I realized that I had placed my bag on a conveyor belt to be scanned every time I entered the subway. Inside the bag was my mother. What did she look like to the square-faced officer sitting behind the screen?

THE POLICE STATION was a one-story building with no particularly striking features except for the wreathed emblem marking the sign. The interior reminded me of an American DMV: a row of receptionists and computers sitting behind partitioned glass. Three windows were occupied by officers wearing light blue button-down shirts with black rectangular strips on their shoulders. The room was empty. Nobody looked up when I entered.

I went to the man closest to me. He had a triangular face and thick eyebrows and his hat was a little too large for his head.

I coughed. Excuse me, I said. I said it again. I sat down on the chair before him. He looked up.

I'm looking for someone, I said.

He waited.

Does he have a name?

Yes.

What's his name?

Li-Yong-Zong.

I'm sorry, there's no one here by that name. His face glazed over; he turned back to his screen.

I mean, I said, I mean I'm looking for a person. I'm—

(how to say *missing person* in Chinese?)

—I'm looking for a person I can't find. A person who is—失踪. He is lost, and I don't know where he is, and I'd like to find him.

You want to file a report on a missing person? He used the words 失踪人员 (shizong renyuan), and I repeated them.

失踪人员, yes, I said. Could you help me find him?

You have to file the report first.

He asked for my ID. I took my passport out of my bag and handed it to him.

You're a foreigner, he said, raising his eyebrows. He used the words 老外 (laowai). Why are you looking for a missing person here?

I was born here, I said, in Beijing.

You have a tourist visa.

I grew up in America.

But you're looking for a missing person here.

Yes. He is missing here, in Beijing. I think.

Did he come with you? Is he a laowai too?

No, no, I don't think so.

So he's Chinese?

Yes. He's Chinese.

The policeman sighed and clicked on the computer, typed in information. He turned the pages of my passport, asking now and then for confirmation that a certain line referred to my date of birth, my surname, etc. He asked for the Chinese characters of my name and I gave them to him.

Name of the missing person?

I gave it to him.

Sex?

Male.

Age?

I looked at him. I don't know, I said.

You don't know?

I don't know, I repeated.

Who is this person? Why are you looking for him?

I explained. My words echoed loudly in the empty room so I spoke quietly. The triangle-faced policeman asked me to speak up. I repeated, He's my father, I never knew him, I only know his name, realizing how ridiculous it all sounded, how little information I had. I said he was last seen in Beijing, to the best of my knowledge, around the time I was born. Arranged like this, as plain evidence for a police report, these facts that had caused me such agony, that made my heart drum against my chest, now appeared like the bad plot of some bad television show. I could hear my mother's voice saying how boring suffering is, how intensely boring it is to feel sorry for yourself. I wanted to leave, to say forget it, but instead I found my voice rising, my eyes wet, my breath fast and shallow. He's my father, I never knew him, I repeated, and repeated it again. He's my father. I never knew him. I wiped my face. I asked for a tissue.

The policeman flitted his eyes to his colleagues. He stood shakily. Suddenly he was no longer a can't-be-bothered bureaucrat but a young man who did not know what to do when a woman cried. His eyes softened, his lips trembled as he spoke.

Miss, miss, he said. Don't cry, please, don't cry.

A woman police officer appeared in his window with a packet of tissues, which he passed to me under the slot in the glass.

Miss, he said. I'm going to try to help you, okay? Stop crying, okay? Just wait here and I'll be back, and I'll try to help you.

好吗? 好吗? he said. Okay? Okay?

He disappeared into a room behind the room. I waited. I was still crying. I could not stop. On my lap the tissues shredded and turned to grains of filth. The room was quiet and cold.

From somewhere behind the glass I heard faint speaking. Some minutes later, the young policeman appeared with an older one, a middle-aged man with graying hair and a square, stone-looking face. The older policeman came around the partition and introduced himself as Officer Shu, the head officer in this district. He invited me inside, and I followed him back through the door where the first policeman disappeared. We went down a hall into a small office.

Tell me what you told him, Officer Shu said when we sat down. His voice was cold and his face betrayed no expression. He sat with his palms flat on the desk and looked at me without blinking.

I told him.

While I spoke he thumbed through my passport, looking at my photo and back at me, tilting it up against the light, peering at the words.

Tell me again, he said, everything you know about him.

I've never met him, I said.

And your mother, she never spoke of him?

No, I said, she wanted me to believe he was dead.

I had never uttered this thought, to myself or anyone else, but as I spoke it now I knew it to be true. I continued, following the feeling of that truth:

—that he had died around when I was born. She never said it, not directly, but I had a strange feeling, it was dark and heavy and it was wrapped around anything to do with my father, and the same feeling also surrounded my early years in China, my birth.

And you were born, he said, looking at my passport, in June of 1988, in Shanghai?

No, I was born here, in Beijing, in 1989.

He looked up, suddenly alarmed.

It's a mistake, I said. I dug in my bag for my birth certificate and handed it over. As I closed the zipper, I saw the envelope of photographs.

Wait—I said—I have photographs. I have photographs of him too.

I handed over the photographs and he thumbed through them quickly, flipping them over, glancing at the name written on their backs. He stacked them like a deck of cards and pushed them back to me. He opened my documents again, looking long at my birth certificate, holding up the certificate and the passport and comparing them side by side.

It's been so long, I said. It's embarrassing, it's so embarrassing. But the truth is I never really thought about him until now.

Why are you thinking about him now?

I clutched my bag against my stomach.

My mother—

My mother left.

I used the words 过世 (guo shi). They meant left earth or left this world or, more literally, passed through worlds or, literally specifically, passed from this world into the other world.

Officer Shu nodded. He rubbed his temples and slumped back into his chair. His hard face slumped too, revealing itself not as soft or kind but simply exhausted. He put down my passport and birth certificate and clasped his hands, then leaned forward, exhaling, and looked squarely into my face. His expression was not mean. He looked like he would've liked to go to sleep.

I'm going to ask you a question, he said, and I want you to think about your answer carefully.

I nodded.

Are you a journalist?

What?

In the pale light of the office, confessing to this older male authority, I would have said anything. I was prepared to say: my mother lied to me my entire life, about the most confusing things. I was prepared to say: I still don't know how she died. I was prepared to say 死, the direct word for death. The edges of the wooden box dug into my thighs. I was prepared to take my mother out for proof.

He repeated his question. Perhaps he said *journalist* in English.

No, I said.

Good, said Officer Shu. You don't have a journalist visa.

Let me give you some advice, he said.

He told me, his voice growing slower and more tired as he spoke, to stop looking for my father. Don't go to another police station. Don't ask anyone else. You're not going to find him, he said. It's been too long. Let it go.

He closed his eyes for a moment. He stacked my documents and pushed them across the desk. He tried to arrange his face kindly, tried, perhaps, to arrange it into the face of a father.

Look, he said, you're still very young. There are many roads to a good life. I'm telling you this for your own good. I'm sorry about your parents. Truly, I am. But forget them and look to the people who are still here—grandparents, aunts, uncles—whoever you have.

I thought about Zhang Bo, something-Guo, the old lady in Shanghai. Only a few times had my mother mentioned anything about her own mother; I knew even less about this grandmother than my father. I opened my mouth to say this but the interview was over, Officer Shu was already leading me out.

You'll stop looking? he said as he opened the door.

I looked back at the waiting room, where my young officer sat staring at an empty computer screen, decidedly avoiding my eyes. My head nodded.

Good.

IT WAS VERY strange, I told something-Guo.

He shrugged as if to say, I'm sorry?

He said, I've never asked the police for anything.

Me neither, I said.

I wasn't suggesting it really, just couldn't think of anything else.

We walked through the cold streets of old Beijing. My head hurt. I had been told to stop, my natural obedience kicked in. But I felt lost; I didn't know what to do instead of what I had been doing.

Hey, something-Guo said, I think it was a courageous thing to do.

He wrapped an arm around my shoulders. He pulled me to him. I was surprised to find my body warmed by the sudden proximity to another. It was a nice feeling. It was the first thing I'd felt in weeks that did not feel like suffering. I leaned into this boy, swelling with gratitude for his presence, his touch. For the first time I considered his face. He was good-looking. He had small and dark and kind eyes.

I was attracted to him. Or perhaps I was attracted to the way he looked at me, to the person I became in his gaze. My pathetic rootlessness, my desperate floundering, my grief—in his eyes they were romantic, they made me beautiful.

I took him back to my hostel room. That night, I slept with my arms around his waist, my wrists pressing his stomach wall, and reassured myself with another body's solidity.

THE WALLS OF the hospital were dark and dense. Fluorescent bulbs pulsed weakly from the high ceiling. On American TV, hospitals were glass-walled, white-tiled, gleaming in abundant light. Here the halls were narrow. The air felt dead. Everything appeared stained with age—the floors, the windows, the doctors' coats. Patients crowded in front of counters, spilling from waiting room chairs to lean against walls and squat on the floor. No one looked at me.

Something-Guo had suggested I visit the place on my birth certificate and I'd listened to him. But I'd expected no epiphanies and I got none. Nurses in pink frocks sauntered down the hall. A young woman led an old woman around a corner. Beyond them, a janitor mopped the floor. It smelled of acrid iron and disinfectant. I gagged. Whoever had been born here seventeen and a half years ago—she was not anyone I'd ever imagined I'd meet.

I walked out into the dull dusk. The clouds glowed orange-gray, and the metal gate of the hospital shined black in the light. Before me, Fuxingmenwai was a concrete river. Cars flew by, kicking up cold dust. I turned and walked, kept walking past one subway station and then the next, until the street name changed. Now the sign said 长安街: simple characters, I could read them without the pinyin. Chang an jie, I thought; 长 (chang) as in long, as in lasting; 安 (an) as in calm, as in still; 街 (jie) as in street, though this was more like an avenue. I said the words again, Changan Avenue, and this time I heard them not in my voice but in the voice of a documentary narrator. *Eternal peace*, this voice said, and then it said another phrase: *gate of heavenly peace*. What an odd translation, I'd not noticed it until now, how grand and dramatic the diction. *Tian* implied heaven but it also just meant sky, and *men* might be a gate but might also be just a door. In Chinese, Tiananmen sounded simpler, even elegant, it could have been calm skies door. Changan Avenue, Tiananmen Square—in the documentary narrator's voice I couldn't hear the grace in either name, only the irony, the threat. I blinked and the avenue appeared as something I had seen before, but from a different angle, and not long at all, not extending as it did now past my periphery, but truncated—cut off by the edges of a photograph.

Are you a journalist?

It was a mistake.

A flash: Officer Shu's tired face, his tired threat to stay away.

SO IT CAME to me, in a whole piece, the content of my mother's lie:

I was born on June 4, 1989, in Beijing.

On the same day, in the same city, perhaps even right here, on this avenue bordering the hospital where I was born, a months-long peaceful demonstration had ended with military intervention. This intervention included the use of tanks and bullets on unarmed civilians. The civilians had been given warning, but it was safe to say no one believed the guns would shoot until they shot and drew blood.

By early morning of that day, the streets were empty and in newspapers all over the world there appeared photographs of tanks lining the boulevards of Beijing.

I had seen these photographs, of course. They were, alongside the Great Wall, among the stock images of Beijing I'd collected while growing up in America. Like much knowledge of history taking place elsewhere, I could not remember when or where exactly I'd gained it, and my understanding was diffuse, accumulated in bits and pieces over time: flashes of imagery, bold-faced headlines, that foreboding tone of the documentary narrator. These, I realized with a stone to my gut, were the exact bits and pieces I'd been afraid to find in Beijing. I had buried them deep. Perhaps I had seen them first in an American textbook, on TV, alluded to in some movie. Perhaps I'd even once noticed that the anniversary of the event co-incided with my birthday. My mother had not been a celebrator of birthdays. She had never spoken to me of June Fourth. So perhaps I had searched this knowledge out myself, in more American books, written in English by Americans for Americans. It wouldn't be the first or last time I asked a nation that wouldn't claim me to tell me about myself. Finally, my mind must have performed the necessary acrobatics to dissociate what little connection my mother had left (the month, the day) from what I had learned, precisely so I would not have to put myself in this position, inside the documentary film, watching a terrible story taking place in a faraway land a long, long time ago and discovering, inside it, myself.

I walked fast. The cold wind whipped my hair. The avenue was six lanes wide with no visible ways to cross. The buildings on either side, set back from the road, provided no barrier from the elements. I stepped past an enormous building and the square opened before me, cold and vast. How the scale of infrastructure here surpassed the ability of my body. Beijing was not designed for humans, I thought—and here my mind completed the idea, even as I heard my other self saying, *What a derivative, Western thought*—but for military machines.

On the edge of the square, staring at the empty expanse, I found myself wanting to be like my mother, wanting to cut away everything. So badly I wanted to be untethered, because to be untethered meant to be undefined, to have a body rinsed of meaning. I didn't want my feet tied up in history. If the father I never knew was dead, like the mother I knew and didn't know—I wanted his corpse to be the property of personal grief, not of national tragedy. I was no hero. I wanted to weep only for myself.

PROFESSOR ZHANG WAITED under the striped French magnolia outside the physics building. He stood with his hands in his pockets, examining the peeling bark. We were meeting for lunch.

He nodded a greeting and we walked together out of the university gates to a small street lined with shops and restaurants. Professor Zhang made small talk, pointing out restaurants that were always busy when it was warmer, a small park, a bubble tea shop his son liked, a good bookstore. I'm glad you came by again, he said. I'd arrived at his office in the morning, breathless, having woken with a sense of urgency, and caught him just as he was on his way to class. It had been a week or more since I had last seen him.

As you know, he said now, continuing his casual tone, I sent your mother many letters, but she never responded to a single one. He paused.

But she did write me years later, after she had married your father. That letter came in early 1991, before the New Year, shortly before your family left for America. I hadn't heard from her in quite some time by then. To be honest, I was worried about her, and about your father. I had begun to assume I would never hear from either again. This letter soothed me tremendously.

He stopped and looked at me. Would you like to see it?

The letter?

He nodded.

We turned into the park. Professor Zhang sat on a bench and I joined him. The thin bare branches of the trees bent in the wind. I took the envelope he held out. The wad of paper inside was thick.

It's been sitting in my office for many years, he said, mixed with a pile of old papers. I've been meaning to show it to you, but I hadn't thought of it in so long I couldn't remember where I'd put it.

The first sentence read: *Yongzong and I had a daughter.*

My Chinese had improved significantly, unraveling like a spool of thread in my conversations with the professor and something-Guo, but many of the following words were illegible. The handwriting was neat and compact—my mother's, I recognized it instantly; the script was in cursive, so the strokes that constituted a word blended together, hiding from me their platonic shape. Still I could not stop looking at the words. Twice the blocks of script were interrupted by equations and diagrams: what looked like mathematical proofs.

I didn't know what your mother was doing when I got this letter, Professor Zhang said. Like I said, I hadn't heard from her in some years. But I was glad to learn that she'd finally found a way to America. The promise of America was why so many of us had decided to study physics in the first place. There was a program at the time for top physics students to study in American universities, called CUSPEA or something like that, and under it you could win admission to a fellowship at physics departments abroad without going through the complicated university application process or even taking the TOEFL. You just had to take one physics exam, in Chinese. Your mother scored high on the exam, of course, and qualified. But she was never very good at English, and she failed the interview.

I remember she was pretty disappointed, though of course she didn't show it. She couldn't shrug off her conception of China as a land of inescapable poverty and shame. China for her would always be identical to the suffering of her childhood, no matter that she had left her hometown, no matter that the country was changing. And yet she kept this storybook vision of America, she believed it was a place where you could make yourself into whatever you wanted. I knew she would get there eventually, and she did.

Of course Yongzong was always a language whiz, he added. I'm not at all surprised that the two of them together did so well abroad.

A gust of wind nearly blew the pages out of my hand. I clasped tight and went through them again, staring hard. On the last page, before the signature, I read the final sentence: *We are finally leaving China, hopefully forever—wish us well.* For a moment, I made Professor Zhang's mistake, and read in the *we* my mother and father. I shook my head and lifted my face to the cold wind. I read the pages again. Legible words and phrases leapt out without context. Again and again, the words 时间 (time), 空间 (space), 未来 (future), 现在 (now, or present), and 过去 (past) appeared. On the second page one sentence was underlined, twice:

如何记住未来与忘了过去?

How to remember the future and forget the past?

The letter was signed 你的朋友, your friend.

I handed it back to the professor. He took it and held it in his lap for a long moment before flipping to the second page. Then he began to read.

What do you make of time? he read. *I mean time in the simple sense, the way we are born knowing it, with the idea of now. In this intuitive understanding of time, the present is real, the past cannot be changed, and the future is ours to make.*

He flipped to the third page.

Einstein once wrote about the death of his good friend: Michele has left this strange world a little before me. This means nothing. People like us, who believe in physics, know that the distinction made between past, present and future is nothing more than a persistent, stubborn illusion. *Einstein was referring to special relativity, of course, but also to Minkowski space and the picture of physical reality as a four-dimensional existence, rather than the more intuitive model of three-dimensional space moving through time. What he means is that the evolution of space through time is only how we humans experience it. He was right about another thing: he died just a month and three days after his friend.*

Did you know Einstein was cruel to his first wife? And probably to his second? He was a bad father too. He had a daughter he never met—no one knew what happened to her. He had two sons. One died in a mental institution, alone.

I have been thinking about thermodynamics, and the fact that the phenomenon of heat—something we so take for granted—is actually a result of probability. But probability as we know it is completely created by the fact of our observation. We only know that fast-moving particles will more likely collide with and transfer energy to slow-moving particles because we have observed it to be so. Probability has nothing to do with possibility. It only serves to limit our perception.

Perhaps you will laugh at me for being such a theoretician. Often I wish I could be more practical, like you.

As Professor Zhang read my mother's words another image of her began to appear—one that I must have hoped existed behind the mother I knew, but which flickered away like an illusion, blinking behind gauze and dim lights each time I tried to see it. In this letter my mother had expressed herself as she never could to me, proficient as I was in neither mathematics nor Chinese. In this letter my mother had found her language, and the beauty and authenticity of the words and phrases and sentences, even as I could not fully grasp their meaning, made me recognize her as a person—truly, as a soul striving, with doubts and desires as tender as my own—like I had never fully done when she was alive and standing in front of me.

Suddenly I remembered a night in one of our American apartments when the cold silence of our living space was broken, and my mother talked to me, almost as a friend, over dinner. Something had happened earlier that day—I had come home, I think, earlier than expected, and found her sitting in the kitchen with her fists clenched on the table, staring out into nothing. She turned and saw me, releasing her hands, blinking. In that moment I saw a strange expression on her face, as if it were at once looking inside itself and draining out into the surroundings. Her lips drooped, her cheeks were soft, her eyes and nose red. In an instant her face reverted to normal—hard and hollow and a little bit angry—and I remembered wondering, bewildered, if she was sick. Only now did I realize my obvious mistake: she had been crying.

There was an unusual mood in our apartment that evening. My mother asked me what I was learning in my classes and I showed her a homework problem I couldn't figure out, something to do with acceleration and force, the distance a cannonball travels against a strong wind. Unlike my mother I had no gift for science, words and sentences made more sense to me than numbers and equations, and usually she was indifferent to my weakness. She'd say my mind was not built for math and state it only as a fact, some mundane discovery she had come upon, like it was raining or the supermarket was closed. But that day she was patient, even gentle. She drew me a diagram and explained how to use the equations. She seemed happy. Newtonian mechanics, she said, are so simple and elegant. If only they were true, the world might be a more bearable place. She then went on to explain why they were wrong, or not quite right, giving me a brief lesson on relativity that went right over my head (I was in middle school). This was shortly before she would give up on academic work entirely. As I put my homework away, she said: Einstein made no significant contributions to physics after general relativity, you know. He devoted his later career to chasing a unified theory, a theory that would harmonize general relativity and quantum mechanics, and he failed. By that time most people thought it was a fool's errand. His reasoning was he could afford it—younger physicists could ruin their careers on such pursuits.

She spoke in a mixture of Chinese and English, fluidly. She continued, her voice growing in anger as she spoke: Because after quantum mechanics, physics stopped asking the big questions, it would peek at God's face but only through a pinprick hole, approaching its most urgent demands from a side door, hoping to gain entry by interrogation of the smallest components—a finger, a nail, a tooth. It's like a game, like trying to trick God into revelation—well, I refuse to play games, I can't believe God is stupid enough to be tricked, the only way to see God's face is to demand it, to stand up and make your intentions clear.

In Beijing, Professor Zhang flipped through the pages of my mother's letter.

There's a lot of this, he said, mathematical acrobatics that I could barely follow at the time, just out of university. Actually, I spent many months going through them. It's possible trying to understand them helped me get through my PhD. They are wild—conceptually—unbelievably wild, mathematically wild too, but also very beautiful. He read again, shaking his head.

So if the passage of time is an illusion created by heat—and this makes perfect sense to me, as they are both measures of change—if humans are simply stupid creatures limited by our nature to experience events chronologically, would this mean that in physical reality we have no control over our lives, that we cannot be held responsible?

He flipped the page again, and finally it was the last one. He exhaled, long and deep. He didn't read the last sentence or the signature. He folded the letter and put it back into its envelope.

It's a very strange letter, he said. Strange and beautiful, the kind of thing only your mother could have made. Of course the most beautiful parts are in the mathematical proofs, which very few people can understand. To be completely honest, it kept your mother in my mind for a long time.

He held the envelope in two hands and looked at it, blinking furiously. He did not give it back to me. He let out a pained laugh.

Maybe one of these days, some museum or library will call me and ask for this letter, and physics students all over the world will study it.

Every time I saw him, I grew more certain that he did love my mother, that he might, in fact, still love her, as one loves those who are frozen in memory. At the very least he wanted very much to know her, fully, to describe how she was, who she was, defining and redefining her in the way of a person who must get to the bottom of something, who would never tire of searching. It was as if he believed that in excavating her soul, he would find, bound tightly inside it, the whole package of humanity, waiting to be unfolded—

WE NEVER WENT to lunch.

I don't think I said anything. I don't think I said what I was thinking: that the letter would never go in any museum, that he was probably the only person left in the world who gave any shits about Su Lan's mind. But I must have betrayed myself somehow, with an expression, a gesture, a silence. The weeping knob in my throat. Perhaps I had been betraying myself this whole time without knowing it. Professor Zhang let out a long breath and looked at me. He said, Where is your mother, really?

I said, She's dead.

I used the direct word, I said, 死.

He said, What happened to her?

I said, I did.

I didn't mean to say it, I didn't even know what I meant. Later, I would try to explain to Zhang Bo while discovering it myself, the rock of guilt I was wedging above my sight: that I was the one who had stopped my mother becoming who she had meant to be. I had resented her for making herself nothing, but had she only done that to raise me, to give me my Americanness? Later, I would open the box of her remains and ask Zhang Bo: What can I make of this? And Zhang Bo, shutting the box with one hand, would tell me about my grandmother. My grandmother who was living alone in my mother's hometown, with no word from my mother in decades. He would tell me how to find her, which trains and buses to take, to follow the one dirt road leading away from town, to look for the lone pine marking my grandmother's house. How it was my duty to go see her.

Bring your mother's ashes back, he would say. It might bring you comfort.

But before that, before we spoke any more about my mother, we sat on the bench beside each other in silence. He stared at the envelope in his hands. I stared straight ahead. The wind blew sharply and branches slapped against branches above. I unclenched my shoulders. I closed my eyes and opened my mouth. Wind came into my lungs, a cold stinging clap. It brought smells of pine, exhaust, and cooking oil, which I tasted in the back of my throat. I listened to it whip through and around me, and to the voices of passing people chattering indistinctly, and felt again submerged in the past, in every other moment when these manifold sensations had passed through my body, and I observed the emotions that accompanied each sensation, floating just out of reach.

Then Professor Zhang was pulling my elbow. I found myself on my feet. He was speaking, quickly, his eyes dancing to avoid mine. He said, Let's go. We have to go.

I followed him.

He took me to the subway station and we got on. We spoke rapidly. I confessed everything. He confessed everything too:

There had been another letter. My mother had sent it to Zhang Bo in late June of 1989, shortly after I was born. The letter was nothing like the other one. It was short, less than one page, and the handwriting was wild, words running into each other, ink dots splattered over the page. Even after he deciphered the words it was difficult to understand—incomplete sentences, exclamations, repeated apologies, repeated pleas. But the gist of it was this: my mother and father had been in Beijing during the government crackdown. My father had disappeared. My mother had looked for him, on the streets, in the hospitals, in the makeshift morgues, without success. She had been forced to return to Shanghai alone. In the letter she begged Zhang Bo to continue searching, to find him.

For weeks Professor Zhang had searched. Upon reading the letter, any bitterness he still held for my father dissolved. He spent every waking moment in the streets, he looked through every hospital room, into the face of every corpse. He asked people he met, he called in favors with anybody of significance, anybody who might be able to obtain information. He even put out an ad in the newspaper.

A month went by and he found nothing. Finally he wrote back to my mother saying he had had no luck. He didn't tell my mother the rumors he'd heard about bodies collected and taken away in trucks, of mass graves and evidence burned. He told my mother to hold out hope that Yongzong was simply lost or hiding somewhere but would return when things calmed down. He offered his friendship and support.

My mother did not write back until two years later, with the letter I had just read.

Around the time of the second letter, Zhang Bo had met the woman who would become his wife. He was very much in love, and the love was doubly happy not only because his future wife loved him back but because once, when he was in love with my mother, he had not believed himself capable of loving anyone else. More than two years had passed since the events of June Fourth. It seemed to him that the country was healing too. The economy was growing, people had more money, found better jobs. Small business in Beijing was booming and everywhere you could see China beginning to develop, becoming a modern nation. In science and technology, especially, the growth was exponential. Zhang Bo had secured a well-paying, respectable professorship. He would soon marry a woman he loved. In the glow of his own happiness he read in my mother's letter affirmation that Yongzong was alive and returned. My mother had encouraged this reading; the first sentence, after all, was *Yongzong and I had a daughter.* For a brief moment he considered it strange that my mother never wrote him explicitly to say Yongzong had been found, but quickly he was able to dismiss it—of course she must have been so happy, so overwhelmed, that she simply forgot.

So when he saw a man who resembled my father in a bookstore on Wangfujing, thirteen years later, his first reaction was of delighted surprise. In fact, the man looked so much like Yongzong that Professor Zhang thought he must be mistaken—time should have done its work. But then he looked closer. Despite the full head of black hair (Professor Zhang rubbed his own graying head), the man did appear to be middle-aged. Certainly he was no university student.

I was so surprised, Professor Zhang said again, not because I thought he was—he swallowed the word—I had assumed from your mother's letter that they were in America together.

Again he tried to justify his misreading of my mother's letter:

Your father and I, he said, we'd had a misunderstanding—an argument—you must understand we were very young. We hadn't spoken in years, so when I got your mother's first letter and heard that he was possibly—it made me sick. Of course, death itself, in anyone—not just one so young, and a friend, and by such an unthinkable—he cleared his throat, began again: My grief was magnified by the unresolved matters between us. Death—even a glimpse—even the possibility of death—reveals the triviality of all other grievances. I had always assumed there would be time to forgive him. So you can imagine the relief I felt when I got your mother's second letter. For the last fifteen years I have imagined your parents exactly as you described them to me, in America, succeeding beyond all expectations, and hearing you confirm these things made me very happy.

He waved me out of the subway train and we transferred lines.

It wouldn't have been improbable for your father to have returned to China for a visit, Professor Zhang continued. In fact, if I remember correctly, I saw the man in the foreign language section, reading an English book. I had gone to the bookstore to get a Japanese manga for my son's birthday; I was on the second floor. But the problem with the doppelgänger in the bookstore was that he looked too much like Yongzong. Even when I saw he was older, about the right age, there was something off about him. I realized that he did not look like he had been abroad. Colleagues and friends of mine who have emigrated—they look recognizably different, even if they are wearing the same clothes and have the same hairstyle, though this is rarely the case. They wear their attributes in a new way. I don't know how to describe it, but you have it. You look like a foreigner, I guessed it the moment I saw you, even though all your features are Chinese.

I must have stared at the man for a long time, Professor Zhang continued, considering all this. Eventually he saw me. I looked into his face. I was convinced it was not him—the physical likeness was undeniable, yes, but the man's eyes lacked the intensity that made Yongzong's face his. It was the one thing I was certain no amount of time could alter. But then the man did something that changed my mind again.

We left the subway and emerged onto another busy street. The traffic screamed.

What? I shouted, running after Professor Zhang as he crossed the intersection. What did he do?

Zhang Bo turned to me and shouted back, He fled.

I followed him, he said some moments later, and then we walked in silence, listening to the cars roaring past.

I KNEW WE were near. The professor's breaths had grown long and slow. He sucked them in with dread. Around us, near-identical five- and six-story buildings lined the residential streets. We stopped in front of one of these buildings.

He has a wife, Professor Zhang said. And possibly, a child.

He did not explain how he knew these things and I did not ask.

We stood and looked at the building. The professor shifted his feet.

It's probably not him, he said after some time.

I'm sorry I brought you here, he said. I don't know what I was thinking.

He made to turn around. I didn't move.

We stood beneath the stripped branches of an old oak, behind a row of hooded motorcycles. Above us a bird sang, its voice thin and cold. But I did not really hear the bird. I did not hear anything. I barely saw. My senses and my mind were suspended in a thick liquid, lifted outside of time.

How long did we stand there? The sun came out, then went behind clouds again. Nobody entered or left the building. Beside me Professor Zhang continued to shift his feet but made no other noise. Now and then I felt him looking at me with an apologetic air. I knew the moment I said the word we could go. But I made no sign and continued to wait, and eventually, there was a stirring inside the building—the sound of a door closing somewhere, followed by voices, then a man appeared in the stairwell, and he was my father.

My father was wearing a shapeless black jacket, zipper open. He had his hands in its pockets. He looked very much like the man in the photographs: wide mouth, square face, my features my mother lacked. He did look older. He was smaller, not only taking up less space (how did I know this, never having seen him in space, but I did) but commanding less of it. Professor Zhang was right about the intensity in the eyes. The man in the photographs had a look that expected—no, demanded—from the world. This one simply used his eyes to see.

The professor stirred beside me. I couldn't even breathe. I watched my father. He stepped lightly, almost hopping, as he came down the stairs, turning occasionally to speak to someone behind him—a girl.

My father and the girl walked across the parking lot together, talking. The girl was six or seven, probably just starting school, the collar of a uniform visible under her red winter coat. She looked like him, more like him than I did, because she was gangly and boyish, with short cropped hair and the beginnings of a masculine gait. Their postures matched: relaxed but upright, not huddled against the cold. As they walked by, my father turned to the girl and ruffled her hair, and she batted his hand away, peeking at him as she did with a little grin.

That's when he looked up and saw me.

Yes, he saw me. We looked at each other, straight in the eyes.

Perhaps his face turned pale. Perhaps his shoulders stiffened. Was there recognition, fear? Whatever was in his body to be discovered, however, was lost, because I discovered nothing, in fact I was plunged into a darkness so intense my sight did not return until they were no more than two figures receding in the distance. I blinked but encountered only a tangle of shape and color and light and dark and the movement of these components, nothing that could be named. In the empty parking lot next to Professor Zhang, I replayed all I'd managed to see: the man and girl exiting the building and walking by, exiting the building and walking by. Suddenly I was the girl, I was watching myself in another version of the past.

Professor Zhang's face was red, his mouth open, his lips blue from cold. It was possible he was weeping. The harsh wind had followed us here, the branches above us swayed about, raining a few remaining dry leaves at our feet. I clamped my coat around my chest and raised my face to the wind. The professor was speaking in a meek little voice, he sounded like a boy:

I wanted to shout out Lanlan's name, just to see . . . I wanted . . .

On a high branch a red-throated bird hopped off into the wind. I watched it dip and rise. I turned back the way we came.

THAT NIGHT, OR perhaps the night after, I do not know, I was visited by a vision of myself from the future. It was not like a scene in a time travel film, in which the older self delivers a warning to the younger self in the most careful terms possible, combatting disbelief and fear. My vision did not try to interact with me or to avoid me, it was not even clearly embodied. It came instead as a sense of who that future person was, a gray cloud of being, accompanied by a feeling of inevitability.

She was from years later, from after I've returned to living, to America and university and the boring but sufferable life. With mild relief I noted that these years would return to her the investigative and reasoning faculties that fled me with my mother's death. She—I, many years later—thinks suddenly of the man I saw in Beijing and decides that he was not her father.

She examines her memory of this afternoon for the first time in many years, observing me now (perhaps this is why I could see her too), and determines that the physical likeness of the man was a coincidence, possibly even my hallucination (what Professor Zhang called hope), because how likely was it that of all the people living in that building, the first and only one to exit would be him. Besides, she knows her father is dead. Her father is dead: in this moment of reflection it becomes clear. This is the only solution to the problem of her history, the only one that sufficiently utilizes all the pieces left behind. By then she has replaced the full memory of this afternoon with the knowledge of history books, which have informed her that her birth hospital was in the district where the most people were killed, that many of the dead have never been identified, that mass graves, mass cremations, all manner of cover-ups in which a body and its evidence could disappear were not only likely but probable.

She imagines then how the events of her birth unfolded, how her father left the hospital for a moment, walking briskly through the front gates, perhaps to buy her mother something to eat, perhaps simply for a breath of fresh air, or to stretch his legs, which, bent under the chair outside her mother's delivery room, grew restless and cramped, and was caught, unwitting—innocent—in the fire. Or perhaps her father, moved by the sight of senselessness, stepped into violence, afraid but unable to stand by and watch injustice—a hero. She imagines these scenarios again and again, and each time they become more convincing, so convincing that when she finally shares them with others, her voice low, her eyes dull, her lips barely moving, these impossible memories will have gained firm territory in her mind, will have become so vivid they must be true.

Liya is surprised, in those first rare moments of divulgence, when, moved by some trick of the light or strange scent in the air, she answers the difficult simple questions (where are you from? who are your parents?) with truth instead of evasion, and is met by a grave and respectful silence, elevating her vulnerability to glamour, heavy and dark. The story about her dead father is a story pleasing to Americans, to Westerners in general, she discovers, and though she recognizes that she is using it to package herself, the pleasure she derives from being a person with solid answers to these questions overrides her doubt. How lucky she is! How attractive this person was to me, this person who, in her lifetime, filled in rootlessness with a story so deep in the mud of history it could be passed as identity—as self! She was the kind of person I'd always dreamed of becoming without a notion of how to do it, a person admired for possessing an authoritative moral center, who, when called to, can speak with assured gravity about past and present, personal and global moral failings, the kind of person admired for seeming to have been born with a knowledge of what is right and what is wrong. She spoke too like she was born with the right to speak, along with the right words—even as I knew she was me I envied her for carrying her history with the dignity of possession. In the presence of other immigrants and especially other Chinese Americans, the children of living parents, she was the one who made the others feel less authentic, who sent them home wishing for a similarly earned peace.

The vision stayed with me as I fell asleep, perhaps it entered my dreams. Vaguely I resisted sleep in order to prolong it, so badly did I want it to be true. Because the alternative was to stay as I was, bombarded by sensory information without comprehension, by emotion and pain without comprehension. I did not know what to do in this state but to keep moving, charge forward to be surrounded by new senses and feelings with the hope that they might replace the current ones and be more sufferable. What vision of a stable future would not be more enticing than this?

THE BEGINNING

SHE IS ON A TRAIN going back in time. The train is a fast train, it leaves the city faster than a jetliner leaving the ground. As the train reaches terminal velocity, the images in the window move faster than their boundaries. To avoid dizziness the human eye must fix on a point in the distance, hook onto the eye of the horizon.

Liya is sitting awake on an overnight train and Su Lan is in a box in her backpack. The box is made of pine and the backpack is on the floor, tucked between Liya's legs. The pine box that has been Su Lan's home for the last month is inches from her daughter's feet. The train turns, the backpack shifts, the hard edge of the box rubs against Liya's big toe—

Su Lan is on her way home for the first time in twenty years.

With her in the bag: twenty photographs of Yongzong, taken during their courtship. Letters from Zhang Bo and one from Fudan University. Behind her, her daughter's laptop in a padded sleeve. Above, a scarf, a half-empty bottle of water, the birth certificate she hated to look at, and the passport with the history she improved. In the linings of the bag, an old cough drop, an empty gum wrapper, a paperclip, and two pens.

They arrive in Yiwu eight hours later. They walk through the train station, through dust and people and suitcases wrapped in twine. At the exit a smoking man scans Liya up and down, ashing his cigarette on the ground. They take the shuttle to Yiwu bus station and weave through the packed lot searching for one going to Dongyang. The engine is rumbling, the door is closing—they swing on as the bus pulls out.

In Dongyang, two hours later, Liya learns that the morning bus to her village has just left. It is eleven A.M. and the next one isn't until three. She buys a ticket. She is ravenous. She eats a bowl of noodles at a stall outside, slurping down the broth. She buys a mantou and gulps it down in big bites. She sits in the waiting room with her feet on her duffel and her backpack on her lap. She falls asleep with her head tilted back, mouth open, arms wrapped around her mother.

An hour later, mother and daughter are still slumped on the hard plastic chair. Liya's sleep is thick and deep. A bus to Hangzhou departs and the waiting room empties. Twenty minutes later, a bus from Hengdian arrives at the same time as another from Yiwu. Passengers pour in. One of these passengers is a boy, barely fifteen, with a close-shaved head and a jacket too big for his bony shoulders. His eyes dart through the station: they land on Liya asleep. In an instant he recognizes that she is not from Dongyang by the way she dresses, the way her body slackens on the seat. He guesses that she is from Shanghai or perhaps even Hong Kong or Japan. He guesses by the way her arms drape around the bag on her lap that though the bag is plain and small, it is valuable to her, and when he walks past her he picks it up without turning his head or breaking his step. His movement is so swift that the people walking behind him don't even blink.

Liya wakes for a moment without opening her eyes. She shifts in her seat, folds her arms across her chest, and falls back asleep. The noise of the influx of passengers is absorbed into a dream she will not remember when she wakes. She snaps up, alert, at 2:55. Her bus is boarding. She grabs her duffel and runs to the gate, digs her ticket from her pocket and boards two steps at a time. It isn't until the bus is halfway up the first mountain, a chilly draft blowing sharp from a window crack, that she hugs her arms around her torso and discovers her backpack is not there. She stiffens. She picks up the duffel, stands, looks under the seat, pats her body, looks over her shoulder, turns around, picks up the duffel again, looks above in the overhead shelf, looks under her seat again. It is a tiny bus, the seats are small and cramped and her neighbor leans away, muttering something in a dialect Liya can't understand. The bus takes a sharp turn and knocks her back into her seat. By this time her backpack is deep in a residential neighborhood in Dongyang, the laptop and passport already sold, the cough drop already melted on the young boy's tongue, the scarf already in the closet of someone else's mother, and the gum wrapper, the paperclip, the pens, the water bottle, the photographs, the letters, and Su Lan already dumped in a garbage pile by the side of a dirt road.

SHE ARRIVES WITHOUT her mother. Her body is aching, her head is humming, the journey has been so long. The road has taken her up and around; many times it did this until it brought her here. Here: far from the edges of her imagination, from the territory of photographic implication. She has entered a landscape painting where mountains are made in gray-hued strokes and trees drawn in sharp tangled lines. From the top a frozen river sweeps down in a beard of white. There Liya is in the far corner, a flick of the brush by the arch of a bridge that leads off the bottom of the scroll.

She crosses the bridge. Before her, frozen farmlands fan out. The sky, punctured, is draining. It is that time of winter afternoon when darkness can slip over in a snap. She passes frosted fields and clusters of dwellings made of wood and mud and stone. Shadows lengthen. Someone calls her mother's name. A woman laughs in an open door. Other bodies appear in other doors, speaking the dialect she can't understand:

Ah Lan!

With a shock she realizes she is wearing her mother's dress, the one from the Shanghai neighbor's shrine. Over her sweater and pants the soft fabric swishes. She hurtles onward to her mother's home, the shadow beneath the lone pine. A single bulb lights the frame of the door. She steps over the threshold. There is the sound of water sloshing, the smell of burned rice, a clutter of furniture and things: table, stool, chair, bed, basket, pot, floor. Firewood stacked high along the back wall. There, for the first time, Liya sees the form of her grandmother's body, outlined in yellow light.

She puts her bag on the packed mud floor. She says, Waipo.

When the body turns, she almost cries out:

Her grandmother's face is her mother's face, if her mother's face could age. The wrinkles are her mother's wrinkles, deepened and set. The way this face looks at her, frowning, with eyebrows raised, is the way her mother looked at her.

Looking at her granddaughter, An also sees Su Lan.

AN IS A woman who doesn't believe in time, so each day is a revelation of what is and has been in store. She moves through time like others move through landscape, accepting new sights with delight or disgust. In this way she can take what happens as it comes. She tries to watch herself too with detached curiosity, wondering what she will do next.

What a way of seeing—it drove her daughter away. Now she approaches the image of her daughter with caution. She has seen this image before, her daughter wearing the same yellow dress, appearing in her door. In her dream Lanlan also sets her traveling bag on the floor. She bends to unzip it and takes out a gift, presenting it in two arms like a child. It is a roll of white cloth, impossibly soft yet strong, at turns like silk and wool. Before An can take it, it unfurls. It covers the table, the stove, the floor, and as it does this it disappears, taking what's underneath it. Lanlan steps back and the cloth billows, draping the walls of the house. There they stand on an empty patch of earth. Lanlan opens her purse. She takes out a tube of lipstick and paints her mouth. She turns to her mother and smiles.

Each time An has this dream she tries to change it—to take the bag, to stop Lanlan from walking through the door—and wakes instead with her arm raised, preparing to strike her daughter or to embrace her.

Is she angry or sorry? Did Lanlan abandon her or did she push her daughter out?

Waipo, the image of Lanlan says again. An narrows her eyes. The image is built like herself, with wide shoulders and a sturdy pose, a good body for climbing and working. Lanlan, on the other hand, was short and frail. There are traces of another in the face too: the square jaw, the dark brows.

An says: You're Ah Lan's girl. Is your mother coming?

Liya says: Uncle Zhang told me to bring her back, and I failed.

The two women speak and listen, though neither understands what the other says. They repeat their messages with different words, stretching out phrases, distorting vowels. Where did she take you? An says, and Liya hears the words *where* and *dirt*, which in dialect sounds like *you*, and tries to explain her journey, the endless trains and buses, how she fell asleep, how she doesn't know where she lost her mother, and from *sleep* and *know* An hears *water* and *eat*, and brings Liya a bowl of porridge, and Liya, surprised, says thanks, which is the first thing they both understand. It is a door: An's look of suspicion softens to concern, Liya's frustration to dull fatigue. Liya looks at An and tries again. An understands: *dust, bone, lost, not.*

She sees her granddaughter's face, at once afraid of the words and resigned to them. She turns away. She walks out the back door and stands in darkness, eyes wide, skin vibrating.

Very unkind of you, she will say to her daughter, the next time they meet. How cruel to die before your mother.

AN HAS SEEN what happens when you try to change the future. The village leaders did this in the years before Lanlan's birth, promising bounty for all. One year they told everyone to stop farming and melt their tools to make steel. Another year they wasted digging the reservoir. The big rice bowl campaign didn't even last a year; for two months everyone ate as much as they craved in the communal dining room before they all ran out of food. Fields grew bare; livestock died. People started dying too. Lanlan's father caught the illness that would kill him.

An's husband was an older man—a widower—he spoiled An with love. Those first years of marriage, she got all sorts of ideas about what life was supposed to be. When the famine came she had to learn how to suffer all over again. She knows how love can break a person, how once you've tasted that kind of happiness it is hard to go on without. You have to know what to do with hope, which is to squash it. You have to tell yourself whatever story you must to rewrite happiness into something ugly, something you don't even want.

Lanlan never understood this. Lanlan, born after the worst of the famine, always acted as if the rules did not apply. For some years An believed it too. Her daughter had left for Hangzhou, then Beijing; her name was on everyone's lips. In those years people were good to An. Neighbors stopped to ask if she had eaten and invited her to their homes. Her leaky roof was fixed for free and her house wired with an electric bulb. People dropped by for news of her daughter. Favors and gifts increased in the weeks surrounding visits. There was talk about how beautiful Ah Lan had grown, how stylish and yangqi her clothes. Parents brought their unmarried sons with baskets of fruit and firewood. For half a decade An had more food than she could eat. Then Lanlan stopped coming back.

The truth is, to this day An has kept that feeling about her daughter. Though she will not say it, not even to herself, she has been waiting for Lanlan's return. And what did she expect? Some kind of triumph, a parade, gold spilling from her shoes? It wasn't hope, it wasn't even fear. Hope, fear, she can't tell the difference anymore.

THERE ARE WAYS to help the dead, An says. She packs a basket with incense, wine, and sheets of thin golden paper. She stares at Liya and shakes her head. Liya understands. She takes off her mother's dress.

THEY GO UP the mountain into the dark. An knows the trail by heart. Liya follows, weaving through bamboo and pine and terraced plots. They stop at a row of graves planted on a mountain ledge. They light incense and pour wine and burn mourning papers. In the sudden light Liya reads the names of her ancestors carved on eroding stone. The flame smolders. They leave for another grave.

In this way they traverse the mountains, lighting small fires, tracing a constellation of their dead. It is cold. Liya is so small in this tremendous dark she might as well be of it. The frozen path rises to meet her feet, stiff leaves brush her cheeks. When the sun rises to reveal the shapes of things, she is sure she will find herself transformed into a rock, a barren tree.

At the last grave everything is set aflame: the incense, the papers, the dress. The wind lifts: ash falls like snow.

What is this feeling? It is like grief but even hollower, the self draining out through a hole.

THE NEXT MORNING Liya wakes to her mother's voice. It is speaking in dialect and it is angry, shouting, accusing. She listens, ear to the sound. She hears how her own Mandarin has been inflected by this language, how its idiosyncrasies seep not only into her mother's accented English but into the logic of her speech. It is a violent logic, not primitive or animal but somehow closer to death, the kind of violence that makes visible things that cannot be seen. So heartbreak appears as actual injury to chest, so grief is solid like stone. What you're longing for will appear before you like a mirror, like hands around your throat.

The more she listens the more she understands. She hears: *How could you?* Then, *Get up, wake up, GO.*

She sits up: sight is a gasp. She is alone. In the one-roomed hut there is no grandmother, no woman-figure from the night before. Morning sun slices in through the wooden slabs, which shrink, black and dank and rotting. Sun lights the writhing traps of cobwebs and on the counter the bowls are white with mold, from which a roach emerges, black shell shining. The air is sour and she is inside a mouth, closing, the earthen floor a tongue, curling, even the door, a square of light, narrowing—

She flees.

Out of the hut and up the path, not stopping to breathe or think. From all sides her mother's name pursues her, reaching out as if to keep her. Here in this place that is not trying to kill you, not exactly, but to keep you dead. And though she is no longer wearing her mother's dress she has become her mother: a teenager, barely, escaping.

Across the bridge a bus idles, door open, and when she swings on, panting, it is Su Lan's voice that comes from her, that says, with force, Go.

SU LAN'S DAUGHTER is on her way to Shanghai and Su Lan is on her way to a landfill, where she will become part of a man-made mountain not far from the mountain where she was born. Su Lan's mother has returned to waiting and the man who was Su Lan's husband is in Beijing, awake, eating slices of white bread by the yellow streetlamp light. Awake, considering a dream that has entered his waking life. In his dream Su Lan travels to the past and chooses the more deserving friend; in his life they wait outside and watch him. The deserving friend snores in a hotel in Hainan, where he has taken his family on vacation. After Su Lan's daughter left, the friend's wife discovered the letter from Su Lan in his briefcase, and though his wife is not a jealous or even sentimental woman, she did not speak to him for two days, not even in front of their son. The friend has resolved to explain to Su Lan's daughter, when he returns to Beijing, and if she appears again, that it is best if they don't see each other anymore. Su Lan's Shanghai neighbor has found her husband. He leads her by the hand and teaches her how to see in the dark.

In Beijing, an old nurse on night shift walks through the main corridor of the hospital where she has worked for most of her life. Six days ago she saw someone who reminded her of someone else, a patient from the past, so much so that she stopped to look again. In fact she was right (it was the patient's daughter, a child once strapped to her chest for a night) but she has forgotten about the child and most other details of the night in question. She has not worked in the maternity ward for fifteen years and remembers little about the patient—not her name, not even her affliction. What remains and won't go away is the woman's bloodshot stare and pale lips, asking if she believes in time. Accompanying this image—the memory of cool air suddenly brushing her damp chest. One memory brings another: that day, she saw a man rising from the dead.

She was standing at the hospital's gate smoking a cigarette. The nurse does not and did not believe in ghosts, but to this day she is sure of what she saw. Lying on the street was a darkness in the shape of a corpse. It rose from the ground and became the shape of a man. As the man shook out his limbs and walked away, he gained depth and color, and when he turned to look back there was even the suggestion of a face. That was what it was, not a dead man come back to life so much as a new, living man born from a lifeless form. It was still creating itself as it walked into the smoke-singed street.

Why was she standing at the hospital gate? Why was the street hot with death? When did she stop smoking cigarettes? Over the years she has used neglect to smudge the intensity from her memory, and mostly she has been successful. But—*Do you believe in time?* The nurse cannot get this question out of her head. She walks past the spot where she saw Su Lan's daughter, and suddenly it occurs to her the reason the patient was so upset—her husband had just died.

LIYA RETURNS TO Shanghai in the dead of night, homesick for the first time in her life. She has been here before. She has hailed this taxi and given this address, she knows exactly what to expect. She can conjure an image of where she is going, and it comforts her, this warm ache of returning to a place briefly left. How sweet the sensation is, desire intensified and softened by its imminent fulfillment.

The taxi leaves her on a dark street. The moon, a thin glow behind clouds, does not illuminate so much as give darkness texture. The shop lights are off; the buildings, too colorful in daytime, are shadows blocking the sky. Appearing thus, as patches of less and more black, the street stretches infinitely. Liya cannot see where it ends. She walks, searching and feeling, toward the entrance of the neighborhood—the pharmacy with the green sign, the arch with the flickering bulb light—she walks and walks and walks. The entrance never appears. She walks the length of the street again, crossing once, twice, another time to the other side, and each time it seems like a darker dark, and each time she does not find it, not by sight and not even by smell, no acrid whiff of the public latrine. Finally she turns onto a lamplit street, orbs pulsing in the blacks of her eyes. Frustration wells inside her, a childish feeling of injustice—if she weren't so exhausted she'd have to fight the urge to cry—she sits on the sidewalk in a pool of rancid light. She closes her eyes.

Somebody touches her arm.

It is a boy, seven or eight years old. He has a long face and a lazy eye, and his bare skin—he wears no coat—is covered in sores. He tugs on Liya's arm.

She does not realize he is speaking. When she finally hears him, his voice is thin and pleading. She pulls back, stands up, walks away. He follows. He repeats his refrain: Ahyi, have pity on a poor hungry boy like me. My mother is sick and my father is dead and we've spent all our money on medicine. Ahyi, have pity . . .

She turns. She picks up her pace. So does he, reciting his story, a tape on steady repeat. Finally she opens her wallet and holds out a bill. He snatches it and disappears. Soon more figures emerge. She is surrounded by three or four or five more beggars with hands out, eyes wide and sorrowful, pleas looping and insisting. Within a minute her wallet is empty and she is again alone.

MORNING IS A relief. Light bathes the expanse of the world: it is so easy to see. She walks down a two-lane boulevard lined with barren baby trees. It is early. Shops haven't yet opened, breakfast vendors are just rolling out their carts. Her head hurts. Her legs ache.

She walks down streets that look familiar and unfamiliar at once, that could be anywhere in Shanghai. Panic has sublimated into unsettled inevitability, fluttering off her sightline like a bird. Would she recognize the neighborhood if she saw it? Does she even remember the correct address? She walks past blocks of bamboo scaffolding, past hammers and drills of demolition crews. She circles the streets until they blend into each other, into one anonymous Shanghai Street, narrow and wide and clean and filthy and old and new and crowded now with human bodies, until the wall of buildings opens and she finds herself facing an enormous nothing:

A crater in the earth, so deep and empty she gulps, looking to the sky for some streak, some smoke of extraterrestrial debris.

The sky is clear. People rush past the sudden desert. At the bottom, a bulldozer crawls. Liya's palm opens, releasing her last belonging, the key to the door that no longer exists. But she doesn't see it falling. She is lifted, lifted as if by a hand outside of time, outside of the time she knows, entering instead the kind of time described by her mother, which spreads out before her as in an open field. In this field *now* is an expanded present and events occur neither in past nor future but simply elsewhere. She floats here, beholding the city—the winding streets and alleys, the grids and curves—

and is struck with the image of someone else searching, running, circling this maze as she. Someone is frantic, longing, trying, to find—her.

No, it is not someone, not someone exactly. It is not a person but the imprint of a person, the inverse of a shadow, a shadow but made of light. It takes the figure of a woman, for a leaping instant she believes it her mother, but in fact it resembles herself. At any moment, she feels, it will turn a corner and discover her, charge into her and fill her.

Liya looks from an airplane window at the curving boundary of ocean and sky below. Impossibly, she is sitting on her mother's lap; they are going to America. Her mother says, Once we believed the earth was flat. We did not think that two people, flying like birds from the same point in opposite directions, would one day find themselves face-to-face. In a similar way we still misconceive of time. Time is not separate from space, they are in fact two aspects of the same thing. Imagine a sphere like the earth, but drawn in four dimensions instead of three. The fourth dimension, the one we have trouble seeing, is time. Imagine two people starting at the same point in space-time, flying around this new sphere, in opposite directions: one travels in the direction of the future, the other in the direction of the past. Just like the people who circle the earth, these travelers will eventually collide.

And so she feels the collision coming, Liya running toward her at full speed. She is dressed nicely, wearing her invented history, as her mother once hoped to wear her new American life. Look how the costume suits her, as Su Lan's never had.

She goes. At the next street she will meet herself, bearing strange consolation, around the next corner she will.

ACKNOWLEDGMENTS

ENDLESS THANKS to Jin Auh for infallible instincts and trusting that the best version of this book was within my reach, to Kate Nintzel for bringing it to fruition and into the world with intelligence and care, and to the formidable teams at the Wylie Agency and Custom House.

Thanks to the Martha Heasley Cox Center for Steinbeck Studies, the Elizabeth George Foundation, the David T. K. Wong Fellowship, M on the Bund Shanghai, Vermont Studio Center, and Hedgebrook for generous gifts of time, space, and means, without which the writing of this book would have been near impossible.

Thanks to dear friends for insights on one or many drafts of this book—Shruti Swamy, Jianan Qian, Simon Han, Sunisa Manning, Christopher Fox—I hope our conversations never end. To Tang Siu Wa, Zang Di, and Yang Xiaobin for character names, and Kate Greene for physics smarts. To my wonderful cohort at Hunter and the brilliant teachers there for nurturing this book when it was barely a seed, with special thanks to Claire Messud for illuminating the possible path forward. To Andrew Cowan at UEA for shrewd and generous reading.

Love and gratitude to everyone at The Ruby and Kundiman. To Emily, Shanshan, Kacie, and many others, for friendship and sanity. To Neel for all of the above. Finally, to my parents and my family, for everything.